HARD TO KILL

A TOM ROLLINS THRILLER

PAUL HEATLEY

INKUBATOR
BOOKS

For Aidan

PROLOGUE

It's hot in the motel room. It's been hot for the last three days. The night comes, and it cools the air. The girls are able to sleep, but never peacefully and never for long.

The men guarding them like to laugh at their predicament. To tease them. To poke them with the toes of their boots or the barrels of their rifles whenever they start to nod off. If they didn't have to be in this room too, they probably wouldn't switch on the AC. The unit, though, is old and beat-up and doesn't work well. The cool air is scant and circulates poorly. The air in the room is thick with heat, perspiration, and fear. Thick enough to choke on.

There are four guards. They belong to Los Perros Locos. The Crazy Dogs. Vicious foot soldiers of the Nogales Cartel. The four men are covered in tattoos. Up and down their arms, on their necks, on their faces. More poke out from under the vests they wear. It's hard to tell what any of the designs are, but that doesn't matter. What they represent is more than obvious enough. It tells the world that they are a gang. A pack. It tells the world not to fuck with them.

Carmen Hernández is being held captive. One of five.

Two of the other girls are dressed similarly to Carmen – dresses, makeup, heels. Like they've been out on the town. Except now the dresses are ripped, and their makeup is running from sweat and tears, and their heels are snapped, and they go barefoot. One girl looks like she has been snatched from her bed, wearing only her nightgown, and the other looks like she was grabbed on the way to the supermarket. She's the only one of them dressed sensibly in jeans and a blouse, and Carmen envies her. Their legs are free, but their wrists are bound with cable ties.

There used to be six of them in this room. That changed last night. The girl who isn't here anymore – another one who looked as if she'd been on a night out, wearing a green dress that sparkled – she tried to escape. She saw an opening to run while two of their guards were having a cigarette, the third was in the bathroom, and the fourth was falling asleep next to the air con.

Carmen could see she was going to try it. Could see how she was psyching herself up. The way her breaths had become shallow and quick. The way her eyes had widened and her pupils had dilated. Her tongue flickered out across her dry lips, wiped away the sweat beneath her nose. Her body began to brace. She started to rise.

Carmen reached out, placed both closely bound hands on her wrist. "Don't," she said, whispering.

The girl looked at her. Looked right through her.

"They'll kill you," Carmen said. "And where can you even go? There's nothing around here but desert one way and the border the other. Neither will make you safe."

"I'm not staying here." The girl shook her head. "I know what they're going to do to us. We're as good as dead anyway." She snatched her arm back out of Carmen's grasp. "I can make it. I'm fast. They won't find me in the dark."

Then she turned away, and Carmen knew she couldn't say

anything else to try to stop her. The heat had gotten to the girl, whose name Carmen did not know. She didn't know any of their names, and none of them knew hers.

The heat, and the situation, and her fear. The girl raised herself on bare feet and dirty legs, getting into position like a sprinter. She chanced one look back at the sleeping guard and another at the bathroom door, which was not fully closed, through which they could hear the other guard pissing. Outside, the two smoking continued on, oblivious, laughing about something.

She ran.

And, sure enough, as Carmen had warned her, she was caught.

At first, Los Perros Locos didn't seem upset about it. They ran her down and they dragged her back, and despite her tears and her screams, they were laughing. The escape attempt had amused them more than anything else. Carmen hoped they would just throw her back into the room with the rest of them and that would be the end of it.

But they didn't.

They mocked the guard who had fallen asleep. They slapped him around the head and made jokes at his expense. The one that had been pissing shook his head at the sleeper, as if he couldn't be relied upon to do this one simple thing.

Then they took the girl around the back of the motel, and they shot her through the head.

Carmen and the others had to dig her grave. It was hot work, even in the night. Carmen was grateful, at least, that the sun was not beaming down on them. She wondered, while she dug, how many other people were staying at the motel. How many had heard what had happened, and how many were watching them now, too afraid to do anything about it. And she wondered, too, how many other girls were buried around the back of this motel, throughout this desert, within a stone's throw of the border.

The fourth day drags on, and Carmen wonders what they are waiting for. She keeps expecting more girls to be delivered, but they never show up. Evening approaches, and shadows stretch across the land. Carmen feels her eyes beginning to close, exhausted from the relentless heat. Hoping, despite everything that might come next, that they will be moved soon. That they will no longer be kept locked up in this room, where no doubt so many have been kept before them, captive, waiting to suffer the same fate.

She's woken by the sound of a vehicle outside. Hears how the sand crunches beneath its wheels, then how it comes to a stop.

"Wake up."

One of the guards kicks the sole of her bare foot. She looks up, sees a grinning face tattooed beyond recognition looking back down at her. "It's time to go," he says.

Carmen feels her body stiffen, feels her blood run cold. The moment she has been waiting for has arrived, and it fills her with dread. She can see it in the other girls, too, plain on their faces. Can feel how they tremble. The one closest to her reaches out, clasps her hand. They're all holding hands, twisting their bodies to do so, desperate for physical comfort.

The guard notices, and he laughs.

The door to the vehicle outside opens, then closes. There are footsteps. The four guards are in the room, hands on their weapons. They grin. A fifth man enters, but he does not look like Los Perros Locos. He wears jeans with a plaid shirt tucked into them, his sleeves rolled up. His face is clean-shaven, and his hair is slickly gelled. There are no visible tattoos, and certainly not any on his face. Carmen wonders who he is. If he is a member of the Nogales Cartel, or if he is a coyote, perhaps, come to transport them across the border.

Carmen assumes that is where they are being taken, anyway. Over into America. Beyond that, she does not know. She grits her teeth, knowing she will find out soon enough.

"I thought there were six," the new man says.

"There was," says one of the guards. The others chuckle.

The man – the coyote, sicario, whatever he is – looks unimpressed. He casts his eyes over the girls.

"To your satisfaction?" the guard says.

The man grunts. He's staring at Carmen. Carmen avoids his eyes. "Some of them," he says. He clears his throat, claps his hands together and turns to the guards. "Let's get them in the truck."

Then the room goes black.

Carmen hears their alarm. One of the guards goes to the window, looks out. "Whole motel," he says. "Looks like a power cut."

Carmen blinks hard, trying to adjust her eyes. She feels how the other girls huddle together, clutch each other. They reach for her, too, pull her toward them with their bound hands.

"Get outside," the man says. Carmen recognizes his voice. Stronger than the others. More authoritative. "Find out what's going on."

They do as he says. Two of them head outside, guns raised like they think it could be trouble. Carmen sees their shadows moving.

"It'll come back on soon," says a guard.

"You get many blackouts here?" says the other man.

"Well, no, but it's not surprising."

The other man grunts.

"You expecting trouble?"

The guard laughs. "What trouble?" He nudges his fellow Perro Loco, who also laughs. The idea absurd that anyone would try to mess with them.

"The Silver Sonora Boys think they have balls big enough."

The guard laughs again. "Fuck the Silver Sonora Boys. They're a joke."

The other man falls silent. He looks toward the door. "Your friends aren't back?"

Carmen looks toward the door too. Peers out into the darkness beyond. With the power all gone, everything looks incredibly dark. She can see stars in the distance.

"You," the man says, talking to one of the guards. "Get outside. Find out where they are."

The guard, the one who hasn't been talking, goes to the door.

Then it happens.

He doesn't get outside. He steps into the doorway, and his body stiffens, almost curls in on itself. He cries out. Drops his weapon. He's pushed back into the room, his feet dragging but his body held upright by the shadow that stands in front of him. It all happens so fast. Carmen sees the flash of a gunshot over the guard's shoulder, hears the loud retort of it in the small room. The newly arrived coyote/cartel member's head snaps back. Blood sprays out the back of it. The remaining Perro Loco screams, starts firing. Carmen and the other girls try to cover their ears, but it's near impossible in their bonds.

The bullets from the automatic rifle thud into the body of the other Perro Loco. Blood spurts from his back, and Carmen understands why the shadow has kept him upright. It's using him as a shield, and as a distraction. The shadow ducks low, avoiding the bullets that tear through the torso of the body it's holding, propping it up with one hand upon its chest. Nearly on top of the last Perro Loco now, it shoves the makeshift shield into him, knocks him back. Carmen sees the glint of a bloodied knife, sees how it was in the stomach of the shield. The shadow raises his gun again, fires twice, kills the last guard.

Then everything is still.

It takes a moment for the ringing in Carmen's ears to calm. It gradually fades away, and she can hear how quiet everything has become now that the gunshots have stopped. The girls to her side are sobbing. They are shaking. Carmen is not. She is doing neither of these things. She's gritting her teeth.

The shadow moves down the line of girls, cuts them loose. He has wiped the blood from his knife off on the body of one of the men he has killed. Carmen watches him. She doesn't think he's a Silver Sonora Boy. He's a gringo.

The girls, freed, flee from the room. The man doesn't try to stop them. Finally, he reaches Carmen. He cuts her loose.

"Who are you?" she says, speaking English.

He glances at her, then gets to his feet. He's bearded, and his hair looks like it needs a cut, but it has been wetted and slicked back to keep it out of his face. He doesn't respond. He starts to turn toward the exit.

"I asked you a question," Carmen says, using the bed behind her to help pull herself to her feet. "What's your name?"

He looks at her again, longer now. He's frowning. Doesn't understand the aggression in her tone or in her face. "Tom," he says. "My name is Tom."

"Well, *Tom*," Carmen says, "they have my sister. How am I supposed to find her now?"

1

Tom has been in Mexico for three months. He stopped at Guaymas first. Took a look around the place where Alejandra grew up. The place she always wanted to return to one day. He scattered her ashes on the beach there. He did it at dusk and stared out across the sea, watching as the sun set and the sky turned the color of fire. He had to admit to himself, when the time came to spread the ashes, that he felt a pang of guilt his brother was not standing beside him. Still, Anthony made his choice, and his choice was not to honor her wishes. Tom will not regret doing the right thing by the woman he loved.

He didn't go straight back to America. There's nothing there for him. He's traveled around, taking in the country. He's picked up a little Spanish. Enough to be conversational, and only if the other person is speaking slowly. He's let his beard and hair grow out, and his usually pale skin has tanned and darkened under the hot sun.

Then the time came when he knew he had to go back. He always knew it would, eventually. Staying in Mexico was not going to bring Alejandra back to him. He'd felt like it brought him closer to her, at first, but that feeling had passed. It was replaced instead by the sinking knowledge that he would never see her again. Her face, her smile, the person who had brought him back safely from so much danger, if only in the hopes of catching a glimpse of her beauty. Of hearing her voice.

He contacted Cindy, a hacker he knows from Lubbock, Texas. She's helped him out in the recent past, in a big way. He's kept in touch with her since. Her skill set is invaluable. She's a good contact to have, especially for a man on the run. He's paid her to keep a watch out for his name. To let him know if he appears on any database. If anyone is looking for him, or expecting his return. When he gets back to America, the last thing he wants is to walk into a lion's den. He sent her another payment, and she sent him a new ID, the Tom Smith cover having been blown back in Cullingworth County while he was making his way to the border. The name on the papers, now, reads David Thompson. Tom has recited this name over to himself, committed all the details Cindy has provided to memory. He works in a bank in New Mexico. He's been on sabbatical. Used up all his vacation days to spend a few months down in Mexico.

So Tom – or, rather, David Thompson – was going home. Heading for the border. He'd found a motel to stay at while Cindy sent him the forged passport and driver's license. It was a rough-looking place. Run-down, in desperate need of some maintenance. Looked to be populated with runaways, outlaws, junkies, and people waiting for a chance to jump the border. Tom didn't mind. He'd stayed in worse places.

Then he noticed the hard cases next door, and though he had his papers by then, he couldn't bring himself to leave. He stayed in his room, by his window, and he watched them. Took particular interest in the girls they kept in the room with them. He'd catch only glimpses of them through the door as it swung open and closed. They were all seated on the floor, and they rarely moved from that spot.

He'd watch for when the men left for cigarettes, catch a further glimpse inside the room, and saw how these tattooed men stood armed with AR-15s. Saw how, when they came outside, they had FN 5.7s tucked into their waistbands.

Tom became sure they were smuggling the girls. Against their will, more than likely. He knew there was a chance these girls had paid to cross the border. That these dangerous-looking men were coyotes, that perhaps it had nothing at all to do with sex trafficking. But he never saw the girls leave the room. Never saw them move around inside it.

And then one tried to escape.

Tom was sleeping at the time. The gunshot woke him. He went to the back of his room, watched from the bathroom as they made the other girls bury her. Then he knew. Knew that these girls were being held against their will.

He made his move.

Carmen Hernández, however, is not grateful for his actions. Carmen Hernández is looking for her sister, Rosa. She tells him about it in the morning. Before then, they're too busy. They go to Tom's car, and they find the other girls staggering through the desert night. They take them home. Luckily, the girls are all from Nogales, and they don't have to go far. Tom tells them he recommends packing a bag and getting out of town for a while. Lying low.

It became clear Carmen had no intention of packing a bag and lying low. They sat in his idling car, the last girl dropped off. "When I take you home," Tom said, "what are you going to do?"

She looked at him, brazen. "I'm going to continue what I was doing before you showed up, and hope that when I show up around those bastards again, none of them recognize me."

"That's a risky game," Tom said.

"I know," she said, glaring. "But it's the only one I can play. I was close – I was so close – and then you showed up and turned it all to shit." Her eyes blazed.

Tom sighed. He could see she was not going to change her mind. Was not going to walk away from this, no matter how dangerous it was. He thought about the guards back at the hotel. Thought about Carmen wading deeper into their ranks, desperate to find what they had done with her sister. A sister who, in all honesty, was possibly dead already.

"All right," he said. "I can't let you do this alone. You're going to get yourself killed. I'll help you find your sister."

Carmen's eyes were still blazing as she looked at him. She considered what he'd said. Her glare softened somewhat. She thought about what she had witnessed back in the motel. Thought about the men he had so ably killed. "All right," she said. "Fine. I suppose it's the least you can do."

Carmen is not from Nogales. She lives in a small town outside the city, but she has a hotel room in the center. They go there first so Carmen is able to shower and change her clothes. She puts on jeans, hiking boots, a white tank top and an unbuttoned checkered shirt. They don't stay long at the hotel.

"Are you hungry?" Tom says when she emerges from the bathroom, fully dressed with her hair tied back.

"I haven't eaten in a few days," she says.

They find a café. Sit inside and take a seat at the rear of the building. Tom keeps his back to the wall so he can see the rest of the room, particularly the entrances and the windows. His beretta is concealed on his right hip, and his KA-BAR is on his left. He's hoping he won't have to use them while they eat.

Carmen has her back to the room, her face concealed. They've ordered huevos rancheros. Before they eat, Carmen nods at the bag on the seat next to Tom. "What's in it?" she says.

"Bullets," Tom says, keeping his voice low. "Phones. Some clothes."

Carmen frowns. "You on the run or something?"

"Or something," Tom says.

Carmen rolls her eyes, scoops up a forkful of egg.

"Tell me about your sister," Tom says.

"She's missing," Carmen says. "I already told you."

Tom raises an eyebrow. "I'm going to need more than that if we want to find her."

Carmen sits back, chewing. "What else do you want to know?"

"Everything. You haven't told me anything but her name so far."

"There hasn't been a chance."

"There's a chance now. Have you got a picture?"

Carmen reaches into her pocket, pulls out a creased polaroid. "It's a few years old," she says. "All the more recent pictures I have are on my phone, and that was taken back at the motel. I don't know what they did with it. It's probably smashed and trashed."

Tom takes one of the burners from his bag and hands it to her. "Use this one for now," he says, then he takes the polaroid from her. It's Carmen and Rosa together. It's hard to tell where they are, where the picture was taken, as the image is occupied mostly by their faces. Rosa looks a lot like Carmen, but it's clear she is the younger sister. Tom hands the photo back. "How much younger than you is she? Three years?"

"Close," Carmen says, sliding the polaroid back into her pocket. "Four. She's twenty-five, I'm twenty-nine."

"You always been so protective? Always been willing to put yourself at the mercy of a cartel to make her safe?"

"She's my sister," Carmen says. "What else am I supposed to do?"

Tom picks up his knife and fork, cuts into the tortilla and the eggs. Someone enters the café. Tom watches. It's an older guy with a cowboy hat and a gray moustache. He talks to the woman behind the counter, and they laugh about something like they're old friends. She has a container ready for him, and she hands it over. He pays, thanks her, leaves.

"So what are you?" Carmen says.

Tom returns his attention to her. "What?"

"Army, Special Forces – I saw how you moved, how you…" She pauses, lowers her voice further. "How you killed those guys back at the motel. You're a professional. That's plain to anyone. So what is it?"

"Nothing. Not anymore."

"Oh? Then what *was* it?"

"I don't want to talk about that," Tom says. He puts egg and salsa into his mouth, chews it and swallows. "It's not that interesting."

"I think you might be downplaying that."

"Think what you like. We should be talking about Rosa, though. How long has she been gone?"

Carmen sighs, takes a sip of water. "A couple of weeks now."

"What happened?"

"She'd come to Nogales for a friend's birthday. She didn't get home. I didn't notice at first. It was the Monday when I got home from work, Mama came to me, asked if I knew where Rosa was. Asked if I knew when she was due home. I could see how worried she was, though. I knew all the things she was too scared to say."

"Rosa still lives with your parents?"

"That's right."

"What work do you do?"

"I don't want to talk about that," Carmen says. She looks at him. "It's not that interesting."

Tom grins. "Suit yourself."

"I will. Anyway, I caught up to the friend whose birthday it had been. She hadn't seen Rosa since the Saturday night. I could see how she was starting to get worried, too, the same way I was, and Mama was. I asked her what had happened, how they'd gotten separated. Ana – that's her name – she said Rosa was talking to some guy, and they went into a bar together. Ana was drunk, Rosa was drunk, all of their friends were drunk. No one was thinking straight. They let Rosa go, and they thought she'd spend the night with the guy they'd seen her talking to. I could have hit her, honest to God. I wanted to hit them all, and I wanted to shake Rosa so hard. I thought she would have more sense than that."

Carmen shakes her head. With her fork, she stabs at what food is left on her plate. "Ana did have something useful, though. She remembered the name of the bar Rosa had gone into."

"What was it?"

"La Perrera."

Tom has picked up some Spanish, but he doesn't know this word. "What does it mean?"

Carmen waves her hand, translating. "Kennel, doghouse, pound – that kind of thing. The name's fitting – it's a club-house for Los Perros Locos. It's crawling with them, save for a handful of girls who don't know any better, or who are impressed by them."

"You went there," Tom says, jumping ahead in the story.

"That's right," Carmen says. She stops stabbing at her food, puts her fork down, done. "I know who Los Perros Locos work for, and I know what the Nogales Cartel do with girls they kidnap – especially pretty ones like my sister. So I put on a dress and a pair of heels, and I went to La Perrera on a Saturday night, just like Rosa." She trails off, staring at the table and chewing her bottom lip.

"And how was it?"

"It was terrifying," Carmen says, looking back up at him. "I pretended to be drunk, but that didn't make it any easier. They were all staring at me. I thought...I thought they were going to rape me. And then, when one of them did put his hands on my shoulder and start leading me aside, I thought that was when it was going to happen." She swallows. "It didn't, though. He was sweet-talking me, which is no less terrifying when it's coming from a face tattooed to look like a skull. He gave me a drink and insisted I drink it. It was spiked. I woke up in the motel room with the other girls. I was the last to arrive."

"And I already know they didn't say where they were going to take you," Tom says, remembering how Carmen had glared at him after the fight in the motel.

"Mm." She still doesn't look like she's fully forgiven him for this. "Why are you helping? You don't know me. You certainly don't know Rosa. You didn't know any of us back at the motel. You have no horse in this race, so why commit yourself to it?"

Tom takes his time answering. He finishes eating first, though there's not much left on his plate by now. Carmen does not rush him. She sits and watches him, and waits.

When he's done, he looks at her and takes another moment. He clears his throat. "I saw what they did," he says. "I saw that you were all in danger."

"That doesn't answer my question," Carmen says.

Tom runs his hand down his beard. "I knew I could help," he says. "And because I can, I should. I have to."

"Says who?"

"Says me."

Carmen looks at him. He can feel how she appraises him,

how she mulls over his words. "Why are you in Mexico, Tom?"

"I'll tell you some time," he says. "But not right now. Right now, we have somewhere we need to go."

"Where's that?"

"La Perrera."

He sees how her face drops. How she'd hoped to never return there. How she'd feared this was exactly what he was going to say. "How can that help us?" she says. "They could recognize me, and they won't talk to you."

Tom pulls money from his pocket, counts off their bill. He smiles at Carmen. "Don't worry," he says. "I'm sure I'll be able to find someone willing to accommodate us."

2

The scene at the motel has been kept private for Pedro Ruiz's arrival. News has not spread of what has happened. The situation has been contained. Pedro used to be a police officer, when he was in his early twenties, until it became clear to him it was a fool's game. The reward did not match up to the risk. He started doing favors for the Nogales Cartel, until those favors became bigger and bigger, and he left the force to pursue cartel employment full time. With it came money, girls, power, and he quickly regretted those five years he spent with the police. He's thirty-eight now, but he's kept in close contact with colleagues from those days. He knows which hands to grease, which means that on the rare occasion an event such as this occurs, the force keeps it quiet, and gets in touch to let him know what has happened.

Pedro steps out of his Audi R8 and removes his sunglasses to look the scene over. It is not quite the chaos he anticipated when he'd first been told there'd been a shoot-out at the motel and five of their men were dead. He'd expected smashed windows, scattered bodies, a broken door, perhaps.

Shell casings. Blood baking under the sun. He walks toward the building, and thinks how if it weren't for the police and his own men gathered around one room, he'd have a hard time telling where the fighting happened.

"Where are the bodies?" he says.

The police all avoid meeting his eye. They look at the ground, into the room, or off into the distance. It's Castillo, one of Pedro's own men, another former policeman, who answers first. "They're inside," he says. "Most of them, anyway. Couple more down the side, propped up. Look like they're just sitting there."

Pedro takes a step to his right, looks down the side of the building. He sees the silhouette of two men in the shadows there. As Castillo says, it just looks like they're taking a seat, grabbing a quick rest out of the heat. "How about the girls?" Pedro says, turning back to Castillo.

"None of them here," Castillo says. "None of them dead. They're gone."

Pedro runs his tongue around the inside of his mouth, over his teeth. The police stroll off, find themselves something more important to be doing away from Pedro and his men. Pedro steps forward, and his men part before him. He steps inside the room, looks it over. The air is thick with the stink of blood and death, amplified by the heat. He grits his teeth but doesn't cover his nose. It isn't anything he hasn't smelled before. He's used to it by now.

"The two down the side," Pedro says, knowing Castillo is behind him. "How were they killed?"

"Stabbed. Both of them. Right through the heart."

Pedro looks down at the three bodies in the room. Sees how one of them has a stab wound in his stomach, but rolls him onto his side with the toe of his shoe and sees how his back has been peppered with bullets. He sees the transporter, Roberto, though it's hard to tell with half of his face missing.

His clothes give him away – more practical and respectable than the low-slung jeans and white wifebeaters of Los Perros Locos – not to mention his lack of tattoos. Pedro leaves the room, steps back out into the relatively cleaner air. "What did the cameras get?"

"Nothing," Castillo says. "The power was cut right before it happened, and so was the feed to the cameras."

"What about the other residents?" Pedro tilts his head toward the other motel rooms. "Have they been questioned?"

"They've been questioned," Castillo says. "They didn't see anything."

Pedro isn't surprised by this. The inhabitants and guests of the motel are not the kind of people likely to see a thing even if it happened right in front of them. They mind their business. They don't want any trouble. They live here because they know they will be left alone. "Who asked them?" Pedro says. "The cops, or you?"

"We did," Castillo says. "So I know they're telling the truth."

Pedro grunts. "All right. Tell the cops they can do whatever it is they want to do. Take photographs or whatever. There's nothing else we can get from this."

Castillo nods, goes to do as Pedro has said.

Pedro returns to his car. His sunglasses are still in his hand. He puts them on, gets inside and turns on the engine in order to pump the air conditioning. He likes to keep the interior of his vehicle cool. It helps him think. All hot air does is make him sweat. It agitates him. He pulls out his phone, calls Miguel Aguilar.

Miguel has been waiting for his call. It does not take him long to answer. "Yes."

"I'm at the motel," Pedro says.

"And?"

"The girls are gone, and the guards are dead, and so is Roberto."

"Your thoughts?"

"It would take more than a few men to overwhelm Los Perros Locos like this, and so fast. More than that, whoever they are, it doesn't look like they lost a single man in the process. All the blood I saw looked accounted for."

"Who do you think is responsible?"

"To kill our men and steal our girls, it must be the work of another cartel. Looking to move in perhaps. It could be the Silver Sonora Boys, but it seems too professional for them – to cut the power to the motel and to the security cameras first... I'm not sure they'd think of that."

"Perhaps they've acquired some new recruits. Ex-Special Forces, maybe, who would have knowledge of such things. I've heard rumors they have a new recruit claiming as much."

Pedro snorts. "They'd have to be desperate to join the Silver Sonora Boys. If they're this good, I'd expect them to offer their services to us first."

"Well, they didn't, and now they must die for it. Find them, Pedro. Find whoever is responsible, and make them pay. Make it messy. Send a message with it – we're not to be fucked with. Kill one of ours, we kill five of yours. You understand."

"Of course."

Miguel hangs up, and Pedro places the phone in the holder built into his car's display. He looks back toward the motel. Castillo and the rest of his men are standing to one side, waiting. The cops have moved in on the room. They're unrolling tape, cordoning off the scene. Pedro catches Castillo's eye, circles his finger in the air. Castillo understands. *Round up the troops, and follow me.*

Pedro doesn't wait for them to get back to their cars. He pulls away from the motel, puts his foot down and speeds along the road, kicking up dust and sand behind him. They'll catch up with him eventually. They always do. In the meantime, Pedro wants to get a head start on his search for whoever is responsible for what has happened at the motel. The best place to start, he thinks, is with the enemies he's already aware of.

He needs to find out where the Silver Sonora Boys are holing themselves up.

3

Carmen directs Tom to La Perrera. Tom drives. When they reach it, he idles on the other side of the road, looks over. The building is nothing special. It could do with a lick of paint, the windows need a cleaning, but other than that, it is nondescript. There's nothing that marks it as the hangout for a vicious gang, save perhaps for the name above the door. As opposed to the rest of the façade, the paint on this wooden banner is fresh. Red lettering against a black background. It gives the impression that it wasn't so long ago that the bar was taken over and renamed.

"Now what?" Carmen says. He can hear how her voice shakes. "Do we go in?"

Tom looks around. Checks the buildings on the side of the street where he's parked. "No," he says. "We watch."

He parks the car around the corner. Tom goes back on foot. Carmen stays inside with the window rolled down, not wanting to go near the bar. Tom looks the area over. He checks down the side of the building, and around the back. Inspects the entrances and exits. The routes to and from the building. Commits them all to memory. Carmen is watching the mirror as he returns to the car, not wanting to be caught unaware.

"Well?" she says, when he stops by her open window. "Did you find whatever you were looking for?"

"Almost." He opens her door. "Come on."

Carmen asks where they're going, and Tom explains on the way.

They go to the building opposite La Perrera and climb the fire escape at the back of it. It takes them to the roof. Tom crawls to the edge and looks down, tells Carmen to do the same. To stay low. "It's a better viewpoint here," he says.

"You can't see inside."

"No, but I can get an idea of who's going in and out. Get a feel for the clientele, and how many of them might be in there at any time. We try to do this parked on the street, and it's just a matter of time before they spot us."

Carmen watches. The front of the bar is quiet, for now. Tom notices how people don't pass directly in front of the building. They cross the road, give it a wide berth.

"And then what?" Carmen says.

"Then I'll go in, and politely ask for directions," Tom says. He grins, but doesn't think she notices. "From what you've said, they're going to notice me as soon as I go in."

Carmen snorts. "Oh, they'll certainly notice a gringo wandering in off the streets."

"I can play the lost and confused tourist very well. I don't want to have to go in there completely blind, though." He looks at her. "I need you to think about the interior. Can you do that? Bring back every little detail you can think of."

Carmen is quiet a moment, then says, "Okay."

"You've got it all?"

She falls quiet again, thinking. Her brow furrows and her eyes move from side to side, going back through her memory, recalling what she saw while she was inside. "I think so."

"Then think harder. I want to be able to go in there and recognize everything as being exactly where you tell me it is."

Carmen breathes in through her nose. She closes her eyes. "I was scared," she says. "And there were so many of them."

"Look beyond them. Try to see all the things you didn't notice last time. I need the layout."

She nods. "All right." Her body starts twisting as she prepares to describe it to him, putting herself back into that room with all those men, retracing her steps in her mind. "You go through that door there and directly in front of you is the bar. The bartender was a big guy, didn't look like one of Los Perros Locos, but didn't look like he was scared of them, either." She thinks.

Tom listens as she talks, though he keeps his eyes on the front of the building. He visualises what she tells him. Commits it to memory, compartmentalises it right next to the image of Rosa's face she'd shown him in the polaroid.

"To the left, there were tables," Carmen says. "But most of the men were standing. Six tables, and a padded bench that went along the back wall. To the right, there's a pool table. It's a bigger space on the right. There aren't any tables there."

"What's beyond that?"

"Nothing. A wall – no, wait. There's a door." She frowns. "There wasn't a sign on it. It must be the back room. A storage room." She opens her eyes. "That's it. That's everything."

"What about toilets?"

"What about them?"

"You haven't mentioned any. What're they doing, pissing in buckets? If not, you've missed a door."

He sees her realize he's right. She closes her eyes. He can see her eyes moving under the lids. "It's to the left," she says slowly, pointing. "To the left of the other door. The storage door." She opens her eyes, nods.

"You sure?"

"I'm sure."

Tom nods. The whole while, he's kept one eye on the building opposite. "How many of them were inside when you went?"

Carmen counts them up in her head. "A dozen, maybe more. But that was a Saturday night."

Tom hasn't seen anyone enter or leave the bar yet. The windows are dark, and it's impossible to see movement inside, if there is any.

"How long are we going to do this for?" Carmen says.

"I need to know what I'm up against," Tom says. "You should get comfortable."

Carmen doesn't look like she's making any effort to get comfortable. She looks restless. "How will you know when you're ready? When it gets dark? When it gets dark tomorrow night?"

"Could be."

Carmen makes an exasperated noise.

Tom looks at her, raises an eyebrow. "I understand the rush, but getting ourselves killed won't help Rosa."

Carmen isn't watching the bar. She sits back, clasps her arms around her knees. "I know that," she says. "I know you're right, but that doesn't make it any easier."

"We'll find your sister, Carmen. You just need to be patient, and to trust me."

She looks at him. There are tears in her eyes. She grits her teeth. "Every minute that passes is another minute they take her further away from me, or worse." She looks down at her hands, wringing them together. "I just hate knowing they have her. That she's...that she's who *knows* where, and she's all alone." She shakes her head. "I hate it."

4

Rosa Hernández does not know where she is. What she does know is that it is dark, and cramped, and that she is not alone.

The room is hot with the heat of the bodies jammed inside. She thinks it's underground – a basement, perhaps. There are no windows, and only one door. It's hard for her to see how many others are in the room with her. Her eyes struggle to adjust. She cannot twist her body into a comfortable position. Her back is against a rough wall, and there are people on either side and in front of her, also battling to twist themselves into positions that could bring some semblance of comfort.

She thinks they're all women. She hasn't heard any voices or sounds that could pass for male. Some of them are crying. Tears that never stop.

There is one toilet. It's in a far-off corner, and it is used without privacy. It's hard to find in the dark, and a lot of the girls don't bother trying. The room stinks with piss, as well as shit, sweat, and fear.

She doesn't know how long she has been held captive like

this. Without light, it's impossible to tell. Men come to throw them food, but there's no way of knowing how long passes between each 'meal.' Sometimes they come with a hose, too. They spray the room down. To clean them, and to keep them cool. The men laugh while they do this. Rosa doesn't know who they are or what they look like. She can't get a good look at them. They wear masks, and they don't talk. Their mocking laughter is the only sound they make.

Rosa fears she knows what is going to happen. Where she, and the other girls, are being transported to. What they will be forced into, what they will be used for.

She remembers going into the bar. La Perrera. She knew as soon as she stepped inside she should not have entered it, but she was drunk and wasn't thinking straight. There was a man, and he was handsome and charming, and he didn't have tattoos all over his face like the rest of them. He bought her a drink. Before she could take a sip, she excused herself, went to the bathroom. While she washed her hands, she was grabbed from behind. Something was put over her mouth, covering her nostrils, too. Chloroform, perhaps. She doesn't know what happened next. Everything went dark.

She woke up in a motel room with five other girls. Some of them were dressed as she was – as she still is. In dresses and skirts, their makeup done and their hair styled. They'd been grabbed, kidnapped, all of them. The men from the bar were guarding them, armed with automatic rifles that looked as though they could tear a body apart under a barrage of bullets in mere seconds. They were kept in that room for days, and when finally they were moved they were tied up, and bags were placed over their heads. Their journey was hidden from them. Rosa doesn't know where the other girls from the motel room are now. They could be here, with her, in the basement. She'd call for them, but she never knew their names.

The door opens, and the men enter. There are more of them than usual, and they don't bring food, or the hose. A ripple travels through the room. The men start grabbing the girls, gathering them up and shoving them toward the door. Then men at the door grab them and push them along, keep them moving. Rosa hasn't been grabbed. Not yet. Her heart beats faster. The spit dries up in her mouth and her breath catches in her throat. The girl to her right reaches out, grabs for her. Rosa gives her her hand. They each squeeze the other's.

The men leave, slam the door. The room doesn't feel so cramped anymore, but this does not bring any comfort.

The men return soon after. They grab more girls, a second group to be ushered to the door and out of the room. The men leave again. They're gone longer this time. Then, on the third visit, Rosa is grabbed and dragged through the door.

The light outside the basement is strong, too bright. It blinds her. She blinks against it, feeling nails driven through her skull with it. She loses her feet and someone has to carry her, bodily hauling her down a corridor with the tips of her toes dragging on the rough ground. Then, before she can recover, regain her eyesight, she feels herself thrown to the ground. Her hip scrapes against something hard and sharp. She looks up, sees that this new room already has some girls in it. Pushing herself up on her outstretched arms, she counts them – seven. She's the eighth. Again, she wonders how many of them were being kept in that basement. Lying on top of each other, breathing each other's air.

"On your feet," someone says, in English, and Rosa realizes they're talking to her. One of the girls in front of her offers her hands, helps pull her up.

"Against the wall," a voice comes, hard to tell if it's the same as the last one. It barks at them. "Line up!"

They do as he says. Rosa slips into the group. Her vision is adjusting, though it remains blurry at the edges. She can see some of the room now. It's a communal shower. The walls are tiled, the spaces between them black with mold. There is a drain clogged with hair in the center of the room, and Rosa realizes this is what she scraped her hip on. The men are wearing masks still. They come toward the girls, grab them, tear the clothes from their bodies. Dump them in a pile behind them and don't stop until the girls are naked, not a stitch remaining. The girls try to cover up, though it doesn't do much good.

The hose is brought into the room. The mouths of the masks the men wear are uncovered, and she can see that the one handling the hose is grinning. He licks his lips.

"Spray them down," says someone behind him. "Clean them off. Get them good – some of 'em stink of piss."

The hose turns on. It spews out freezing cold water that there is no escape from. It runs up and down the line. The girls scream. Rosa is one of them, the shock of it hitting her skin at such force. It drives the air out of her lungs, feels like it might crack her ribs. It hits her in the face, fills her eyes and mouth and nose, and she'd fall if it weren't for the wall behind her.

Then, finally, it ends. The hose is shut off and they stand where they are, dripping and trembling. The men don't let them dry.

"*Move*," one of them, the barking one, says.

The men usher them out of the room in single file. One of them slaps Rosa on the ass. Her teeth are chattering. Tears stream down her face, though it's impossible to tell among all the rivulets of dripping water.

They're brought into a room. The floor is varnished wood, and it is warmer here than where they have just been. They continue to shiver with their arms wrapped around themselves. Rosa feels goosebumps rising on her arms, all over her body. She shakes so hard she worries she might catch hypothermia.

The room is already occupied. There is a woman here. Rosa becomes aware of her out the corner of her eye. She steps in front of them all now. The woman is white and looks to be in her late fifties or early sixties, though she wears a lot of makeup as though she is trying to disguise this fact, trying to make herself look younger. Her blonde hair, with wisps of white mixed throughout, is tied back from her face with a clip at the back of her head. She wears a gray pantsuit with an ostentatious fox-fur scarf draped over her shoulders, though it's far too hot for such a garment. Her heels make her much taller than the naked girls lined up before her.

She's looking them over. Her face is impassive at first, but it soon begins to change. An eyebrow rises, her tongue runs around the inside of her mouth, over her teeth, making her top lip bulge. She looks each of them up and down. When her eyes lock with Rosa's, Rosa looks away. She can feel her appraisal, though. Feels how her eyes run over every inch of her body, from top to toe. How she stares at Rosa for longer than the others.

"Turn around," the woman says. Her voice is firm, and has a raspy quality like she's a lifelong smoker.

The girls do as she says. Again, Rosa can feel her eyes on them, up and down, on their backs now, on the way their buttocks shake as they tremble.

"All right," she says. "Turn back."

They do. The woman steps forward now. She steps right in front of Rosa. Rosa keeps her eyes lowered, and tries not to whimper. The woman reaches out, grabs her face. She's rough. She forces Rosa's mouth open, looks inside. Twists Rosa's face from side to side, up and down. Inspects her teeth.

The woman lets go, and Rosa's face aches. Her jaw clicks.

"That one," the woman says, pointing at Rosa. Then she points at two others: "And her, and her."

"Yes, Ms. Snow," one of the men says. The men come forward. They grab Rosa and the other two girls Ms. Snow pointed at, and they take them from this room. Rosa glances back. The other girls are led out another door.

Ms. Snow sees her looking. She smiles, just a small tugging up at the right corner of her mouth, and Rosa thinks it is the most terrifying thing she's ever seen.

5

Tom has watched through the night. He waits until dawn, when, by his reckoning, there are only a few men left inside the bar. He tells Carmen to hold back, to wait outside and watch the door. To only come inside when he tells her.

Tom steps inside. He moves lightly on his feet, looks left and right. The layout is as Carmen described, is almost exactly as he pictured it in his head. The area to the left looks empty. Directly in front, the bartender is not present. Tom sees an ashtray on the counter, an open box of matches next to it. Tom checks inside the box. There are a dozen matches left. He pockets the box. Off to the right are three Perros Locos. They're playing pool. They haven't noticed him.

He goes into the left room first, KA-BAR out, to make sure it is as clear as it at first appears. It is. He returns to the door. Checks the three others are still playing pool. One of them is gone. Tom waits, watches, but he does not reappear, and the men are not alarmed. Tom assumes he has gone to the toilet.

He opens the door again, motions Carmen inside. Points

for her to stand to one side, out of view. She does as he says, steps to the left.

Tom locks the door. One of the men at the pool table hears it click into place. He turns back, sees Tom. He raises his eyebrows. Laughs to get the attention of his friend, points Tom out to him. He says something, but the only word Tom catches is 'gringo.'

The third man returns from the toilet, buttoning up his jeans. He frowns, sensing something has happened, then he looks Tom's way.

"Good morning, gentlemen," Tom says, stepping forward. "I hope you all understand English. My Spanish isn't the best. Anyway, I'm sure you're all wondering who I am and what I'm doing here." Tom looks each of them in the face in turn, smiling. "I was hoping you'd be able to answer some questions I have."

The three Perros Locos look at each other, then burst out laughing.

The one closest to Tom, laughing hardest, is the biggest of the three. His muscles shake with his movements, veins bulging against his skin. Behind him is the other man who was playing pool. He is smaller, but he has a mean face and unblinking eyes. The man who has arrived last, from the bathroom, is the smallest. He looks no less vicious than the rest, but Tom settles on him being the one he can make talk the fastest.

The biggest man, closest to him, steps forward. "Think you is in the wrong place, gringo," he says in broken English.

Tom makes sure to keep smiling. "No, I'm right where I'm supposed to be."

The big man frowns at his smile. "All right," he says. "I'll play along. Ask your questions."

"The girls you kidnap from here. Where do you take them?"

The big man's face drops. "Who the fuck are you? FBI? CIA?"

"Not anymore."

The big man looks back to his friends. "Get this fucker," he says. It's in Spanish this time, but Tom's able to understand.

The three move in. The second man wields his pool stick. He's the only one of the three visibly carrying a weapon, though Tom doesn't doubt they likely have knives and handguns hidden on their persons, perhaps tucked into their waistbands or strapped to their legs.

Tom is armed, but he doesn't want to pull the Beretta. Wants to keep this quiet.

The big man reaches him first, swings for him with a right hook. Tom is faster. He ducks under it with ease, then drives his elbow back into the man's kidneys. The big guy drops to a knee, but the second man is already coming in, swinging the cue. Tom catches it with both hands, holds it tight. He moves through to the third man, the one he wants to keep alive. He's charging, too, but Tom cuts him short. He lashes out, kicks him in his left knee. Blows it out. The man's knee twists to the side and his eyes go wide as he realizes what has happened. He collapses, clutching his leg and screaming.

So much for keeping things quiet.

The second man pulls on the cue, trying to wrest it from Tom's grip. The bigger man is back on his feet, coming in from the right. Tom jabs the cue up into his face, crushes his nose with the thick base of it, then headbutts the second man. This breaks his grip on the cue. Tom keeps hold of it, uses it to sweep the big man's legs out from under him. Plants him flat on his back. The second man charges again, face bloodied. Tom strikes him across the stomach with the cue, doubling him up. Brings it down over his back, breaking it and putting him down. With one broken, jagged end, he goes to the fallen big man, drives it down into his chest. The big man's body goes tense, he shakes, both hands clasped around the wood. Then he stills, a drop of blood running from the corner of his mouth. He falls back, eyes still open.

Tom turns. The second man is still down, but he's stirring. Tom stomps a boot down on the base of his neck. The sound of it breaking is as loud as a gunshot in the room, even over the sound of the third man's screams.

He's the only one left, now. He pushes himself back along the ground, his left leg dragging uselessly. The screams die, replaced by panicked coughs and gags. His eyes never leave Tom, closing in on him.

Tom presses a boot just below his dislocated knee, exerts pressure. Before the man can resume screaming, Tom clamps a hand over his mouth, silences him. "Do you want to talk?" he says. "Or do things need to get worse?"

Tom lowers his hand, lets the man speak. His voice shakes. In English, he says, "Fuck you."

Tom sighs. He stands up, takes his boot off the knee. Turns to look back at the door, to check the rest of the room, make sure no one has come running, and he sees Carmen. Sees how she has stepped to this side of the bar now. Sees how her eyes are wide, sees the near-disbelief in her face at what she has just witnessed. "Into the back," Tom tells her.

It takes her a moment to gather herself, but then she nods, hurries past them both and toward the back room. Opens the door. While she does this, Tom reaches down, grabs the last man by his collar, bunches it up in his fist and starts dragging him across the ground toward the door.

The back room is for storage. Shelves with various bottles, as well as cleaning equipment. There are a few kegs stacked in the corner. Tom goes back through into the bar and gets a chair. He sets it down against a wall in the back room, then hauls the man up and sits him down in it. He pulls the man's shirt up over his head and uses it to tie his hands together in front, pulling the knot as tight as it will go. He closes the door that leads into the bar, drags one of the shelves in front of it to block the way. The rear door is still clear. It leads out into an alleyway. At one end of the alley is a brick wall. This is the side that leads out onto the main stretch of road. Anyone who wants to come in the back way will have to take the long way around. Tom has already checked this out on his recon. Directly opposite the rear door, on the side of the building opposite, is a fire escape. When they leave here, they will climb up it. Escape via the roof of the building.

Tom wants to work on their survivor fast, though. He wanted to keep this quiet, but the screaming may have gotten some unwanted attention already. Possibly from the missing bartender, wherever he may be.

Tom stands in front of the injured Perro Loco. The man spits at him. "Tell us where the girls are being taken," Tom says. He doesn't have the time for preamble. Knows it will take a lot to make this man talk, and he wants to get down to business.

The man answers him in Spanish. "*Jodate.*" *Fuck you.*

Tom grabs his knee, squeezes. "Answer my question."

The man's face twists, but he refuses to scream this time. He starts spitting rapid-fire Spanish, too fast for Tom to understand. Tom lets go of his knee, steps back. He turns to Carmen. "You're going to have to translate," he says.

She hesitates. "Do you...do you want me to tell you what he's saying now?" Her expression says it's nothing pleasant. Tom thinks he can hear some references being made to his mother.

"No," Tom says. "I get the gist." He reaches into his pocket, pulls out the box of matches he found on the bar. He pops it open. Makes sure the man can see everything he's doing. He slides out one of the matches. Holds it up in front of the man's face for him to get a good look. "If you talk now, I won't have to waste breath telling you what I'll do with this."

The man is silent. Surly. His lips purse shut.

"Are you aware of how sensitive the skin is beneath your fingernails?" Tom holds the match steady. "People have been exploring it since the medieval times. They'd grip the nails with red-hot pliers and they'd twist. It's called denailing, and it's painful." Tom waits a beat, lets his words sink in. "I don't have any pliers with me. I have matches. If you don't start talking, I'm going to force the bottom of this match under the fingernail of your right index finger, all the way down to the cuticle." Tom pauses, looks into the man's eyes. "And then I'm going to light it, and I'm going to let it burn down. And if you still won't talk, I'll do it to your other nine fingers, and then I'll move on to your ten toes. And if you're still holding out after that? Well. Then we'll *really* get creative."

The man's eyes are wide. He swallows.

In reality, Tom does not have time to go over ten fingers and ten toes. He's hoping to spook the man into talking faster.

The man doesn't, though. Not yet. "Have it your way," Tom says.

He grabs the man by his bound hands, strikes him across the face with his elbow to daze him while he does so. He grips the man's right index finger, as promised. The man tries to curl it, to protect it, but Tom encloses it with his fist and keeps it straight. He holds the matchstick and forces the bottom of it under the nail. It takes some twisting and forcing to make it fit. It gets under. He pushes it in deep. The fingernail cracks. The man is screaming so loud Tom's ears begin to ring.

The match is in place. Tom straightens back up, gives the man space to see his finger, to see what has happened to him.

The man is breathing hard. Carmen is, too. Tom glances at her. She looks like she's going to be sick.

Tom pulls a lighter from his pocket. "I picked this up in Texas," he says. He grabs the hand again, lights the match. "I took it from a dead man."

The man stares as the match burns down, the flame getting closer and closer to the tip of his finger. Tom holds him by the wrist, stopping him from shaking it out.

The man spews something in Spanish. Carmen has to clear her throat before she can translate. "He says he'll answer your questions," she says, speaking fast. "He's begging you to blow the fire out."

Tom looks at him. "I'll blow it out when you talk. Where are you taking the girls?"

Eyes wide, staring at the flame, at his bleeding finger, the man spits his words out. Carmen translates as he goes, hurrying to keep up. "He says they transport them over the border, into Arizona. They hand them off to their American partners."

Tom's eyes have never left the man's. "Who are the Americans?"

"He says he doesn't know," Carmen says.

"I'm not so sure I believe you," Tom says.

"I don't know!" the man says, crying out in English now. He starts crying. "I promise! I don't have anything to do with that – I just know they go to America! I don't know who the Americans are, and I don't know where they send them after that!"

Tom holds his wrist, squeezes it tighter. Lets the match continue to burn. "Are you sure about that?"

"Yes!"

"Tom, he doesn't know," Carmen says. She sounds like she's about to cry, too. "He doesn't know. Stop it now. Put the fire out."

"She believes you," Tom says to the man. He leans in closer, looking deep into his eyes. "I'm not sure I do."

The man's mouth trembles. Spit hangs from the corner of it. Snot runs from his nose. Tears are streaming from his eyes. "No se," he says, likely feeling the heat of the flame now. "I swear, I don't know."

Tom waits. Waits until he can smell flesh beginning to burn.

"Please," the man says.

"Now I believe you," Tom says. He lets go of the man's wrist, pulls out his KA-BAR and stabs him through the chest. He doesn't bother to blow out the match.

Carmen stares at him. She looks like she's seen a ghost.

"Let's go," Tom says.

She shakes her head. "You're a –" She makes a sound like she might be sick. "You're a monster," she says, horrified. She turns, and she flees.

6

The escape route Tom had planned out, up and over the roof of the building behind the bar via the fire escape, goes to hell as Carmen runs away down the back alley. Tom follows, catches up to her, grabs her by the arm before she can escape the end of the alley.

"Get the fuck off of me!" she snaps, snatching her arm back from him. She follows it up with something in aggressive Spanish, again too fast for Tom to comprehend.

Tom holds his hands up. "All right," he says. "I'm sorry I grabbed you, but chances are Los Perros Locos know about all the screaming, and they're coming here now. You knew the escape plan."

"Fuck your escape plan," Carmen says, spittle spraying from her lips. "And fuck you!"

Tom goes to the end of the alleyway. Checks the road and the streets. There's no one coming. Not yet. "Let's go," he says. "We can talk about this somewhere else."

"I'm not going anywhere with you," Carmen says. "You're as bad as *them*."

"Come to the car," Tom says, keeping his voice calm. "We

need to get out of this area right now. You don't want to be around me anymore, fine. We can talk about that in the car. We finish talking and you still feel the same, I'll take you wherever you want to go, and that'll be that. You don't ever have to see me again."

Carmen stares at him. She grinds her jaw, thinking. "Fine," she says, spitting the words through gritted teeth.

They leave the alley, cross the road, head to where Tom has left the car a couple of streets away. Carmen will not walk beside him. She holds back, not wanting to be near him. Tom lets her do what she wants, so long as she keeps up. He looks around as they go, checking the area for Los Perros Locos, or anyone else who looks as though they might want to catch up with them.

They reach the car, and Tom starts driving. They get a couple of blocks between themselves and the bar when Carmen says, "Let me out here."

"We haven't talked yet," Tom says.

"There is nothing you could say that I'd want to hear," she says. "Not after that."

Tom spots a parking lot. He pulls over into it, slides into a space at the back under the shade of a tree. "You weren't expecting that. I get it," he says. "I probably should have prepared you better for what I might have to do."

She snorts.

"When you're dealing with people like this, people who wouldn't think twice about torturing you just for fun, you have to be prepared to go to the same extreme lengths as they are."

She stares at him. "How many people have you killed, Tom?"

He stares back at her. "I don't know," he says. "I stopped keeping count."

"Who are you?" she demands. "And I don't care if you

don't want to talk about it right now. I want to know, *right now*."

Her face is hard. Tom notices how she keeps one hand on the door handle, ready to get out and bolt at any time. "I was US Army," he says. "During my last tour of Afghanistan I rescued some injured men from behind enemy lines and kept them alive on our way back to base, and rather than give me a medal, they recruited me into the CIA. I was part of a black ops team. We operated in extractions, assassinations. Torture."

"But you're not CIA anymore."

"Technically, they could say I never officially was."

Carmen is silent now, digesting his story. "The CIA – they taught you how to do things like that?"

"A lot of it I picked up as I went."

Carmen's mouth twists while she chews on her bottom lip. "I'm starting to think you're more dangerous than the people who took my sister."

"That's a good thing, right?"

"I don't know..." Carmen shakes her head. "I just don't know." She runs her hands down her face, closes her eyes and shakes her head. Tom wonders if she is seeing what he did to the man, how he tortured him. If it is playing over in her mind, over and over. He wonders if it will bring her nightmares.

"How about we make a compromise," Tom says. "Going forward, I'll calm my methods, and in return you won't run off when you see something you don't like."

Carmen takes a deep breath. She's resolved. Has made a decision. "I think it's best you go play hero somewhere else, Tom. The kind of help you're offering, I don't think it's the kind of help I want."

Tom waits a beat. "How are you going to get into America?" he says. "Do you have papers?"

Carmen hesitates.

"No? What are you going to do instead? You know they won't let you over the border without the proper documentation. Are you going to pay a coyote to take you across? Do you really think that's your best course of action?"

"I'll figure something out."

"I'm sure you will. You seem resourceful. You'd gotten pretty far already, before I met you. But what about when you're in America? What then?"

"I'll figure it out. I told you."

Tom doesn't want to let her go alone. He knows that if she does, she'll likely get herself killed. "You asked me why I was in Mexico," he says.

"I asked," Carmen says. "You wouldn't tell."

Tom takes a deep breath. "There was a woman I knew. A woman I loved. She was from Guaymas." He reaches into his pocket, takes out the photograph he's keeping there. He holds it up to Carmen, lets her see. "Her name was Alejandra. She loved someone else, though. Loving that person...it got her killed. I came here with her ashes, to scatter them. It's what she wanted – to come home."

Carmen studies the picture, then looks back at him. Tom returns it to his pocket, next to the Santa Muerte pendant.

"I thought that being here, in her country, I thought that would bring me some kind of peace. I thought, in some way, that it could get me closer to her, even if she's not here anymore."

"And?" Carmen says. "Did it?"

Tom shakes his head. "No. I can't put her to rest, not within myself. She's always going to be there, a big part of me that can't get over the grief of losing her. A big part that can't stop blaming myself for not being there to keep her safe."

"And, what? What's that got to do with me?"

"If I let you go on alone, you *will* get yourself killed. Probably your sister, too. I can't let that happen. You asked me why I'm helping you."

"You answered that one."

"Yes, I did, and what I said was true, but maybe it wasn't the whole truth. Maybe the whole truth is that I look back over my life – the killings, the tortures, and all the rest of it – and I don't see much that I can be proud of. I don't see much of anything that Alejandra would be proud of. Nothing that honors her memory. Nothing that brings down that tally I stopped keeping track of a long time ago."

Carmen leans back in her seat. Her hand slips from the door handle. "You know, I'm not as helpless as you might think."

"I know that," Tom says. "And I'm sure moments will come when I need you to keep me alive, too. We've got a better chance of doing that together."

Carmen nods. She looks reluctant still, though less so than she was before. "You're going to calm things going forward?"

Tom nods.

Carmen sighs. "Okay," she says. She repeats it, louder this time. "Okay. Then let's go to America."

7

The Silver Sonora Boys think they're a bigger deal than they are.

It doesn't take Pedro long to track them down. They're young. Amateurs. He spreads word through the city, tells his contacts to be on the lookout for the SSB. It doesn't take long for word to get back to him. Pedro has eyes throughout Nogales.

They're hiding out in an abandoned tenement building on the outskirts of Nogales. Pedro takes his best men – Castillo, Mendoza, and Moreno, whom he took with him when he left the police – and a half a dozen other foot soldiers to make up the numbers. They watch the building first, get an idea of how the Silver Sonora Boys are guarding it. They barely are. They have a couple of men outside, walking the perimeter, guns obscured under their jackets. Little else.

"They're not utilising the space they have," Castillo says. He stands next to Pedro. They're in the top floor of a building opposite, watching through binoculars. Mendoza and

Moreno are nearby. "They should have guards at the windows, snipers. They should have men on the roof."

"They're amateurs," Pedro says.

The SSB have been attempting to move in on Nogales Cartel territory for the last two years. They think of themselves as a threat, but they're little more than a nuisance. In their heads, they are at war with the Nogales Cartel for control of Nogales itself, but this isn't entirely accurate. They've staged hit-and-run attacks. They've killed off a useful sicario here and there, and they've attempted kidnappings of family members – but the key word is *attempted*. They were not successful, and lost some of their own men in the efforts. And while their attacks on Nogales Cartel headquarters and convoys have been costly and problematic, they've never caused the kind of issues that the Nogales Cartel have been unable to rebound from.

"You remember I was telling you I'd heard one of their newest men was ex-Special Forces?" Castillo says.

Pedro snorts. "You said it yourself – they don't have anything covered. Do you really believe they have an ex-Special Forces in their ranks? Could be he's told them that's what he is, to impress them, but he's a liar. The proof is right in front of us, and it *isn't* staring back at us."

"My point exactly," Castillo says.

"The attack on the motel looked different from their usual M.O.," Mendoza says, stepping up beside them. "*That* looked like the work of a professional. Could be the SSB are improving their tactics. Maybe their Special Forces claimant isn't such a liar after all."

Pedro looks at him. "Well," he says, and lets the word hang for a moment. "We'll find out soon enough, won't we?"

They attack at night. Pedro sends the foot soldiers in first. They take out the guards with ease. Slit their throats to keep it quiet. They get inside the building. Pedro is at the rear. He follows his men in. He hears gunshots, screams. By the time he gets inside, the ground-floor rooms have been cleared. The air smells of gunfire and blood. "Is there anyone else in the building?" Pedro says.

"We're sweeping it now," Moreno says. "We'll know soon enough."

Pedro nods, then heads into the thick of the bloodshed.

There are a dozen men lying dead in the room. After tonight, it looks as though the ranks of the Silver Sonora Boys will have been thinned so drastically they will now be no more than an afterthought.

Pedro can also smell marijuana in the air and can see empty beer and tequila bottles scattered around the room. Some of them have been smashed in the gunfire. The Boys were having a party, it looks like. Enjoying themselves.

They should have been watching their doors, and their windows.

Four of them are still alive, kneeling with their hands clasped atop their heads, AR-15s poking into their backs. Pedro looks the men over, and he smiles at them. He sees how they shake. Sees how sweat runs from their brows.

Pedro doesn't say anything yet. He steps back, and he waits to hear that the rest of the building is clear.

He does not have to wait for long. Mendoza calls down to Castillo via radio, lets him know they've been through the rest of the building. Castillo tells Pedro. Pedro nods. He turns to Moreno. "You have the camera?"

Moreno nods. He pulls it out, ready. He doesn't start recording yet. He'll know when to begin.

Pedro steps in front of the men again. "Well, well," he says. "I had been led to believe one of your men was ex-Special Forces."

The man on the end, his lower lip trembling, catches Pedro's eye and tilts his head toward the man on his right.

He's likely hoping this betrayal will save his life, or at least grant him a quick death. Pedro has no intention of giving him either, not until they've answered his questions.

"You," he says, looking at the man indicated. "It was you, was it? And you managed to survive the massacre, eh?"

The three others are looking at the man now, the one who claimed to be Special Forces. They're realizing for themselves what Pedro already knew – there's nothing special about this man. Never was.

"Exactly what 'Special Force' were you?" Pedro says. The man's mouth opens, closes, opens, closes. He starts to make noises, starts to stammer. "Quiet," Pedro says, without raising his voice. "These idiots might believe whatever lines you fed them, but I will not."

The man's lips clamp together, so tight the blood instantly drains out of them.

Pedro steps back, addresses the four. "Recently, members of Los Perros Locos were killed at one of our motels, and the girls they were guarding were taken away. We've taken restitution for the murders of our allies –" Pedro motions to the dead bodies surrounding them "– and now we want the girls back."

Mendoza returns to the room. Pedro signals to him. "Show them what's hanging from your belt there."

Mendoza steps forward, pulls his machete loose. He holds it in front of the kneeling men's faces.

"Tell me where the girls are," Pedro says, "or we start hurting you, and then we start cutting you into pieces, bit by bit."

One of the men breaks, starts crying out. "We didn't attack any motel!" he says. "We didn't take any of your girls!"

The one who gave away the ex-Special Forces is furiously nodding along, his eyes closed tight.

Pedro steps back and flicks his head, directing the men

standing to the sides of him. They come forward, throw the four prisoners down and set about them with boots and fists.

Pedro walks away, finds a space to sit on a sofa next to a dead Silver Sonora Boy. He inspects the cushion for blood first. There is none. Settled, he looks back to the beating. Moreno has started filming. He's moved in closer, catching the sight of men being kicked in the face and the head, of having their testicles stomped on. He gets up close to capture skin splitting and then gushing blood, and so the audio will pick up on the sounds of bones cracking and breaking. To hear the sounds of these men crying out, screaming, begging for mercy.

Pedro lets this go on for a while. By the time he signals for them to stop, to step back, the prisoners are broken and bleeding. Their faces are swollen, and their eyes are filled with blood.

"Where are the girls?" Pedro says.

None of them answer. They sob, and gasp for breath, and they moan in pain, but none of them speak. Too scared of what their answers may bring them.

Pedro looks at Mendoza. Mendoza stands ready, machete still in hand, squeezing it. Pedro raises a finger. "One at a time," he says. "Piece by piece."

Mendoza shows his teeth in something that might be a smile. He nods, takes a step forward.

Pedro's phone begins to ring.

Mendoza looks at him, an eyebrow raised. "Wait," Pedro says. He answers the phone. It's Gabe. A Perro Loco. Pedro listens as he tells him what has happened at La Perrera. Pedro can feel all eyes in the room on him, waiting, expectant.

"Understood," Pedro says. He hangs up the phone, slides it back into his pocket. He places one hand on the arm of the tattered sofa, prepares to pull himself back to his feet. He takes a deep breath. It feels like the room breathes with him.

Pedro stands, crosses the room to stand in front of the prisoners again. "Gentlemen," he says, "seems you weren't lying. Apologies for disrupting your evening." He turns, goes to leave the room. Passing Mendoza, he nods. Mendoza steps forward, machete raised. Moreno follows him with the camera.

8

Tom and Carmen lie low in a hotel, waiting for night before they attempt to cross the border. They've been to a store, and Tom has bought dark clothes for them. All black. After, they went to a supermarket and bought food and water, brought them back to the hotel to eat and drink while they rest and wait.

Tom stands by the window, watching the street below. Evening comes, and the daylight begins to fade. It gets cooler. The streetlamps start to come on, and neon signs in the windows of the businesses opposite.

Carmen is behind him, cross-legged on the bed. The dark clothes they have bought are spread out on the bed in front of her. She clears her throat. It's been a while since they last spoke. Since the car, when he persuaded her not to continue on her own.

"You were in the army?" she says.

"I told you that," Tom says without turning away from the window.

"I'm trying to make conversation," Carmen says. She blows out exasperated air. "Why'd you join?"

Tom turns around now. There is a table next to the window, with two chairs. He pulls one of them out and sits down. He can face Carmen, but he can also keep one eye on the street below. "I was young," he says. "I wasn't sure what else to do. My father…he's a survivalist, and he raised my brother and me to be survivalists, too. We spent all our weekends at it. We lived in New Mexico, and sometimes he'd drive us out into the desert and leave us there to find our way home. Sometimes he dropped us off together, and sometimes he dropped us off separate, so we'd have to do it alone."

"That sounds awful," Carmen says.

Tom smiles, like these are fond memories. "Not really," he says. "Dad wouldn't have done that if he didn't think we'd be able to handle ourselves. Anyway, to answer your question, after our upbringing, it felt like a natural progression to join the army. I already had some training for it."

"Where was your mother during all this?"

"She died when I was nine. Cancer. It was just us and Dad after that."

"Oh, I'm so sorry." Carmen grimaces. She fingers the black sweater that she will be wearing in a few hours. "You have a brother?" she says.

Tom nods, but doesn't elaborate.

"What's he called?"

"Anthony."

"And did he join the army, after your survivalist upbringing?" She grins.

Tom shakes his head. "No… Anthony – Anthony took a different path. He's younger than me, and I think he took our mother's death harder. I don't think he ever got over it, not really. And I think a part of him resented how our father raised us. He got older, and he started to rebel. He fell in with bad crowds. He'd get in trouble." Tom shrugs. "We haven't spoken in a while. He's not very happy with me right now."

"Oh? How come?"

Tom thinks of Alejandra. Of her stolen and scattered ashes. Ashes that also contained Anthony's unborn child.

"It's complicated," he says. He changes the subject. "You haven't told me what you do."

Carmen smiles. "I'm a teacher."

Tom raises an eyebrow. "Oh, really?"

"Yup. Elementary school. I get them while they're still young."

"That's very impressive," Tom says. "Where do they think you are right now?"

"They know my sister was taken," Carmen says. "I'm on sabbatical. In all honesty, I'm not really thinking about my job right now."

"That's fair. Do you like it, though?"

"I love it." She smiles. Tom can see the sadness in it – the sadness that she wishes she were still teaching now, that nothing had changed. The hope that one day things will go back to normal. "There's nothing like it," she says. "And I want to get back there, back to my students and my old life – but I'm trying not to think about those things. Not while I'm here."

"I'm sure your students miss you, too," Tom says. "I'm sure you're a very good teacher."

"Well, it certainly hasn't taught me how to put matchsticks under a man's fingernails, but it's satisfying in its own way."

Tom smirks. "You're very brave, coming after your sister like this."

"Brave, or stupid," Carmen says. "There's a very thin line. I just couldn't sit by and wait and just *hope* for news of her. I had to do something, even if it was the dumb thing." She continues playing with the sweater. She chews on her lip. "It's not the first time I've had to get Rosa out of trouble. It is the *worst* situation she's found herself in, though."

"I assume she doesn't have a sensible job shaping young minds."

Carmen smiles that same sad smile. "No, not quite. Rosa has always... She's always been the wilder one. Perhaps like your brother. She's never really held down a job – she drifts from bartender to waitress to secretary. I don't know what she's planning on doing with herself."

"She sounds a lot like Anthony."

Carmen nods. "I just know that whatever her plans may be, I'm pretty damn sure sex trafficking and prostitution don't figure into them." She falls silent, looking down at her fingers twisting up the sweater. She lets go of it and looks up at Tom. "Let me ask you something," she says.

"Sure."

"About Alejandra."

Tom pauses. "Okay."

"Do you keep that picture of her in your pocket all the time?"

"I try to," Tom says. "Along with a pendant she gave me."

Carmen raises an eyebrow. She's unaware of the pendant.

"Santa Muerte," Tom says. "Alejandra said it would keep me safe."

"She must have cared for you a great deal."

Tom doesn't answer this, but he hopes so.

Carmen continues. "Aren't you worried her picture will get damaged, that it will fade? Especially with the heat here. The sweat of your leg could soak through your pocket, ruin it."

"Perhaps," Tom says. "But the truth is I don't really need to look at it to see her face. It's always in here." He taps his temple. "I just like to keep the picture as a piece of her, just like the pendant. More than that, I found out the hard way not so long ago how easy it can be for the things that are important to you to be stolen if you don't keep them close enough."

Carmen hesitates before she asks her next question. "Do I remind you of her?"

Tom cocks his head. "How do you mean?"

"Do you see her in me, is that why you're helping? I know you said you wanted to honor her memory, but I can't shake the feeling it's perhaps something more than that. We're both Mexican. We have similar hair, similar eyes. Perhaps there's more to your assistance."

Tom looks at her. He pictures Alejandra in his head, compares the two. "No," he says. "I meant what I said. You don't look anything like her, Carmen. And you're not her. I know that. You don't remind me of her."

"Okay, good," Carmen says. "Because I'd hate to think you were fetishizing me in some kind of Alfred Hitchcock-*Vertigo* way."

Tom can't tell if she's joking, but he laughs regardless. "Hand on heart, I am not fetishizing you. I'm not going to ask you to change your hair or your clothes, and when we're in America, we're not going to go diving in San Francisco Bay."

Carmen raises an eyebrow, spreads her arms out over the black clothing spread on the bed. She's laughing, though.

"Alejandra did not dress in all black to take part in clandestine border crossings," Tom says. "And as I recall, didn't it turn out the Kim Novak character was the same woman in two different guises?"

"It's been a long time since I saw the movie," Carmen says. "I didn't have you pegged as a movie buff, Tom."

"I'm full of surprises," Tom says. "You do remind me of someone, though."

"Oh?"

"Her name was Sally Blevins. She had some trouble with her sister, too."

"And what happened?"

Tom turns his face to the window, keeps an eye on a car with blacked-out windows as it passes below. It keeps going, turns out to be nothing. "It's a long story," he says, turning back.

Carmen holds out her empty hands. "We have time," she says.

9

It's late when Pedro reaches La Perrera. By this time the bar is usually busy, filled to bursting with members of Los Perros Locos. The music is pumping loud, and the drinks are flowing. Pedro has only been a few times before. The bar is not his idea of a good time. Los Perros Locos living up to their name. They are wild. They're as prone to fight each other if no one else is available. The last time he was here he saw them brawling, smoking crack. He saw some of them fucking women in the corners, in open view of everyone else.

The bar is not so lively tonight. It is silent, and it is mostly empty save for the three dead bodies inside. They've been laid down together side by side in the center of the room. One of them has signs of torture on his hand. Pedro kneels down beside him, sees the remnants of a matchstick poking out from under his fingernail. The thought of it makes him shiver, and clench his fists.

Pedro has brought Castillo with him. Gabe is waiting for them in the bar, standing with the bartender, the only other signs of life present. "Where were you?" Pedro says to the bartender.

"I was upstairs," he says. "Sleeping."

"And you didn't hear anything that went on down here? That man was tortured. I doubt he was quiet while it was happening."

"I wear earplugs," the bartender says. "It can get noisy in here, and I don't want to be disturbed."

"You must have had them in deep," Pedro says.

"I'm a heavy sleeper. Sometimes noise gets through, sometimes it doesn't. This morning it didn't."

"This happened this morning?" Pedro says, turning to Gabe.

Gabe's face is tattooed with *Los Perros Locos*, in gothic scrawl. Surrounding it are small guns and knives, and a couple of teardrops under each eye. "These are our men," he says, jabbing a finger at the ground. "He killed them here, and he killed them at the motel, and we want his fucking blood." Gabe's eyes are ablaze. His jaw works, his teeth grinding together.

"You should have called me," Pedro says.

"We called you as soon as we found what had happened at the motel," Gabe says. "And what good did that do us? You're still looking. We wanted a chance to find him ourself. I called you..." He breathes hard. His shoulders heave. "I called you because we can't."

Pedro's eyes narrow. "You keep saying *he* and *him*. Do you know something I don't?"

The corner of Gabe's mouth twists upward. It could be a smile, but it looks too wicked. "There's a camera."

"There is?"

Gabe points behind the bar. "You won't see it. It's well hidden. We keep it pointed at the door, in case of events like this. If someone comes at us, we want a good look at who it is."

Pedro's mind races. "You have footage? You know who it was?"

Gabe nods.

"And it was just one man? Alone, he did all this? Killed three Perros Locos – tortured one of them?"

Gabe and the bartender exchange glances. "Not totally alone, no," Gabe says. "There was a girl with him, but she held back. He did all of this" – he waves his hands around – "by himself."

Pedro looks at Castillo. Castillo raises his eyebrows. "Show us the footage," Pedro says.

Gabe and the bartender lead him behind the bar, up the stairs and into the apartment where the bartender lives. They go into a small room where the cables from the camera come through the wall and connect to a television. The screen is paused. It shows the doors into the bar, both closed.

"Bring them up," Gabe says to the bartender.

The man sits down, hits play. They watch as the door opens, as a man steps inside and looks the room over. Then he disappears off to the left. He comes back a moment later, opens the door again and ushers a woman inside. He hides her in the room to the left of the entrance. The man locks the door.

"Pause on their faces," Pedro says.

The bartender does.

Pedro looks at Castillo. "I've never seen either of them," Castillo says.

Nor has Pedro. "A gringo," he says. "The girl is a Latina, though." He turns to Gabe. "And you think this is the man who attacked the motel?"

"The Silver Sonora Boys admit to it?" Gabe says.

"No."

"No, and I'll bet you were real rough asking them too, right?"

Pedro nods.

"Adds up," Gabe says. "I don't know what he wants from us, and I've got no one here to ask about it, either."

Pedro thinks of the tortured man, his index finger blackened by a burning match. "I need to make a call," he says. "Castillo, get a printout of their picture. We'll need it."

Pedro leaves the bar, goes out to his car. He calls Miguel.

"Is this good news?" Miguel says.

"Not entirely," Pedro says. "But perhaps a little."

"Speak, then."

"First, the Silver Sonora Boys are done for. You'll get the footage soon, and then so will everyone else."

"That *sounds* like good news," Miguel says.

"They had nothing to do with what happened at the motel."

"Mm," Miguel says. "That's not so good."

"There's been an attack at La Perrera," Pedro continues. "Three of them have been killed. Looks like one of them was tortured. There's a camera, though. We're assuming the guy who hit La Perrera is the same who took out the guards at the motel."

"*The* guy?" Miguel interrupts. "Just one?"

"That's what it looks like. A gringo. There's a girl with him, Latina, but she doesn't get involved."

"One of the girls taken from the motel?"

"I don't know. Maybe. There's none of our men left alive who would remember what those girls looked like."

Miguel is silent. "One man..." he says, letting the words hang in the air. "And how many of Los Perros Locos has he single-handedly killed now? Seven? Eight?"

"Something like that."

Miguel chuckles. "I thought they were supposed to be

tough. I took them on because of their reputation. Now they're being picked off by one man – a gringo, no less? We may have to review our relationship with them. Anyway, you have footage of this man? And the girl with him?"

"Yes," Pedro says. "Castillo is getting it now."

"Circulate the picture. Send it to all of our contacts, both in Mexico and the US. Find out if anyone recognizes them, knows who they are. Find out why he's doing this, what he wants. And then find *him*."

"Yes."

"And then you know what to do."

"Of course."

Miguel hangs up. Doesn't bother saying goodbye. Pedro puts the phone away, looks up toward the front of La Perrera to see Castillo emerging. He gets into the passenger seat, holds up the image he has printed out.

"Little fuzzy," Castillo says, "but clear enough."

Pedro nods. "Make copies and spread them out." Pedro starts the car's engine. "Let's find this motherfucker."

10

It's dark. Close to midnight. The area near the border fence is quiet. The buildings are dark; the road is quiet. Tom and Carmen are wearing the all-black clothes they bought earlier. They don't head straight to the fence. They hold back. Tom watches. There is a border patrol Jeep on the other side, in America. He times its passings. It crawls by every ten minutes, a flashlight hanging out of the passenger side, shining through the fence into Mexico.

"How long are we going to wait?" Carmen says.

"One more pass," Tom says. They crouch low down the side of a building, where the beam of the flashlight doesn't reach them. Tom has been waiting to see if anything changes in the routine. If the ten minutes shortens, for example, or if another Jeep appears from the other direction. It hasn't happened yet.

"Feels like we do a lot of waiting around," Carmen says.

"Necessary waiting around," Tom says. "Never rush into anything. Not if you can help it."

Tom wears his backpack. It has his usual burner phones, his Beretta and ammo in it, but it also contains their change of clothes. They've left the car behind, parked at the hotel. They traveled here on foot. They have everything they need. If it didn't fit in the backpack, it got left behind.

They wait. Ten minutes pass. The Jeep returns. Makes its sweep. Tom leans out at the corner of the building, watches as it continues on down its route. He moves. Ducks low and runs to the fence. Coils of barbed wire are looped on and around the top of it. Tom climbs, KA-BAR out. He starts cutting through where they are bound to the fence. Tears coils of it loose, pushes them aside so he's able to continue climbing. He reaches the top, a pathway cleared behind him. There is no barbed wire on the American side. He drops down into Nogales, Arizona. Stays by the fence while he waits for Carmen. Sees her crossing toward him, mimicking his run. He checks the time. Seven minutes have passed while he worked his way through the barbed wire.

Carmen climbs. She reaches the top, prepares to swing her legs over. One goes wide, catches in the barbed wire. "*Shit!*" She tugs on it, tries to tear the loop free from her trouser leg.

Tom checks the time. It's been nine minutes. The Jeep will be returning.

He starts climbing up the fence, meets her at the top. Knife in hand once again. "Hold it still." Carmen does as he says, raising her captured leg so he can reach it. He cuts the barbs loose, tears through the fabric of her pants to get her leg free. He can see, in the moonlight, where some of the barbs have scraped against her shin and calf. She's bleeding.

"The Jeep!" Carmen says.

Tom doesn't bother to look. He knows it's coming. It's due.

They drop back down into America together as the sound of the Jeep's engine gets louder, racing toward them. Its main beams come on, capturing them in its glare. A voice comes through a speaker. "Halt!" it says. "Stay right there!"

"*Run*," Tom says.

They burst away from the fence, staying together. Carmen sticks by his side. The cuts in her leg aren't deep enough to slow her down. The Jeep roars after them. Tom races for an alleyway he spotted when he dropped down the first time. It's too narrow for a vehicle. They reach the darkness there and keep running. The sound of the Jeep screeches to a stop behind them, one of its doors opening and slamming as one of the men gets out to pursue on foot. The Jeep roars back into life, screeches away, hoping to cut them off at the end of the alley.

Tom hears the footsteps of the man behind, pounding down the alleyway after them. Tom reaches a corner, presses himself up against the wall. Listens as the man gets near. He's nearly upon them. Tom sticks his arm out, knocks the man down. He lands hard on his back. Tom hears how he gasps. The air has been driven out of him by the impact. He rolls side to side, trying to push himself up. Tom leaves him. The man is just doing his job. He doesn't need to hurt him any further than he already has. By the time he's able to get to his feet, they should already be gone.

Carmen has kept running. Tom catches up. Grabs her by the arm and drags her to one side as the end of their current alleyway opens out onto a main road. "They'll have called for backup," Tom says, both of them breathing hard. "We need to clear this area as soon as possible."

"What do we –" Carmen swallows, gasps, continues "– what do we do?"

Tom points. "Go to the end of the alley," he says. "The Jeep is coming around. It'll be there soon. Go out onto the road and give yourself up."

"*What?*"

Tom places his hands on her shoulders. "Trust me." He

turns, runs in the opposite direction, hoping that Carmen really does trust him enough to do as he has said.

He reaches the main road at the other end of the alleyway, peers out. It's clear. He can hear the Jeep's engine. It's heading toward where he sent Carmen. He follows, reaches the corner building, peers around. Carmen is in the middle of the road, hands raised in surrender, eyes squinting against the headlights pointing right at her.

The Jeep slams to a stop. The driver's door opens, and the border patrol agent gets out, gun raised. "Hold it right there! Don't fuckin' move!"

Carmen stands very still with the gun pointed at her.

"Where's your friend?" the agent says, creeping forward. "Huh? There were two of you. Where's your friend?"

Carmen says something in Spanish.

"Huh? Speak English, damn it! Where is he?"

Carmen keeps talking in Spanish. Keeps him distracted.

The man steps forward, waving the gun. He's getting worked up. "On the fuckin' ground, beaner! On the fuckin' ground, *now*! I swear to Christ, I'll put a fuckin' bullet in you!"

Tom creeps up behind him. Gets close enough without making a sound, then moves fast. He comes in from the side. In a split second, he spots the gun is a Glock 19M. He grabs the gun in both hands and pushes the barrel to the side, away from Carmen. The gun goes off. The bullet hits a wall to the side of the alley exit, tears a chunk out of it. Tom feels the slider hot in his hand now, unable to eject the spent cartridge. He reaches down, presses the button for the magazine release. Feels its sharp edge dig into the pad of his finger as he presses down. The magazine hits the ground with a clatter.

The border patrol agent looks up at Tom in alarm. Hands busy, Tom headbutts him. The agent stumbles back, releasing his empty Glock. A hand goes to his face, to where Tom's forehead connected with the bridge of his nose. Tom follows through, brings the handle of the gun down over the top of his head. Again, the blow isn't hard enough to knock the man out, but it's enough to put him down. Keep him incapacitated. Tom throws the empty gun aside. The agent groans on the ground.

"In the Jeep," he says to Carmen. She drops her arms and runs over, dives into the passenger side. Tom gets behind the wheel, and they speed away from the scene.

11

Gerry Davies is alone in his office. It's lunchtime, and he's sitting back in his chair, eating a meatball sub. He doesn't go to the canteen anymore. Feels like he barely leaves his office. Dares not to part from his computer. Even at the end of the day, he takes his laptop home with him, leaves it switched on at all hours. There is an alarm on it, turned up loud.

The alarm begins to sound.

Gerry gives a start, almost falls back in his chair. He drops the sub back into its wrapper, then sucks the sauce from his fingers. The alarm continues to sound, shrilly ringing in his ears.

"God fuckin' damnit," Gerry says, wiping his hands on his trousers now. Doesn't want to get sticky fingers all over his keyboard.

Finally, he's able to hit mute. There is only one reason why the alarm would sound. Gerry checks it, sees if it's anything worthy of note. He's had a few false alarms.

He sees the picture that has been flagged. His eyes go wide.

Gerry runs from his office, laptop clutched under his arm. He races down to Senior Special Agent Eric Thompson's office, pauses outside to catch his breath. It takes longer than it should – his nerves are fraught. It takes him a while to get his composure back. People passing him in the corridor eye him curiously. There are a few raised brows. Gerry nods at them, forces a smile, tries to act like everything is all right despite his flushed cheeks and the sweat on his brow. While he waits, he takes a piece of gum from his pocket, starts chewing furiously. Eric will not be happy if he turns up with food in his teeth and his breath smelling of meatballs. Eric Thompson is a fastidious man. Gerry makes sure to tuck his shirt in before he knocks on the door.

"Come," Eric says.

Gerry swallows hard, grits his teeth. He steps inside. Eric is behind his desk. He doesn't raise his head, not at first. He's signing some paperwork. There are stacks of folders neatly aligned in front of him. He lifts a sheet, signs the next page. He slots it inside a nearby folder, then adds this one to one of the piles. Makes sure it's straight. Only then does he see who has come to his office. He looks Gerry over, tilts his head.

"I got a hit," Gerry says, realizing as he speaks how breathless he still is.

"Oh?" Eric raises both eyebrows. "Close the door. Take a seat."

Gerry sits down, places his laptop on the desk and opens it up. He notices how the action disrupts some of the folder stacks on Eric's desk, and nearly upends a pot of pens. Eric glares at this. Gerry pretends he doesn't notice, hopeful that all will be forgiven and forgotten once Eric sees the footage.

"This just came through," he says, turning the laptop around and hitting play.

Eric watches. Gerry knows what he sees – footage taken from the dashboard of a Jeep. Split screen: one of the cameras showing inside the Jeep, the two agents; and the other showing outside, through the windshield. A man and a woman climbing over a border fence. They run from the approaching vehicle. They escape down an alley. One of the agents gives chase. The Jeep continues on. There's nothing to see.

Eric looks up. "Is all this necessary?"

"It's literally just come through," Gerry says. "I came straight here. I knew you'd want to see it. I haven't had a chance to edit it down."

The Jeep comes to a stop. There's a woman in the middle of the road, hands raised. The driver gets out, gun pointed at her. Whatever happens next is off camera. There's a gunshot. Then, the woman drops her arms, starts running toward the Jeep. Someone gets in behind the wheel. Eric leans forward. The Jeep drives away. The man notices the camera on the dash. The woman asks him what he's doing as he tears it free, killing the feed.

Eric begins to smile, and Gerry knows the footage has ended. He turns the laptop around, rewinds it to when the man and the woman are inside the Jeep. He pauses it on their faces, turns it back to Eric. "This is the first alert I've had on the facial recognition I set up for Tom Rollins in about three months or so. This footage was relayed back to the border patrol headquarters down there in Nogales, Arizona, and the software picked up on it."

Eric is staring at the screen, the small smile still playing over his lips. "Tom Rollins," he says. "Returned at last." Tom has grown a beard, and his hair is longer, but it's him. Eric would recognize him anywhere. He's been staring at his picture and reading up on his past activities for the last six months, ever since he foiled an attack on a synagogue in Dallas.

Eric looks up. "You said this was Arizona?"

Gerry nods. "Nogales. Looks like they came over from Nogales, Mexico."

"Who's the girl?"

"I don't know. Is she important? I could probably find out."

"Do that," Eric says. "It could help us. Forewarned is forearmed."

Gerry nods, goes to stand, to pick up his laptop.

Eric stops him. "Print this picture," Eric says. "What he looks like now, and the girl. I want a copy. When you get back to your office, find out who she is and continue tracing their movements. I want to know where they are at all times."

"I'll try my best," Gerry says, dreading what he has to say next, "but Tom is aware we're watching out for him. He's avoided us for this long."

Eric runs his tongue around the inside of his mouth. "Set up facial recognition for the girl, too," he says. "Tom may be savvy about covering himself, but the girl perhaps not. And if they've crossed together, chances are they're traveling together. She could lead us to him." Eric looks at her again, on the screen. "Seems he has a thing for Mexican women, doesn't it?"

Gerry frowns, doesn't understand.

"Never mind," Eric says, waving him away with a flick of his wrist. "You know what you need to do, so leave me now. I need to make a phone call."

12

Tom and Carmen didn't go far with the border patrol Jeep. It wasn't exactly inconspicuous, covered as it was in its agency logo. Tom drove it into a ditch, then burned it out in order to destroy any trace of them from inside the vehicle.

They're hiding out in a hotel now. They've changed back into their regular clothes, the all-black ensembles dropped into a dumpster at the side of the building.

Tom sits by the window, keeps an eye out for cop cars, or border patrol. "It's hot for us here," he says. "I didn't spot that camera fast enough. They'll have our faces."

Carmen sits on the edge of the bed, leaning forward. "So what do we do?"

"We can't leave Nogales without checking it out first. Rosa could still be here, and if she's not, there should still be a trail, telling us where she's gone."

Carmen is silent, chewing on her lip.

"So we'll wait 'til dark," Tom says.

"Feels like we're always waiting for dark."

"It's a good cover. It's also a necessity – we're going to have to talk to streetwalkers, and they aren't exactly renowned for being easy to find in the middle of the day."

Carmen swallows. Tom knows what she's thinking. She's worrying about her sister, about where she could be and what she is going through.

Tom keeps talking, keeps her mind occupied. In forming plans, they're being proactive. Being so will keep Carmen distracted. Keep her from overthinking Rosa's predicament, and fearing the worst.

"We'll go to brothels, too," Tom says. "We'll ask questions, see if anyone knows anything. Hey, we might get lucky."

Carmen raises her face, looks hopeful. "You think so?"

Tom does not. Not really. "Sure," he says, but he knows it's unlikely the cartel is transporting girls from Nogales, Mexico, just to keep them in Nogales, Arizona.

"She could be close by," Carmen says. "She could be near us right now, and we don't even know it."

"Could be," Tom says. He watches the road and remembers the last time he did the same thing in Mexico, not more than twenty miles away from where he now sits. He has not been in America for a few months now. This is his homecoming. When Cindy had sent him the papers containing his new fake identity, he hadn't expected he'd make his return by climbing over a barbed-wire fence and then being pursued by the border patrol.

"We might have to track down whoever the cartel's US contacts are," he says. "If we don't get lucky and find her here, and we have to go further afield, it's going to be handy to know who to ask."

"*Ask?*" Carmen says.

"In the nicest way possible," Tom says.

"No matchsticks this time," Carmen says. "Never again. I'm not sure that's an image I'll ever get out of my head." Her mouth twists, and she clenches both fists, like she can feel the pain she witnessed. "Where are they?" she says. "Do you still have them?"

"I've got them," Tom says. "If I come into possession of something that might prove useful, I keep hold of it. That's why I have a lighter even though I don't smoke."

"I heard you say you took that lighter off a dead man," Carmen says. "Did you kill him?"

"Not that one," Tom says. "Found him that way." He sits up in the chair, stretches his back. "We're going to have to cover a lot of ground," he says. "We're going to need another car." He stands, looks down onto the road again. "I'm going to go out. I shouldn't be too long. Maybe an hour." He grabs his bag before he goes. It's on the bedside table.

"What if they come looking for me here?" Carmen says.

Tom knows she's talking about the border patrol. About cops. He shakes his head. "They don't know we're here," he says. "If they did, they would've turned up a long time ago now."

Tom shoulders his backpack, reaches for the door handle.

"What are you going to do?" Carmen says. "Are you going to steal a car?"

Tom looks back at her. "No," he says. "I'm going to buy one."

13

Rosa still does not know where exactly she is, but by now she is fairly sure she is in America. She doesn't get to see much, but what little she *does* see and the accents she hears seem only to further confirm her suspicions.

She and the other girls who were picked out by Ms. Snow have been moved somewhere new. Before they left they were given clothes to wear – gray tracksuit bottoms and baggy gray sweaters. No underwear, no bras. Dirty, scuffed sneakers that looked as though they had been worn dozens of times already. Sacks were placed over their heads, their ankles and wrists were bound, and they were stuffed into the back of a truck and driven. It felt like they were driving for a long time, but in the dark, with the rhythm of the vehicle, Rosa felt herself drifting in and out of sleep. When they arrived wherever they are now, the cable ties on their ankles were cut and they were led inside, rough hands on the insides of their arms. Rosa has bruises in the meat of both biceps, close to her elbows.

They're in a room now. It's nicer than the basement, at

least. The air is clearer. It does not stink. There are two king-size beds that the girls are able to share to sleep. The window, however, is barred, and the door is locked from the outside. Meals are brought to them twice a day – lunchtime, and in the evening. The portions are never very big. They're made up mostly of vegetables, and a couple of slices of ham. Sometimes they get half a boiled egg, too. Likely the people holding them captive do not want them to put on weight while locked up in a room where they can't get any exercise.

The men who bring the food do not wear masks. They're white, and the little they say is in English.

The girl Rosa shares her bed with is called Juana. Rosa recognizes her from when they were lined up in front of Ms. Snow. Rosa wonders where they took her from. She was not in the motel room with her back in Nogales.

Juana does not speak English. On the rare occasion the men bringing food start barking orders, Rosa has to translate for her.

"I think we're in America," Juana whispers, in the dark while they lie in bed. The girls in the other bed are sleeping. Neither of them snore, but Rosa can hear their deep breathing.

"I think so, too," Rosa says.

"Where do you think they've taken us?" Juana says.

"I don't know," Rosa says. They both keep their voices low, knowing there's more than likely a guard outside the door, and for all they know, he might understand Spanish. They don't want him listening in. "I fell asleep in the truck. I lost track of time."

Juana giggles, though there's not much humor in it. "Me too," she says. "This place…apart from the bars on the windows, it feels like a hotel."

Rosa agrees. She's wondered, in the few days they've been kept here so far, what the rest of the building looks like.

There's nothing to see out the barred window, nothing that gives away what kind of building they're in or where they actually are. It's facing a brick wall.

"What are they...?" Juana trails off. Rosa thinks she knows what she's going to ask, but struggles to think how she could be so naïve. "What are they going to do with us?"

Rosa pauses before she answers. She's lying on her back. Juana is on her side, facing her. Rosa rolls now, so they're face-to-face. "Juana," she says, "how old are you?"

Juana has a baby face, but Rosa knows such looks can be deceiving. However, Juana hesitates.

"Juana?"

"I'm seventeen," she says, biting her lip.

"How did they take you?"

"I was at a bar. I had...I had a fake ID." She looks miserable, regretting what she has done.

"Where were you?"

"Obrera."

"Is that where you live?"

Juana nods. "I wasn't even far from home, not really. Just a few blocks. I think they picked me up when I left the bar. I was drunk. I... I don't really remember anything."

Rosa knows that it wouldn't make a difference if the cartel had known what age Juana really is. This is probably the first time anyone has asked her. "What do you *think* they're going to do with us, Juana?" Rosa says. She doesn't mean to sound harsh, but she doesn't know how else to tell the girl what is happening.

Juana doesn't answer. She lowers her eyes, and Rosa knows she already has a good idea.

"Have you...?" Rosa searches for the right words. "Have you ever been with anyone before? A man? Or a woman, perhaps?"

Juana doesn't look up. She shakes her head a little, and a tear falls from her eye.

Rosa reaches out, takes her in her arms. She holds her close, squeezes her against her body. Juana buries her wet face into her chest, her sobs muffled against her skin.

The next day, the men come into the room earlier than the usual mealtimes. There's two of them. Neither of them are carrying food. Instead, they carry guns. "Stand up," one of the men says. "Line up against the wall." He points with his weapon.

The girls do as they're told. They stand in front of the barred window. Juana stays close to Rosa. She's trembling. She reaches out, grabs Rosa's hand. Rosa locks her fingers through Juana's. Keeps their entwined fingers hidden behind their bodies.

The men stare at them. It feels like minutes tick by. Nothing happens. The door to the room remains open. Rosa can't see much of the hallway outside. She sees a dirty carpet, and a wall with a stain on it.

Then someone else comes into the room. Rosa recognizes her. The woman who picked them out, took them as her own. Rosa hasn't seen her since she was selected.

The woman looks them over. She's wearing a black dress with tights, high heels that make her as tall as the men with the guns standing either side of her, and the same fox-fur scarf Rosa first saw her in. There is a sour look about her face, like she was sucking on a lemon before she entered the room.

"My name is Shelley Snow," she says, the same authority in her tone that Rosa remembers from the last time. "You shall call me Ms. Snow, if you need to call me at all. You work for me now."

Rosa feels Juana's grip tighten.

Shelley Snow begins to pace up and down in front of the girls, like an army general inspecting her troops. "You will commence your employment here in this hotel," she says. "You will be broken in here, and I'll see what you're made of."

She looks at Juana when she says this. Rosa hears how Juana stifles a whimper. Sees out the corner of her eye the way she stands straight, trying to look strong. "If I am impressed by your work, you will move up the ranks. I like to rank my girls into tiers. The work you do here will determine where you rank. Will you become one of my favorites, and be rewarded accordingly, and treated accordingly? Or are you simply here to make up the numbers and be visited hourly by every Tom, Dick, and Harry off the street?"

She stops pacing in front of Rosa, looks her in the face with a small smile at the corner of her mouth. Rosa avoids eye contact. She sees the smile, though. Sees how the earlier bitterness is gone now. Instead, it has been replaced by hunger.

"I feel, as I look you over now," Shelley Snow says, "that I already know into which tiers you are all going to fall." She's still in front of Rosa, still staring at her. "I'd like to be pleasantly surprised." She steps forward, right in front of Rosa now. Rosa flinches. Shelley notices it, and her hungry smile widens. She reaches out, strokes a finger down the side of Rosa's face, then along her jaw. "My, aren't you a pretty one," she says. "I have such high hopes for you."

Rosa closes her eyes, does not answer. Juana squeezes her hand again, this time offering comfort rather than being in search of it.

Shelley turns away, starts leaving the room. She stops by her guards, speaks to one of them. "Get them cleaned up and into some better clothes," she says. "It's time to put them to work."

Shelley leaves. She doesn't close the door. It remains open.

The men usher them out of the room, lead them down

the hall. One of them is at the front, occasionally turning and walking backwards to keep an eye on them. The other is at the rear, making sure they don't try to fall out of line.

Up close, walking on it, the hallway carpet isn't as bad as Rosa had first thought. It's blood red in color, and thick. If she were barefoot, it would probably feel quite comfortable, and warm. There are patches where it looks as though things have been spilled, and even a few spots where it looks like cigarettes have been dropped, their flame burning into the fibers before they were either plucked up or stomped out.

The doors down either side of the hallway are all closed. Rosa can hear that they are not all empty. She can hear what is happening inside them, too. The sounds make her stomach sink. Make her heart pound, and her jaw clench. Juana is behind her. She cannot see if Juana hears them too, but assumes she must be able to. Can't begin to imagine the fear she is feeling. The dread that will be building in the pit of her stomach.

The guards take them to a bathroom at the end of the hall. There's a shower. They start the water running, and tell them to strip down. The guards watch them as they do so. They shove each of the girls under the water one by one. The first girl shrieks. The water is still cold. By the time Rosa gets under, the stream is lukewarm.

"Be sure to clean behind your ears," one of the guards says, leering, close to her. "And between your legs."

When she's out of the water, she's handed a dirty towel to dry herself with. Then she's led away, wrapped only in the towel, by a new guard she did not notice arrive. The girls are separated now. Juana is left behind, in the bathroom still. Her turn under the water.

The new guard escorts Rosa to a room, opens the door and motions her inside. There's a dress laid out on the bed, and a garment so thin and small Rosa isn't sure if it qualifies as underwear. "Get dressed," the guard says. "You'll have company soon."

Rosa hesitates. "My...my hair's still wet." She doesn't know why she says it. Doesn't know why it's the first thing that comes into her head.

The guard shrugs. "He won't care, and neither do I." He stares into her eyes, makes no attempt to look at her naked body barely covered by the towel. "I'm sure Ms. Snow made it very clear to you how she wants things to be, but just in case it didn't get through, I'm going to make it extra clear. Behave yourself while you're in here. Do what's asked of you, anything and everything, with no complaint. That clear?" He doesn't give her a chance to answer. "And put some fucking effort in. Here's a tip for you – some of the girls who come here don't make any effort. Like they think that might get them off the hook or something, get them cut loose. Doesn't work like that. You don't put the effort in, we'll just find ways to make it so you do."

Rosa is silent. She has to remember to keep breathing.

"Now get dressed," the guard says, then smirks to himself and adds, "Not that it'll be staying on for very long." He starts to close the door. "I'll be right outside," he says. "I'll hear everything, so don't go trying any funny shit."

The door closes. Rosa stares at it. She tears her eyes away long enough to look down at the dress. It's plain and black, and looks as if it will fit about as well, and cover her as much, as the underwear.

She wants to cry, but she doesn't. She can't. Tears won't help her, not here, not in a place like this.

14

Tom and Carmen cruise the nighttime streets in the car Tom has bought. It's an old Ford, faded silver in color. There are specks of rust on the doors and along the rocker panel. It was cheap, and it's inconspicuous.

They look for girls. Find where the streetwalkers congregate and park down the road from them, and they watch.

"She's not one of them," Carmen says.

"Be patient," Tom says.

"I get real tired of hearing you say that."

"And I get real tired of having to repeat it." Tom grins without turning to her, his eyes never leaving the gaggle of girls who stand on the street corner. Some of them stand together, smoking cigarettes and talking. Others are more proactive, standing at the edge of the sidewalk and popping their hips at the cars that pass by, winking at them, licking their lips. A couple are standing back from the others, leaning against the side of the nearest building, their arms wrapped around themselves as if they're cold, even though it is a warm night. Tom and Carmen have their windows down.

Tom wonders if they're junkies, in withdrawal. Desperate for their next hit.

"Some of the girls will be elsewhere," Tom says. "They'll be in cars. They'll be with customers."

"So how long do we wait?" Carmen says.

"Until we're sure," Tom says. "Until we're sure the girls we've seen so far are the only ones who work here. Until we're sure Rosa isn't going to turn up in an hour's time, climbing out of someone's car."

Carmen settles back in her seat. The night crawls on. Tom keeps one eye on the girls and another on the mirrors, watching the cars and pedestrians that pass by. Keeps his eyes peeled for cops. They don't seem to come this way. He hasn't seen a single one yet, neither driving nor on foot.

Sometimes other girls return to the corner, or a car stops and hurriedly drops one off. Whenever they do, Carmen sits up, leans forward, desperate for a good look at their face. She is disappointed each time. "Do you think anyone's looking for any of those girls?" she says. There are black girls, white girls, Latina and Asian.

"I don't know," Tom says. "Maybe. Maybe some of them like what they do. Maybe some of them have run away from the people looking for them."

"Mm." Carmen settles back into the seat. "I just want her back," she says, and her voice almost cracks. Tom spares her a glance now, takes his eyes away from the girls and the road behind them. Her face is hard, her jaw clenched tight, but there is a sheen to her eyes. She's holding back tears. She's been strong so long, but it's catching up to her now.

"We'll find her," Tom says. "We will."

Carmen takes a deep breath through her nose. "Rosa is four years younger than me," she says, shaking her head and sitting up, chasing away the tears and the tremble in her voice. "We had a brother."

"Oh?" Tom picks up on the past tense.

"He was two years younger than me. His name was Francisco." She stops, gathers herself, and Tom isn't sure if she's going to continue. He doesn't prompt her. "He was six when he died. I was eight, Rosa was four. Rosa was at home when it happened, still clinging to our mother's skirt, wouldn't leave her side. Francisco and I, we were just playing..." She stops again, blinks hard. A car pulls up to the corner, and a girl gets out. She's Latina. Carmen leans forward again. The girl turns, and she's laughing about something. The girl is familiar, but she isn't Rosa. They've seen her already on the corner. They watched her get picked up. This is her triumphant return.

Carmen sighs. "We were outside of town. There was a cliff there, and we were playing close to it. We weren't on the edge of it or anything, and we'd been there so many times before, and I just wasn't thinking... Francisco fell. We were just playing, and I only looked away for a second, but then I turned back, and he was gone. I knew what had happened, instantly. I didn't see it, I didn't hear it, but I knew he'd fallen over the edge. Then he started to scream." Carmen closes her eyes, recalling the sound.

"It wasn't a long drop," she says. "It could only have been about twenty feet, but he was so small, and there were rocks at the bottom, and..." She covers her mouth with her hand. "His bones... He'd broken so many of his bones in the fall. He couldn't move. He was just lying there, screaming. I could see...I can *still* see how some of them were popping out through his skin. He saw me looking down at him, and he started crying out for me, calling my name. I couldn't get down to him. I tried, but there was no way down. I told him I'd go to get help, and he was begging me not to leave him, but I had to go. We didn't have phones, and even if we had, there wouldn't have been any signal out there.

"So I ran home. I went as fast as I could, and I got my

father, and I was crying so hard, and I could barely breathe after running so far that I almost couldn't speak. He finally understood enough of what I was trying to tell him, and he threw me in the car and got me to direct him back to the cliff. When we got there..." She stops, doesn't finish. Tom doesn't need her to. He knows what happened next. He knows what they found.

"I'm sorry that happened to you," he says.

"It didn't happen to *me*," Carmen says. "Not the worst of it, anyway." She wipes her eyes, still determined not to cry. "For the longest time, all I could see in my mind, and every time I closed my eyes, was his broken little body. When I tried to sleep, I'd hear his screams. It was like he was calling to me. For the longest time, I was sure he was haunting me, and I'd watch at my bedroom window, certain I'd see him approaching through the dark."

"It was grief," Tom says.

Carmen nods. "He was my responsibility that day, out by the cliff. I shouldn't have looked away. We should never have been there anyway. It was a stupid place for us to go, and a stupid accident happened. My parents never blamed me, not outright." She looks at Tom. "But I know they were thinking it. How could they not? It was my fault. I should have been looking, and I wasn't." She turns back to the girls. "I can't let them lose another child."

"Rosa is a grown woman," Tom says. "You can't be expected to watch over her all the time."

Carmen grunts. "I'll get her back to Mexico, and then we'll see about that."

Tom checks the time. They've been watching the corner for four hours now. It's getting close to dawn. As if in response to his noticing the time, Carmen yawns.

Tom starts to get out of the car. "Wait here," he says.

Carmen gives a start. "The hell I will," she says, following him out.

Tom doesn't stop her. They approach the group of girls together.

"Evening, ladies," Tom says when they're close enough. He smiles. "Or morning, as the case may be."

The women, some of them talking in a huddle, all turn to his voice. The ones talking fall silent and spread out, each of them looking Tom and Carmen over.

"My, my," one of the black women says, "a couple, huh? Been a while since I was last with a couple." Some of the other girls chuckle.

"As much as that sounds like a pleasant way to spend what's left of the night, that's not why we've come over," Tom says. He addresses the black woman. She was the first to speak, and she carries herself with an air of importance. Tom has a feeling she is someone these other girls look up to. A kind of leader amongst them. "We're looking for someone."

Carmen reaches into her pocket, pulls out the picture of Rosa. "My sister," she says.

The hooker takes the picture, inspects it. She shakes her head, hands it around to the other girls. "She looks just like you," she says to Carmen, "but I ain't seen her. Anyone else?"

The picture makes its way back to Carmen. No one speaks up.

"Sorry," the hooker says. "What happen, she run away? Looks a little old to be running away."

"She was taken," Carmen says.

"We don't suppose you might happen to know anything about Mexican girls being smuggled over the border and put to work?" Tom says.

The hooker's eyes narrow. She shakes her head. "Can't say as I do." She turns to a couple of the Latina girls on the corner with them. "You two heard anything about that?"

They both shake their heads. One of them speaks, says, "Ain't heard about it, but it doesn't surprise me, either." She has a Californian accent.

"Who's smuggling them?" the black woman says.

"Cartel," Tom says. "Someone on this side of the border's probably involved, too. We don't know who."

The hooker grunts. "If they wanna keep a close eye on them, they likely ain't gonna put them to work on the streets. More likely keep them in a brothel. Keep 'em indoors."

"A brothel?" Carmen says. "Do you know where we can find it?"

"Shit, course I do," the hooker says. "I know where you can find all of 'em." She gives them details and locations. Carmen punches the information into her phone, then thanks her profusely.

"How much does this information cost?" Tom says.

"Nothin'," the hooker says. "I don't charge for giving directions." She looks at Carmen, tilts her chin at her. "Good luck finding your sister."

They head back to the car. Tom turns it, drives back to the hotel. "We'll hit them up tomorrow," he says. "It's getting late."

"It's getting early," Carmen says, looking at how the sky is slowly beginning to lighten.

The streets are still quiet when they get back to the hotel. Inside, people are still sleeping. The porter on the desk barely looks up as they pass through the small foyer. He's watching a television hidden under the counter. Its glow casts a sickly light upon his face.

"So tonight wasn't a total bust," Carmen says as the elevator takes them up to their floor. "We should've just spoken to the girls sooner, though."

"We needed to be sure Rosa wasn't there," Tom says.

The elevator doors open. They step out into the hall, head

along to their room. Halfway along, Carmen turns her head, opens her mouth, about to say something. Tom presses a finger to his lips, cuts his eyes at her so she knows not to make a sound. She frowns, looks down the hall. Looks to the door of their room. It's closed. She leans in close, whispers, "What is it?"

Tom points in front of their door. There is a small piece of paper, folded many times into a tiny square. Tom wedged it into the doorjamb when they left. It's no longer in the jamb. It's on the ground, close to the baseboard.

Carmen moves her head around, searching. "What?" she says, keeping her voice low. "What are you pointing at?" She can't see the paper.

Tom motions for her to step back and to stay quiet. He keeps one eye on the door, in case it should open. "Someone's in our room," he says.

15

In Lubbock, Texas, Cindy Vaughan wakes early. She never sets an alarm. She's always up before dawn.

She doesn't get straight out of bed. Instead, she stretches. Her arms above her head, the tips of her fingers touching the wall, and her toes poking out from under the bottom of the blanket. She yawns while she does so, and feels how her spine pops. She rolls over the edge then and gets to her feet, stifling another yawn. She sleeps in underwear and a Killing Joke T-shirt. She strips them off in the bathroom before she gets into the shower, humming to herself while she washes. When she gets out, she feels fully awake. She puts on fresh clothes and heads through to her front room, where her computers are.

She doesn't go directly to them. She puts on some music first. Opts for Front Line Assembly, and plays it *loud*, neighbors be damned. They haven't complained yet. She gets a glass of water from the kitchen, then settles in at her desk. Fires up her laptop to find she has an alert. She downs half the glass of water, then clicks on the alert. It doesn't take her long to see what it's for.

Tom Rollins has returned to America. He hasn't been subtle about it, and he hasn't come as David Thompson – the fake identification she sent him.

"Why do I bother?" she says, thinking about the work that went into the forging of Tom's documents, the creation of his new persona.

There is footage. It has been circulated internally within the border patrol down in Arizona. She can see Tom, along with a woman she doesn't know. Tom's beard has gotten thicker, and his hair is longer, but she recognizes him. There is some text beneath. It explains how Tom (unnamed in the text) has snuck an illegal into the country, then attacked two agents and stolen a government vehicle. The vehicle was later burned out. All agents are warned to be on the lookout, and to be warned that the individual involved is considered highly dangerous.

This is how she knows he has not returned as David Thompson. David Thompson would never need to steal a Jeep from the border patrol. David Thompson would very calmly, and very *legally*, cross the border in his own vehicle.

Cindy checks to see how far the notice has reached. How many other agencies throughout America it has been forwarded to.

Cindy frowns, checks again.

It hasn't. This surprises her. She figures the border patrol in Arizona must be keeping it in-house, wanting to track Tom and the woman down themselves. Still, though, this shocks her. Something like this would ordinarily be forwarded to at least the local law enforcement and more than likely the FBI, too.

Cindy leans back in her chair. She folds her legs and rests an elbow on the arm of the seat, props her head up in her hand. She turns the music up louder. It helps her think.

She checks the FBI. They have sophisticated firewalls,

and it takes her a while to break through them. When she gets inside, she searches for Tom's name. An encrypted communication comes up. She can't see who it's between. Not yet. She cracks her knuckles and delves back in.

The message is from Senior Special FBI Agent Eric Thompson. Cindy reads it through, her eyes moving quickly through the text.

"*Shit.*"

16

Tom is outside the hotel. Carmen is still inside, still in the hallway outside their room. She knows what she needs to do.

The fire escape that runs down the side of the building looks in need of maintenance. Some of its holdings are rusting over, and it creaks as Tom makes his way up. He takes his time as he nears the window to their room, avoiding the creaks and rattles. He ducks low when he reaches it, peers in from the corner. The room is in darkness. He can't see the person inside.

He pulls out his burner phone and his Beretta. Sends a message to Carmen's phone – 'NOW.' Puts the phone back into his pocket and holds up the gun. Watches. Carmen makes her move. Tom sees the door to the room thrown open. Carmen is not in sight. She has jumped back into the hallway.

The door opening has shown Tom all he needs to see. The man in their room emerges from the shadows to Tom's left, a Springfield XD held in two hands before him, raising it toward the door.

Tom shoots through the glass, catches him in the back high up toward his right shoulder. The man goes down. Tom puts his elbow through the window, aiming for the shattered area where his bullet has already gone through. He climbs in, avoiding the shards of broken glass.

The man is pushing himself back up one-armed. He's reaching for the Springfield. Tom kicks the gun away. The man is white. Tom doesn't recognize him. The man swings with his left arm, his right hanging useless. Tom avoids his sloppy attack, grabs him by the wrist and twists, spins him around and presses down into the back of his left shoulder with the butt of the Beretta. "And who might you be?" Tom says.

The man grimaces, bent double. He avoids looking back at him. "Fuck you." He spits the words.

"Who sent you?" Tom says.

The man's right arm isn't as useless as Tom first thought. He grabs a push knife from a holster down by his ankle, twists and jabs at Tom's stomach. Tom lets go of his arm, leaps back, away from the blade's sharp jabs. The man is quick to advance, switching the knife to his left hand. He slashes wildly, clearly right-handed and struggling with his precision.

Carmen appears in the doorway. "Stay in the hall!" Tom says.

The man gets in close before Tom has a chance to turn the Beretta on him. Cuts him across the forearm, causes him to drop the gun. Tom feels blood running down his arm, dripping from his fingers. The man continues to advance, his right arm pressed to the side of his body and his left still swinging out with the knife, hoping to make further contact. He backs Tom up against the wall. Tom lashes out, kicks him hard in the chest. Tom takes a cut across the thigh for his efforts. It draws blood, but it's not deep.

The man rolls back with the kick, hits the ground on his behind, and starts pushing himself along, scurrying away. His eyes dart side to side. Tom can see that he's searching for the Springfield. Tom pulls out his KA-BAR. The man reaches his gun, grabs it in his right hand, wraps his left around his wrist to help him hold it up, to steady it.

Tom throws the KA-BAR. It buries itself into the man's neck up to the hilt. His eyes go wide as blood begins to pour from his mouth, and pump out around the blade. He drops the Springfield with a thud. Tom stoops to pick his Beretta back up. The man is dying, will soon be dead. He can't get any information out of him.

"All right," he says, calling to Carmen. "You can come in, but you ain't gonna like what you see."

Carmen steps tentatively into the room. She sees the man's convulsing body on the ground, and she quickly looks away.

"Close the door," Tom says. "Did anyone hear anything? Anyone come running?"

Carmen does as he says. "I don't think so," she says. "No one came into the hall."

"Doesn't matter," Tom says. "We need to move. We'll take the fire escape. Grab your things."

"Who was *he*?" Carmen says, jerking her thumb back toward the man, who is now lying still. Dead.

"I don't know," Tom says. "I didn't get a chance to ask properly."

Carmen sees that he is bleeding. "You're cut," she says, stepping forward.

"It's nothing," he says. "They're not deep. Come on, we need to go."

Carmen doesn't have much that she needs to gather up. She grabs her things while avoiding looking back at the dead body down the side of the bed. She pauses, listening. "Is that your bag?" she says.

Tom hears it too. There's a buzzing. He grabs the bag, reaches inside for the vibrating phone. It has a piece of paper taped to the top of it with the name 'Cindy' written across it. There are already a few missed calls from her. He answers.

"Oh, thank Christ," she says.

"Cindy," he says, "what's up? You sound worried."

"That's because I *am* worried, Tom," she says. "God help me, I'm worried over *you*. I spend all that time putting together a fake ID for you, creating a fake persona, and what do you do? You come sneaking into the country and get yourself caught on camera."

"Yeah," Tom says. "Sorry to waste your time."

"Uh-huh. Who's the girl, anyway?"

Tom looks at Carmen, wonders if she can overhear. She's watching him, listening to his side of the conversation. She looks confused, wondering whom he's talking to and what about. "A friend," he says to Cindy.

"She sure is pretty."

Carmen doesn't react to this, and Tom knows she can't hear Cindy's side. "She sure is," he says. "What are you calling for, Cindy? I get the feeling it's for more than just to slap my wrist."

"Oh, you're very right about that," Cindy says. "Because I'm not the only one who saw that footage. Are you familiar with Senior Special FBI Agent Eric Thompson?"

"I believe we've been in contact," Tom says.

"Why doesn't *that* surprise me? Seems like he's got a real hard-on for you, my friend. He's got one of his boys tracking you down in Nogales there, and he's sent a hitman there via his directions. Oh, and this guy wasn't cheap. Agent Thompson has spent a *lot* of money on him."

Tom looks toward the dead hitman. "We're acquainted," he says.

"For real? Well, shit. Seems like he got out in front of me."

"Seems that way. Didn't I pay you to let me know about this kind of thing *ahead* of time?"

Cindy pretends she didn't hear the question. "He's dealt with, I assume?"

"Yes. Eric wasted his money, you ask me."

"Efficient as ever, huh?"

"I don't get paid by the hour."

"You don't get paid at all. What's the girl's story?"

"She's lost her sister," Tom says. "I'm helping her find her."

Cindy is silent.

"You still there?"

She clears her throat. "Yeah," she says. "Yeah, I'm still here."

She sounds a bit off. Tom doesn't understand. "You all right?"

"I'm fine. What happened to her sister?"

"Cartel kidnapped her."

"Shit. *Shit.*"

Tom frowns. "Something up? You sound shaken."

"I'm fine, I told you." She clears her throat.

"All right," Tom says. "I need you to do me a couple of favors."

"A couple? That's more than usual." It's hard to tell if there is sarcasm in her tone. She sounds a bit more like herself.

"I think they'll be small favors, for someone of your talents."

Cindy chuckles. "You've buttered me up. I'm listening."

"First things first – my friend, her name is Carmen Hernández. She's a schoolteacher. Can you get online and hide that information? If people are coming after us, I don't want them able to see who she is and what she does."

"Easy." There's a pause. "What's her sister's name?"

"Rosa."

"Okay."

Cindy doesn't say anything further, so Tom continues. "Second one might be harder. Can you send Eric a message for me? But only if you're certain it can't be traced back to you."

"I can do that."

"Great. I'll send you the message."

"I look forward to seeing it."

They say their goodbyes, and Tom hangs up the phone. He quickly punches in his message, sends it, then drops the phone back into the bag. He looks at Carmen. "You good to go?" he says.

"Who was that?" she says, tilting her head.

"Cindy," Tom says. "She's a friend. You'd like her, I'm sure."

"Uh-huh. You told her my sister's name?"

"Mm." Tom nods. "She asked." He doesn't mention how she'd sounded off, how something seemed to affect her.

"I heard another name," Carmen says. "Eric? Is that right? Who's Eric?"

"We've never met," Tom says. "But we've spoken on the phone."

"That didn't answer my question."

Tom goes to the window, pulls it open so Carmen will not have to crawl through the broken glass. He brushes away the remaining shards. "Eric is a man who is not anywhere near as dangerous as he thinks he is," Tom says.

17

Eric Thompson comes from old money. Descended from oil barons, his home reflects this. The interior is kept in whites and creams, and the ground of the foyer through to the kitchen is tile, to keep the house cool. There are a few paintings on walls dotted throughout the mansion, and a couple of statuettes in marble of Roman nudes. There are acres of land between himself and his nearest neighbors, many of whom are new money. Football players and CEOs of tech start-ups. Eric hasn't seen the interiors of their homes, but he can only imagine the garish designs and the walls adorned with pop art. When it's dark he can see how some of them have their lights on all night, and if he passes by close enough he can hear the awful music that is pounding inside. They have parties. Half-naked women screeching as they are thrown into pools. An orgy of decadence that Eric wants no part of, that has no place here.

If Eric didn't want to, he wouldn't have to work another day in his life. He likes to. It keeps him occupied. It gives his day purpose.

And it brings power.

His father's influence got him into the FBI. Everything else has been of Eric's own doing. One day, he plans to be head of the FBI. He won't remain in Texas forever. A few more years and he'll leave the state, move on up in the world.

A few more years, and one pesky problem that should be dealt with soon enough.

Eric's ascension had been planned for much sooner. Months ago, in fact. The bombs would have gone off in Dallas, killing Senator Seth Goldberg in the process, one of the many among the thousands of dead. Then, Eric would have dispatched his team to take out the people 'responsible' – the neo-Nazi cell he'd carefully arranged as the fall guys for the Dallas attack. If everything had gone off without a hitch, he'd already be on his way to Washington.

As it stands, things did not go as they should have. Someone got in the way.

Tom fucking Rollins.

Eric doesn't curse much, but in this instance, it feels warranted.

Tom has added a few years to Eric's career projection. Now Tom needs to die. He potentially knows too much about Eric's own involvement in Dallas. For that, he needs to be eliminated. Eric can't take any chances.

He stands at the back of his house, french doors wide open as he breathes in the evening air. He can see the lights from one of the neighboring houses off in the distance. Can hear the noise that passes for 'music' emanating from it.

He's trying to be calm. Trying to be patient. Waiting for his hitman to get back in touch to tell him the deed has been done. Eric had hoped the mission would be accomplished the night before, but he understands these things take time.

The sun is beginning to lower. Eric steps back inside the house, closes and locks the doors. He paces the floor, jaw clenched. He goes upstairs. At the top, he stands at the end of the hall and looks down to where his wife's room is.

Much like his career was set up by his parents, so was his marriage. Eliza is also descended from wealth. It was a marriage of convenience, both for their parents and for each other. For their parents, it opened up a whole new world of business opportunities and relationships. For Eric and Eliza, it kept their parents off their backs.

Eric knocks on her door, then steps inside.

Eliza sits at her vanity table. She's curling her hair. She turns back to see him, an eyebrow raised, surprised. He doesn't usually come to visit. "Eric," she says, her tone cordial. "What can I do for you?"

"Nothing," Eric says. Eliza looks like she is preparing to go out. "Just wandering the house."

She continues to curl her hair. Turns back to her mirror and looks at him in its reflection. "Something on your mind?"

"Should there be?"

"It's the only time I've ever known you to *wander*," she says. "And it's the only time you ever come to see me."

Eric leans back against the doorframe, hands in his pockets.

"It's also the only time I ever see you slouch," she says. "Something to do with work?"

"Yes."

"Then I won't probe further." Eliza knows Eric likes to keep his business to himself. She never pries.

Likewise, Eric keeps out of her affairs. They sleep in separate rooms. They hardly ever see each other around the house. She tends to her business, and he tends to his.

Since their marriage, they've made love only a handful of times. A bland, perfunctory act on the rare occasion they're both feeling in the mood. At first, in the early days, they thought it was expected of them. They did it thinking they should, perhaps in order to sire a child. Neither of them enjoyed it very much. Eric has become aware, over time, that he is asexual. He has little interest in women, and no interest in men. He gets by just fine without indulging in his baser urges.

Eliza, on the other hand, has no interest in doing it with *him*.

Eric knows why she's getting dressed up, and why she's going out. He knows what her intentions are. It's quite possible he won't see her around the house again for another couple of days, if not longer. She has boyfriends. Sometimes she goes out and finds new ones. Eric does not interfere.

He looks around her room. He can't remember the last time he was in it. It currently smells of hairspray, and underneath that there is the sweet scent of perfume. Her bed is made, and laid out on it is a red dress, and underwear of the same color. Eric notices there is no bra. Eliza continues on as if he is not present. She's not dressed. She wears a silk nightgown tied at the front. Her makeup is already done. She finishes her hair and stands, slips off her gown and reaches for the thong.

Her body is tight from hours spent in the gym. Her breasts are high and firm, from the implants she had inserted a couple of years before. The scars on the underside where they were put in are barely noticeable. No cheap rush job by a talentless hack who leaves behind large, revolting scars, as Eric is sure many of the football players' girlfriends will have.

Eliza sits down, rolls stockings up each of her legs. "I've called a taxi," she says without turning. "It should be here soon."

Eric pushes himself up from the doorframe, keeps his hands in his pockets. "I'll leave you to it," he says.

Eliza looks at him in the mirror again. "Do you want to

talk about something, Eric? I still have a little time." She stands, pulls the dress over her head.

"No," Eric says. "That's all right."

Eliza straightens out the dress. "How do I look?"

"You look...very nice," he says, wondering if he should say 'beautiful.'

Eliza grins and rolls her eyes, and he knows he should have. She picks up a handbag from her dresser and kisses his cheek on her way past. "Well, I hope whatever is troubling you soon resolves itself," she says. "I'll wait outside. The taxi will be here any minute."

She walks off down the hall. Eric watches her go. Neither of them bother to say goodbye.

He doesn't go to his own room. He goes to his study instead, to distract himself with work. He settles into the leather seat behind his large mahogany desk and checks emails, then starts reading through paperwork. Before he knows it, a couple of hours have passed, and he realizes this is what he should have been doing all along. Rather than fretting and troubling himself over a situation he has minimal control over, he should have thrown himself into his work. Kept his mind and his hands busy.

He leans back in the chair, stretching his back and rubbing his eyes. It has gotten dark outside, and in the room. He turns on the lamp at the far-right corner of his desk, and notices he has a new email.

Eric's stomach sinks. It is not from an account he recognizes. It's not from the hitman he hired, either.

Eric bites his lip, opens the message. The email is addressed to him. It clearly comes from a fake account, and he imagines it will be hard to track, though he'll put Gerry to work on it regardless.

It's a short message, only two sentences, but it hits him like a hammer:

'Your hitman failed. I'll be seeing you soon. -TR'

Eric stares at the message, reads it over and over. He tries not to panic. Takes deep breaths to maintain his composure.

Tom Rollins is already an issue. Tom Rollins just became a bigger issue. Eric knows he has to get him before Tom can get to *him*. That was supposed to be the purpose of the hitman, but it seems he wasn't worth the money Eric paid him.

Eric needs someone better. Someone more on Rollins's level. Someone, perhaps, who has prior knowledge of Tom Rollins. Someone who may have an axe to grind. Hell, he needs a *team* of someones.

"Well," Eric says, speaking the words out loud to comfort himself. "Plan B it is."

18

Tom has assumed that Senior Special FBI Agent Eric Thompson is the man behind the attempted attack in Dallas. Has assumed that he is the man he spoke to on a diner phone shortly after said attack was thwarted. He knows that this puts him and Carmen in a difficult predicament, now that Eric knows where he is and will likely be sending more hitmen after him. He has resources at his fingertips, and Tom has no idea how many dirty agents.

They've left the hotel where Tom killed the hitman, left the body where it lay down the side of the bed. No time to clear up, to dispose of him. They checked in under false names and paid in cash. There were no cameras in the hotel – Tom checked. There's nothing to trace them back to that room. They've checked into a new hotel, though this is simply a base of operations. They've kept moving since they left the last one.

Tom has switched vehicles, too, knowing there's a chance Eric, and the men he sends next, will know its details.

He wants to find Rosa fast. To send her and Carmen back home so he can deal with whatever is coming next without putting them in danger. He tried sending Carmen back to Mexico, where it's safer for her, telling her he would continue alone and return Rosa to her. Carmen has refused to leave his side. "I'm not going anywhere without my sister," she says.

"You're in danger with me," Tom said.

"So what's new?"

"I don't know who he's going to send, or how many."

"I'm not going anywhere, Tom."

He didn't waste time trying to dissuade her. They started visiting the brothels the hooker told them about. They went inside posing as a couple, voicing an interest in Latina girls to join them in a threesome. The Latina girls were brought out for their inspection. None of them were Rosa. Tom and Carmen would pick one at random, take her to a room. Inside, they paid the girl extra to answer their questions, and to pretend they had sex with her. The girl would be confused, but she'd shrug and take the money. They asked her if she knew anything about the girls being brought up from Mexico by the Nogales Cartel, and where they might be going. She didn't. Neither did the girl in the second brothel. They hung around in the rooms for twenty minutes after, to make it look believable. Tom could see the disappointment and the frustration growing in Carmen. They weren't getting anywhere. Their leads were swiftly drying up.

In the third, they get something.

After Tom finishes asking her their regular questions, she goes stiff. She looks back at the door, stares at it like she's scared someone could be standing outside, listening in. She turns back to them, gritting her teeth, her face pinched. She nods.

Carmen is standing against the wall, likely expecting this trip to be another dead end. She leans forward when the girl responds in the affirmative. The girl is sitting on the end of the bed, with Tom standing in front of her. The room is very similar to the ones they have been in already at the other brothels. The red curtains are drawn closed to cover the window. The bed is made, but the sheets are creased and crumpled. On the bedside table there is a bowl filled with condoms.

"You *do* know about it?" Carmen says, trying to keep her voice low but clearly excited they might be about to get something they can work with.

Tom motions for her to lower the volume of her voice. He turns back to the girl. "What's your name?" he says.

"Emilia," the girl says, glancing at Carmen.

Tom pulls up a seat from the corner of the room. He sits down in front of Emilia. "You know about the Nogales Cartel?" he says.

Emilia nods. She closes her eyes. When she opens them again, Tom can see tears. She wipes them. She swallows hard. "They...they took me," she says. "They brought me here."

Tom can hear how Carmen is holding her breath, biting her tongue, desperate to dive in and start peppering the girl with questions.

"Did they take you from Nogales, Emilia?" Tom says.

She nods. She tries again to wipe the tears out of her eyes, but they will not be dispelled.

"How long ago?"

She looks up to the ceiling, remembering. "I...I don't know," she says. "I'm not sure. I think...I think a year? Maybe longer?" She shakes her head. "I don't know." Her voice is breaking, threatening to be overcome by her tears.

Tom watches her. She lowers her face, and teardrops fall from her eyes down to the shag-pile carpet below. Tom holds a hand out to her. She stares at it, then clasps it with both of her own. Tom places his other hand over the top, looks into her eyes. "Emilia," he says. "Do you want to go home?"

She nods, tears flying from her face. "Yes," she says.

"I'll take you home, Emilia," he says. "When we leave this room, you're going to leave with us."

He can see in her face how her emotions are battling. Hope struggling to be controlled by pessimism. "But – but Alan," she says.

"Who's Alan?"

"He guards us. He's in charge of us here."

"What's he look like?"

"He's big," she says. "He's so big…" Her voice trails off, her hope overcome by fear. "He has no hair. He…" She struggles to think how else to describe him.

Tom saw him when they came into the brothel, before they were shown the girls. The muscle, similar to the other men he'd seen in the other brothels. He was stood to one side, leaning against the wall, trying to look tough while he sipped from a can of soda. "Don't worry about Alan," Tom says. "We need to ask you some questions, and then we're all going to leave together."

"Tom," Carmen says.

He looks at her.

"What do we do with her when we get her out?" she says. "I don't want to leave her here either, but we have to be realistic. We can't go back to Mexico, not yet. It's going to be hard enough risking the crossing when we have Rosa."

"We'll put her in a motel in town, one near the border," Tom says. He turns back to Emilia so she is included in the conversation. "And we'll give you money to stay there and buy food. Then, once we have Rosa, we'll take you back to Mexico with her."

Emilia nods. Anything to be out of the brothel.

"Do you know Rosa?" Tom says. "Rosa Hernández? She would have arrived in America not so long ago."

"I don't know her," Emilia says. "I'm sorry."

"That's all right," Tom says. He's still holding her hands,

still comforting her. She's beginning to look like she's calming. "Do you know what happens when they bring the girls into America?"

She nods. Takes a deep breath. "They pay the border patrol so they can smuggle us into the country without any trouble."

Tom can feel Carmen's eyes on him. He looks her way, nods once.

"I don't know if it's all of them, or just a few. I suppose it doesn't really matter. Once we're over, some of the girls are kept here in Nogales, and others are transported elsewhere. I don't know how far they go. They could be spread out all across America, maybe."

Carmen takes a sharp breath.

Tom lets go of Emilia's hands. She's engaged in her telling now. She doesn't need comforting anymore.

"Before we're divided up, though, there's a woman comes to see us," Emilia says. "A madam, I guess. She picks the girls she likes best – the prettiest, I think – and she takes them away with her. I don't know where they go, though. I don't even know the lady's name."

"She could've taken Rosa," Carmen says.

Tom nods. He stands. "Is that everything?" he says.

Emilia nods, and winces like she's worried it might not be enough.

"That's a big help, Emilia," he says. "Thank you. Now let's go."

She hesitates. She does not make any attempt to stand. She looks too scared.

Carmen steps forward and holds out her hand. "I can't imagine how you must feel right now," she says. "I know this must be hard, and it must be scary, but it's going to be okay. I promise."

Emilia looks at her. Her tears are returning.

"Stay by my side," Carmen says. "We'll get you out. You won't ever have to see this place again."

Emilia takes a deep shuddering breath. She takes Carmen's hand and gets to her feet. Tom can see how she holds Carmen's hand tight, how her knuckles have turned white. Carmen looks her in the eyes and nods, then draws her close to her, holds her at her side.

They leave the room.

There's no sign of Alan, not at first. They walk down the hall, and toward the foyer and the exit, without incident.

Alan is in the foyer. He *is* a big guy. He's talking to one of the girls, leaning against the wall and looming over her. He sees Tom, Carmen, and Emilia passing through. Does a double take.

"Hey," he says. His voice is deep.

Tom turns to him. Motions for Carmen and Emilia to keep going.

"Hey, hold it," Alan says, stepping forward. "Where the hell do you think you're going?"

"She's going home," Tom says.

"This *is* her home," Alan says, stopping in front of Tom and rolling his shoulders.

"Her real home."

"The hell she is." Alan looks over the top of Tom's head. "Emilia – get back in your fucking room, right now."

Tom hears how Emilia whimpers behind him. He has no doubt she wants to do exactly as Alan says. Probably Carmen is having to hold her in place by the door.

"Right now, Emilia," Alan says. "Right now, and no one else needs to know."

"She sounds scared of you, Alan," Tom says. Using his name gets his attention. Alan looks back down at him, sneering. "Now, what'd you do to make her sound so scared? You ever hurt these girls, Alan?"

"I'm about to hurt *you*, motherfucker."

"Uh-huh." Tom is unfazed, and Alan can see it. It makes him falter a little. To compensate, he tries to make his face meaner. "You give them a slap when they step out of line? Maybe more than that?"

"The girls know to behave themselves," Alan says. "Same way you're about to find out."

"I've got somewhere I need to be, Alan," Tom says. "But I'm thinking that when I'm done there, I might come back here. Pay you a visit. Ask the girls here what they really think of you, and their working conditions." He looks past Alan, to the scantily clad woman he was talking to. She is watching with wide eyes, unable to believe that someone could be talking to Alan in such a way.

Tom goes to turn.

"Where the fuck do you think –" Alan doesn't get to finish what he wants to say. He reaches out, places a hand on Tom's shoulder, clearly with the intention to spin him back. Tom is anticipating this. Turning his back was a fake-out. He wraps his right hand around the index finger of Alan's left, the hand upon his shoulder, and wrenches it back until he hears it snap. Alan's sentence is cut off by his alarmed cry. So surprised, he hasn't realized he's in pain yet.

Tom turns with the finger he's still wrenching back. Keeps hold of it while Alan's left arm bends and begins to twist back. Tom kicks him in the side of the leg, brings him down to his knee, shortens his height advantage significantly. Alan's still crying out, the pain in his hand beginning to register. Tom punches him across the jaw, silences him. Blood flies from his mouth, and at least one tooth. Tom lets go of his broken finger, and Alan topples, using his right hand to stop himself from falling completely. Tom grabs him with both hands on the back of his bald head and drives his knee up into his face. His nose crunches. He probably loses another couple of teeth from the impact. He goes down, turns as he's falling, and lands on his front. Tom takes hold of his wrist and presses a boot against his shoulder.

"This is to make sure you behave yourself until I get back, Alan," Tom says, then breaks his arm.

Alan screams.

Tom leaves him there and heads back for the door. The girl Alan was talking to is watching still, unable to tear her eyes away. Emilia looks the same.

The three of them leave the brothel together, go to their car. Emilia climbs in the backseat, and she's crying as they pull away. She's smiling at the same time. Tears of joy. Of relief. Tom and Carmen don't try to stop her. Don't try to comfort her.

"Sounds unlikely that Rosa is still in Nogales," Tom says to Carmen. "We'll put Emilia here in a motel, give her some money to tide her over, and then we'll have to pinpoint where exactly Rosa has been taken."

Carmen nods. She's silent for a few blocks while they drive through the deserted nighttime streets. When she finally talks, she does so haltingly. "Did…did you… Did you mean what you said back there?" she says.

"What part?" Tom says.

"About going back to the brothel, after we've found Rosa. To make sure the girls are all right."

"Of course," Tom says, looking at her with an expression that makes it clear it would be unfeasible for him to not follow through on something he's said he will do. "I might have to go back to the others, too," he says, returning his eyes to the road. "See how things are run there. It looked like they all had an Alan. I'll need to check if they have the same bad attitudes."

"All right, then," Carmen says. She sounds impressed.

19

Pedro goes alone to Miguel's mansion. The guards on the gate recognize him. They wave him through.

There are guards throughout the grounds, dressed in black suits and wearing sunglasses, armed with MP5s. The driveway that leads to the main house is long, decorated either side with cacti, interspersed with marble nudes. Pedro can feel eyes on him all the way down. He parks his car at the end of the driveway, in front of the steps that lead up to the house's entrance. There are two men standing either side of the door. One of them steps forward as Pedro approaches. "You know the routine, Pedro," he says.

Pedro does. He spreads his arms and his legs, and the guard pats him down. Pedro leaves his gun in the car whenever he comes to Miguel's.

"Clear," the guard says, straightening up. "Senor Aguilar is at the back of the house. He's expecting you."

Pedro steps inside, walks straight through the foyer and the kitchen. The inside of the house is cool with air conditioning. On the way, he passes Miguel's latest girlfriend. Pedro nods at her, though he can't remember her name. She smiles. She's a sweet girl, and more than half Miguel's age. She's wearing a black bikini and her hair is wet and swept back from her face. She's been swimming in the pool out back, and will more than likely be returning to it after she finishes taking a drink from the refrigerator. Pedro makes sure not to let his eyes linger over her taut body any longer than is polite, any longer than is likely to get him noticed – not just by the girl, but by Miguel, or his guards.

Miguel stands out on the patio, hitting golf balls out into the desert. There is an armed guard standing off to his left, and another to his right. "Pedro," he says without looking up, setting his stance and preparing his club. "What have you got for me?" He hits the ball. He watches it sail out across the sand with eyes narrowed against the sun.

Pedro watches it go, too. Miguel's girlfriend has left the kitchen, has left the house via the side door and is walking along the rim of the pool off to their right. She dives in. Pedro avoids looking right at her. "We have a lead on our man from the motel," he says.

Miguel turns now, leaning on his club. "Oh?"

"He's in America. We floated the picture to our friends in the border patrol, and they had a picture to show us in turn."

"What was he doing?"

"Climbing a fence into the country, along with the same girl he was with at the bar."

"Did they catch him?"

Pedro shakes his head.

Miguel clicks his tongue against his teeth. "Do they at least have a lead on him? Know where he's going?"

"No," Pedro says. "But they had a name."

"Don't keep me in suspense, Pedro."

"Tom Rollins."

"Should I know it?"

"No. He's ex-army, ex-CIA."

Miguel raises an eyebrow. "Who's he affiliated with now?"

"No one, so far as we're aware. But apparently there was an attempted terrorist attack in Dallas some months back, and he stopped it."

Miguel frowns, pondering this. "So what does he want from us? Just a Good Samaritan, desperate to play hero?"

"That's my guess."

"He's made a terrible mistake."

Pedro nods his agreement.

"What about the girl?" Miguel says. "Did they know who she was?"

"No."

"A lot of fucking good they do us," Miguel says, turning his head to the side and spitting.

"Mm. However, we do know now that they're both in America. We don't know where exactly, but I'm sure I'll be able to pick up on a trail. I can hunt him and the girl down. I want to go to America, go after them. With your permission."

Miguel considers this. "I'll be going to America soon," he says.

Pedro is aware. "Yes."

"I don't often go north of the border," Miguel says. "This is a big deal. For me. For all of us."

"I understand," Pedro says, being sure to always keep his tone subservient.

"Do you think there is a chance this Tom Rollins could potentially jeopardize my trip?"

"Possibly," Pedro says. "We don't know what he wants, and we don't know what he's going to do next, but we *do* know that he's already brought us enough trouble. Could be he has some kind of vendetta against the Nogales Cartel that we're not aware of."

Miguel turns, looks out across the desert in the direction he has been hitting the balls. Turns to his right, looks to the pool where his too-young girlfriend is now climbing out of the water again and stretching herself out on a lounger to bask beneath the sun. He turns back to Pedro. "Go to America," he says. "Find him, and find the girl, and deal with them. And I want it done fast, Pedro. I want it dealt with before I go north. We can't take a risk on anything interfering with my trip."

Pedro nods. "Of course," he says.

"Take your best men."

Pedro doesn't have to think about this. "I'll take Castillo, Mendoza, and Moreno."

"Will the four of you be enough?" Miguel says. "We've seen what he's done to Los Perros Locos, alone."

Pedro grins. "We're not Los Perros Locos," he says. His subservient tone slips somewhat as he adds, "We're not vicious amateurs. We're professionals."

Miguel looks at him, and Pedro worries he may have stepped out of line.

Then, Miguel laughs. "Indeed," he says. "Go then. Find them. I have every faith in you. Make sure the next time I see you is back here, and not in America."

Pedro nods, then walks back through the house. In his car, heading back down the long driveway, he calls Castillo, lets him know they've been given the go-ahead.

They're going to America.

20

Eric believes firmly in the old saying, *Know your enemy*.

Over the last six months, since his plans in Dallas were foiled, Eric has spent his time reading up on Rollins. Has read up on everything about him he's been able to get his hands on, everything that has allowed him to explore Rollins's past. Knows that he was in the army. Knows he was raised by a survivalist, doomsday-prepping father out in New Mexico. Knows that his brother has regularly been in and out of trouble. Knows, too, that he was black ops in the CIA, and that he went AWOL after a mission in Afghanistan.

It took a lot of influence, a lot of greased palms, and a lot of favors for Eric to get his hands on the report from that final mission.

The mission itself reads as straightforward enough. Aaban Ahmadi, an Afghani warlord, was assassinated in his desert fortress home. Eric had to delve deeper, to both call in and offer further favors to find out the story behind the story. Turns out Ahmadi was not alone in his home. It was not just he and his men. There were women and children present, too. Whole families. They were killed. Everyone on the ground was killed.

Eric has wondered if perhaps this didn't sit right with Tom Rollins. Why else would he abandon his unit, go AWOL, make himself a wanted man?

There's the complaints Rollins lodged, too. Complaints against Captain Robert Dale, his unit commander. They were dismissed, and no records were kept.

Eric has gotten the names of the rest of the unit. Led by the captain, it also comprised Simon Collins, Nathan Sapolsky, and Ezekiel Greene. Eric has reached out to Captain Dale. Testing the waters. Dale has agreed to meet. Has given Eric a location and told him to come alone. The location is not in Texas. Eric has had to travel north and east, to Arkansas.

The spot is a picnic bench in a wooded area. There's no one else around. Eric has been sitting alone for the last half hour. He had to park his car down the hill and continue on foot. Luckily, he's dressed for the occasion. Hiking boots and jeans, a plaid shirt with a windbreaker. The hill was steep. Eric was breathless by the time he reached the bench.

He's had more than enough time now to regain his composure. He looks back down the hill, but no one is coming his way. He looks up it, sees no one coming down, either. The minutes pass by. He starts to wonder if a joke is being played on him. If perhaps Captain Robert Dale has no interest in meeting with him, regardless of the subject matter, and is just sending him on a wild-goose chase for his own amusement instead.

Something in the trees opposite catches his eye. Eric watches. A man emerges. Eric recognizes him from pictures. Captain Robert Dale.

He's a broad man with a severe buzz cut. His face is clean-shaven. He wears combat trousers and a khaki T-shirt, a black jacket over the top. He's smiling, but it's mirthless. It looks cruel. The kind of smile worn by a small child while torturing animals.

"Eric Thompson," he says, stopping by the picnic table with his hands in his pockets.

"Captain Dale," Eric says.

Dale smirks. "Call me Robert," he says, sitting down. "I'm going to call you Eric."

"Fine," Eric says. "You were in the trees the whole time?"

Robert shrugs. "Making sure."

"Of what?"

"You are who you say you are. That you came alone."

"I've been open about who I am," Eric says. "What would I have to hide?"

"Never be too careful," Robert says. His humorless grin never leaves his face. Up close, it looks more sadistic. Eric would not like to know what is running through his head. "You said you wanted to talk about Tom Rollins."

"That's right," Eric says.

"So shoot."

"Very well." Eric clears his throat. "I'm sure you're aware, Tom stopped an attempted attack in Dallas six months ago. Since then he's surfaced in a small town called Brenton, down in Cullingworth County, and then he disappeared off the grid. Seems he's been in Mexico." He watches Robert while he talks, gauging his reactions. It's hard to get a bead on the captain. His face never changes. It's impossible to know what he's thinking.

"Why should I care where he is?" Robert says.

"He's a wanted man," Eric says. "Wanted for abandoning your unit."

Robert doesn't say anything to this.

"What happened in Afghanistan, Robert?"

"Which time?" Robert says. "I've been to Afghanistan a

lot. More than any one person should ever have to, and that goes for the folk who live there, too."

"You know what time I'm talking about, Robert. Don't pretend like you don't."

For the first time, Robert's grin falters. "We had a mission," he says. "We accomplished that mission."

"And Rollins? What happened that caused him to go AWOL?"

"Fuck Tom," Robert says, his grin gone completely now. "He's a pussy. He knew what the job was, but he was too much of a fuckin' bleeding-heart liberal to see it through the way it needed to be. Him and Zeke both, pair of fuckin' bitches."

It's Eric's turn to grin.

"What's so fuckin' funny?" Robert says.

"Nothing's funny," Eric says. "But you just said everything I was hoping to hear."

Robert starts looking left and right, up and down the hill, like his initial suspicions were correct and this is a setup.

Eric puts him at ease. "I have a job, Robert, and I think you're the perfect man for it."

Robert frowns, waiting for an explanation. "Should I assume it's something to do with Tom Rollins?"

"That's exactly right," Eric says. "I want you to hunt him down, and I want you to kill him, and I will pay you handsomely to do so."

Robert's smile returns. Eric doesn't find it so terrifying anymore. Now, he sees in it everything he wants from a man he's sending in to do his dirty work.

"So you want me to be your mercenary, huh?"

"If you want to put it so crudely, yes," Eric says.

"One hundred K," Robert says.

Eric takes a moment, like he's considering the amount. He

was prepared to offer more, but he doesn't let this show. "One hundred K," he says, nodding.

"Sounds like you got yourself a deal," Robert says.

"Half up front," Eric says, trying not to sound as giddy as he feels. "Half on completion of the job."

"Wouldn't expect it any other way."

"Will you be going alone, or with a team?"

"Simon and Nate will want in on this, too," Robert says.

"Good. The more the merrier. I'll be sending someone along with you."

Robert raises an eyebrow. "Who?"

"Gerry Davies. He's a whiz on computers. He'll track Rollins for you, lead you right to him."

"He ever done fieldwork before?"

"No, but I'm sure you and your men will break him in gently." Eric smiles. "I'll let Gerry know." He reaches a hand across the table. "I'm sure it will be a pleasure doing business together, Robert."

Robert takes his hand, grips it tight. "Likewise," he says.

21

Tom isn't able to get as close as he'd like to the border patrol headquarters. The entrance is guarded. Everyone passing through has to produce ID. The parking lot is fenced in. The building is set back, away from the cars. There are cameras in the parking lot and on the side of the building. Tom can't get close to the building. Can't go behind it, either. The view there is blocked by a wall and laden with more cameras.

He parks across the road, hides the car down an alleyway, and watches the parking lot. He wishes he had binoculars, but it's dark and the streetlamps are on, which helps. He and Carmen sit low in their seats. They're alone again. Emilia is safe in a motel near the border. Tom has left her some cash for food and advised her to stay in the room as much as she can until he comes back for her.

"So what do we do?" Carmen says. "Wait until the next time they try to bring some girls up? We don't know how long that's going to be."

"That's not what we're doing," Tom says. "It's like when

we went to La Perrera. We have to watch first. See what we're dealing with."

"Uh-huh. You're not planning on going in there all guns blazing, are you?"

Tom grins, eyes never leaving the lot. "No. I have a much subtler approach in mind."

"Are you going to share it?"

"I've messaged Cindy –"

"Your hacker friend?"

"That's her. I've asked her to run background checks on the agents, find out which of them have an extra income coming in. See if she can trace it back to the Nogales Cartel."

"And then? She's going to send you their pictures?"

Tom grins, thinking of the lack of picture functions on his burner phones. "She's going to send me their names, their details, and the registration numbers on their cars."

"And then..." Carmen trails off. Tom knows why. Understands the alarm in her voice, too. She expects him to torture again. She's flashing back on the matchsticks.

"And then I'll pick which one I'm going to follow," Tom says, "and very politely ask some questions of."

Carmen looks like she has her doubts, but she doesn't press it.

22

Ezekiel 'Zeke' Greene is at home in Shreveport, Louisiana. He's on vacation. The time off was unexpected. A couple of days ago he got a call from his unit commander, Captain Robert Dale, telling him to take a couple of weeks off.

"What's the occasion?" Zeke said.

"I got some personal business I need to attend to," Robert said. "I've already told HQ. Our unit's going dark for a couple of weeks, maybe longer. I'll be in touch when we're ready to roll again."

Zeke tried to ask further questions, but Robert hung up on him before he could.

Something about the explanation didn't sit right with Zeke. Personal business? Zeke couldn't imagine what Robert's personal business might consist of. He'd never heard him talk about family before, or even friends, and he struggled to imagine him taking any time off to deal with anything that may have happened to them. Robert, Zeke knows, is a stone-cold sociopath. The man is only happy when he's working –

when he gets to hurt, or kill. When he's able to indulge in his baser urges.

The only real personal business Zeke can imagine him having to deal with would be to do with his extracurricular activities. He thinks about the drugs and weapons Robert has smuggled back from overseas over the years. He wonders if it has anything to do with that.

Zeke tried ringing Robert's lackeys in order to get a clearer picture. Nathan hung up on his call, but Simon answered.

"The captain's gonna be busy for a coupla weeks, that's all," he said. "Nothin' to worry about."

"Uh-huh," Zeke said. "Busy with *what*?"

"Personal stuff."

"You going with him?"

Simon laughed. "You worry too much, Zeke. Be cool, man. Enjoy your time off. Tell the kids Uncle Simon says hi."

Zeke has no doubts – whatever Robert is doing, Simon and Nathan have gone with him. This knowledge gives him an uneasy feeling. If the three of them have gone together, it can't be for anything good. As he originally suspected, it could be to do with the drugs, or the guns, but he has a suspicion it's something bigger than that.

"You gonna try to at least enjoy *some* of this unexpected vacation?" Naomi says. "Or are you just gonna walk around with your face all mopey like that the whole time?"

They're at the park, sitting on a bench and soaking in the sun. Zeke looks at Naomi. His wife of six years. Before them, hanging from the bars and coming down the slide respectively, are their children. Tre, five years old, and Tamika, three. Tamika reaches the bottom of the slide and jumps up, clapping her hands, looking to her parents to make sure they have both seen her. Naomi smiles and waves at her, and Zeke claps his hands in return. Tamika runs back to the line at the rear of the slide and prepares to go down again.

Not to be outdone, Tre starts calling out. "Mom! Dad! Look! Look at me!"

They do so. Tre is hanging upside down, his legs hooked through the hoops. "Tre, I swear to God," Naomi says, "get yourself the right way up before you fall down and break your neck."

Zeke sees an opportunity to put his wife at ease. He shivers exaggeratedly.

She looks at him, raises an eyebrow. "What's the matter with you?"

"Just that tone there," he says, "and what you said – it was like you turned into my momma for a second."

She gives him a look. The look that always lets him know he's said something he shouldn't have.

Zeke grins. He reaches out, squeezes her thigh. "You know I'm just playing with you, baby."

"Mm-hmm."

"You're right," he says, settling back on the bench and watching his children play without letting his thoughts drift off and concern themselves with Robert, and Simon, and Nathan, and what they might be doing. "I'll try to enjoy myself more. Ain't like a vacation just falls in my lap every day."

"Exactly," Naomi says. "Enjoy this time with your children. And, y'know, with me." She raises her eyebrows.

"That's just what I'll do," Zeke says, smiling. He raises an arm and puts it around Naomi's shoulders. She rests into his hug, the back of her head on his shoulder so she can still see the kids. Tamika is coming down the slide again, and will no doubt want another round of applause at the bottom. "Tre, you heard what your momma said," Zeke says. "Don't go hanging upside down no more."

Zeke allows himself to relax. To be in the moment. Here, in this park, with his family. The comforting weight of his wife against him, and the sweet laughter of his children playing in front of him. He doesn't think about the other three members of his unit. Doesn't concern himself with where they've gone or what they might be doing. If anything, he should be worrying about when they return and they need to go back to work. About the things they'll do when they're back overseas, and how he'll need to turn a blind eye, once again, to what's right in front of him.

Tom had the right idea, he thinks to himself. Even if it did put him on the run. Even if it's not something Zeke could do himself, because of his family, his responsibilities. Tom was right to get out when he did.

23

Robert impressed upon Simon and Nathan the importance of not letting Zeke Greene know where they are going, or why. Zeke is a friend of Tom's, and if he caught the first inclination that the bastard was in danger, he'd do something to warn him, or help.

"One problem at a time," Robert told them. They knew what he meant. Zeke Greene is a problem in and of himself. A high-and-mighty black boy who regularly needs to be taken down a peg or two, until he remembers his place.

Robert has told his men – his true men – that the day will come. "We'll know the right mission when we're on it. Something goes wrong, the bullets are flying – oh shit, ol' Zeke's caught a bullet right through the back of his fucking head. Ain't *that* a crying shame?"

They meet Gerry Davies in Arizona. Eric flies him down. They pick him up in Nathan's van. Gerry looks out of his depth. A deer caught in the headlights, all wide-eyed and nervous, struggling with his baggage. Barely says a word. Out of place among this battle-hardened unit already geared up with combat trousers and boots, Kevlar vests. Their heavier weapons are stored in the van, though they all carry a Glock and a KA-BAR.

"So, Gerry," Robert says, "tell us about yourself." Robert rides in the back with Gerry and his bags. Gerry clutches one of the bags to his chest like precious cargo. It's flat, and shaped like a laptop.

"Um," Gerry says, wiping sweat from his temple.

Nathan is driving the van. Simon sits up front with him. Simon turns. "So you're gonna find our prodigal brother, huh?"

Gerry swallows. He nods. "I'll try my best."

"*Best* might not be good enough," Robert says. "We want him found, Gerry. That's the purpose of this whole mission, ain't it? That's why your boss brought us in. That's why he sent you here to us."

"How much'd he tell you, anyway?" Simon says, eyeing Gerry. "He tell you what we're gonna do when we find Tommy?"

"Tom Rollins is a danger to our national security," Gerry says, sounding like he's repeating something that has been said to him over and over again, "no matter what the papers say, or what Senator Seth Goldberg thinks."

Robert laughs at this. "Sounds like he knows, Simon," he says.

"Oh, surely does," Simon says. "This your first time out in the field, Gerry?"

Gerry nods.

"Yeah, you look like it."

"Don't worry, man," Nathan calls over his shoulder, not wanting to be left out of the hazing. "We'll keep you safe. Ain't that right, fellas?"

"Oh, we'll look after him all right," Robert says. "Especially if he does his job as well as Eric thinks he can. Speaking of, we still got another hour 'til we get to Nogales.

You wanna spend that time productively, get yourself set up? Maybe give us some kinda idea where to start looking, so we don't have to waste our time once we get there."

Gerry flinches, then quickly starts unzipping the case he's clutching to his chest. "Yes, of course, of course," he mumbles.

"I wanna watch this boy work," Simon says. "See if he's all as impressive as he's been cracked up to be."

"We all wanna see if that's the case, Simon," Robert says. He watches Gerry with unblinking eyes, and Gerry feels his stare. His hands fumble as he starts up the laptop. Nathan hits a pothole and the whole van shudders, and Gerry gasps as the laptop almost slips out of his lap. He scrambles to catch it. Simon laughs at the sight.

"Come on, Gerry," Robert says. "Let's get some hustle in that muscle."

"What muscle?" Simon says.

Gerry pretends that he doesn't hear. Focuses all his attention on the laptop, his fingers dancing over the keys. He's sweating harder now, despite the cold air that Nathan has circulating through the van.

"You set up yet?" Robert says.

"I'm set up," Gerry says.

"Well, all right," Robert says. "Now we're getting somewhere. Find our boy, Gerry."

Gerry doesn't look up from the screen. His hands move fast, rattling the keys. Simon raises his eyebrows, impressed at the speed. He looks at Robert, nods.

Time passes. Robert watches him work. Watches the screen. A girl's face keeps appearing. Robert recognizes her from the recent picture of Tom that Eric has supplied him. "That's the girl he's with," he says.

Gerry grunts in the affirmative.

"Who is she?"

"I don't know," Gerry says.

"All that fancy typing and searching, and you ain't even got her name?"

Gerry grunts again. This time, it's not clear what it means. He clears his throat. "I'm going through recent security footage," he says. "Getting hits on the girl. Tom knows to cover up. They either haven't realized I can search via the girl, or else she keeps forgetting to hide her face."

"So what are they doing?" Robert says. "Where are they?"

"I'm finding that out," Gerry says. "I'm working up to what's most recent."

Robert leans in closer to see the screen clearer. To see what Gerry sees. He sees footage of Tom and the girl going inside a building. "What's inside?"

"I don't know," Gerry says. "There aren't any cameras inside."

"What's the building?"

"I don't know," Gerry says, for the first time starting to sound annoyed. "I'm trying to find that out." The van jolts, hitting another bump or a pothole. Gerry grits his teeth. His eyes bulge out of his head as he looks toward Nathan. "Can you *please* try to stop all the bumping around? This will all be a lot faster and easier if I'm not being shaken around from side to side all the damn time."

Nathan chuckles. "I'll do my best, Gerald."

Gerry shakes his head, mutters something to himself that Robert can't make out. He types furiously, raising his knees to bring the laptop closer to his face.

Minutes pass by. Then, Gerry makes a noise. "Huh," he says.

"What?" Robert says.

"The building they went inside – it's a brothel."

Robert raises an eyebrow. "That so?"

"I never knew Tom to have a woman in all the years we

knew him," Simon says. "A brothel makes sense. He had to be getting it from somewhere."

Robert ignores him. Gerry has brought up new footage. Tom and the girl, entering another building. Gerry fast-forwards. They leave it together half an hour later. "Another brothel?" Robert says.

Gerry nods. "Yeah. Same night, too."

"The same night?" Robert strokes his chin, staring at the screen. "What are you up to, Tom?" he says, watching his former unit member on the screen, bearded now and with hair longer than Robert has ever seen on him. "What the fuck are you doing?"

24

Tom is alone. He's left Carmen back at the hotel, told her not to answer the door unless she knows it's him. He explained to her what he was going to do, and she understood that she had to stay behind.

Cindy gave him a list of names. Gave their details, too – their addresses, car makes and models, and registration plates. Tom picks the agent who lives closest to their hotel. His name is Jonas Pringle. Tom takes the bus to his street the night before. It's a nice street. It's lined with trees that obscure the fronts of the houses. Jonas Pringle's driveway is lined with high bushes. No one can see as Tom goes to Jonas's car with a wire clothes hanger taken from the hotel. He twists it into the shape he needs and slides it down the window, uses the hooked end to work the lock mechanism until the lock on the inside of the door pops up. Tom lets himself in, relocks the car, and settles down low in the backseat. He pulls out his KA-BAR. Keeps it in hand all through the night.

It's not a comfortable way to lie, but Tom has slept on rougher surfaces. He's able to twist his body into a shape that allows him to grab a few hours of sleep. He wakes early the next morning. Birds are singing in the bushes that line the driveway. The sun is rising and the interior of the car is beginning to warm up. It's not yet hot.

Jonas leaves his house at seven thirty. Tom hears the door open and close. Jonas lives alone. Unmarried, no children. It was all in the information Cindy gave him. Jonas gets into the car. He's a short, round man with a moustache. He's forty-three. He carries a thermos containing what smells like coffee. He takes a sip, then puts it on the passenger seat. He smacks his lips. Puts the key in the ignition. Before he can turn it, Tom makes himself known.

"Good morning, Jonas," he says, KA-BAR sliding over Jonas's shoulder and pressing into the side of his neck.

"Holy fucking shit Jesus!" Jonas jumps in his seat. He feels the cold steel of the blade against his neck and goes very still. His eyes go to the mirror, trying to see who is behind him.

"Did I give you a fright?" Tom says. "Sure sounds like I gave you a fright."

"Who the – who the –" Jonas stammers, trying to get his words out.

"Doesn't matter who I am," Tom says, anticipating what he's trying to ask. "What matters right now is who *you* are. And, more importantly, what you know."

Jonas starts to shake his head, but he stops when he feels the knife. "I don't know anything, sir," he says. "I don't know who you think I am, or what I might know, but I can guarantee you've got the wrong man."

"I ain't so sure about that, Jonas," Tom says. "Every month you receive a thousand-dollar deposit into an offshore bank account – what's that? A tax-free bonus courtesy of the US government for all the swell work you do down here keeping illegals from crossing the border?"

Jonas purses his lips, doesn't answer.

"It's some kind of bonus, ain't it? Or, more precisely, a

payment. And it doesn't come from the US government. Comes from the Nogales Cartel, doesn't it?"

Jonas swallows.

"Come on, Jonas," Tom says. "You can tell me. We're friends here, ain't we?"

"I don't even know who you are," Jonas says.

"That's right," Tom says. "You don't. But I've got a knife at your neck, don't I? So it's probably best you do everything you can to stay on my friendly side."

"What do you want from me?"

"I've already made myself clear," Tom says. "I have some questions, and I want answers. And I believe you're the man to give them to me, Jonas."

"I'm gonna – I'm gonna be late for work –"

"I'd say that's the least of your concerns right now. We're just gonna sit right here, hidden amongst these beautiful bushes, until you tell me what I want to know. Firstly – the Nogales Cartel. What do you know about them?"

"I don't know anything about them."

Tom moves the KA-BAR from the side of his neck to his throat. Applies pressure.

"I swear!" Jonas says, body rigid. "I swear to God!"

"Don't know anything about them, yet you're taking their money."

"I ain't the only one!"

"I know that, Jonas, but you're the one I'm asking questions."

"They pay us to use the border. They pay us to keep their competition out. I've never even met them, not a single one. Someone else set it up. I was just brought in to help out."

"Help with what? Transporting girls?"

Jonas is silent.

"How'd you manage to get hold of those girls without ever meeting a single member of the cartel?"

"I'm not at the border," Jonas says. "I see them later. I...I transport them. That's all."

"Transport them where? Where do they go?"

"Different places. Most of them stay local. They get sold to brothels. They go to whoever buys them."

"Who's the madam who gets first pick?"

Jonas thinks for a moment. "Oh," he says. "That's Shelley Snow. She picks the prettiest girls. The ones she thinks she can make the most money out of."

"And where's she take them?"

"She has a brothel up in Tucson."

"Where is it?"

Jonas tells him. Tom commits the address to memory.

"Well, Jonas," Tom says, "it was a tough ride getting there, but it sounds like you've told me all I need to know." He notices how Jonas's body sags in relief.

"Think you can take the knife away?" Jonas says.

"Not yet," Tom says. "No, first you and I have to go on a little drive. We need to pick up a friend of mine, and then the three of us are taking a road trip north, to Tucson. It's only, what, an hour away, right? Give or take. Shouldn't take us long to get there."

"What? I – I – I can't go. I can't leave. I –"

"Yes you can, Jonas. And you are. You're gonna drive us right to Madam Snow's brothel, because I'm not taking a chance on you telling your friends what we've spoken about here, sending advance warning to Madam Snow to let her know we're coming."

"I don't even know what you want there!"

"We want one of her girls, Jonas," Tom says. "Hell, while we're there, we're probably gonna take all her girls. Send them home. And now you know. We're in this together now, Jonas. Accomplices."

Jonas closes his eyes, squeezes them tight. "Fuck," he says. "*Fuck.*" He trembles in his seat.

Tom slides his Beretta from his side, presses it into Jonas's seat so he'll feel it in his back. He jolts, and Tom knows he's felt it. "I'm gonna take the knife away, Jonas," Tom says. "But now there's a gun in your back, so don't try anything you're gonna regret, you understand?"

Tom takes the KA-BAR away, and Jonas nods.

"That's good," Tom says. "Start the engine. I'll give you directions."

25

Carmen has struggled to rest alone in the hotel room.

Tom told her not to leave it, and to avoid being seen. She's done as he said, but she's suffered a fitful sleep. All night long, she's heard noises outside the room's door. Footsteps up and down the corridor, pressing on creaking floorboards. Other guests at the hotel, no doubt, but they've made her heart leap into her throat each time.

Even now, in the morning, she doesn't feel much better. She has no idea when Tom will get back.

She's woken early. She kills time. Has the television on, though she barely watches it. Paces the floor. The noise in the corridor outside the room is not so regular in the day. She wonders what all those people were doing up so late at night. It's a cheap hotel, though, and she doesn't have to wonder too hard.

She glances out the window, searching for any sign of Tom. She can't see him. She spots a black van parked down the road. Its front seats are empty. She doesn't think anything of it, not at first. Resumes her pacing. Takes a seat on the end of the bed and tries to watch the television. She can't focus. She goes to the bathroom. Their room is on the corner of the building, and the window is on the side. It looks down into an alleyway below, mostly empty save for a couple of dumpsters. She remembers when they first checked in and Tom pointed out the room's escape routes. He paid a lot of attention to this bathroom window, and the pipe that ran down the side of the building next to it.

"It's strong enough," he said. "It'll support our weight, if it has to."

Carmen leaves the bathroom, crosses to the small kitchen to get a glass of water. Standing, drinking, her eyes drift to the window and fall upon the black van again. It's still there. She watches it from the kitchen. Puts down the glass and goes closer to the window, watching it all the while. She conceals herself behind the wall, peers out to see it. The front seats are empty still, but she notices how the van is shimmying a little. Like there are people in the back of it. She watches, waits to see if anyone gets out, or if anyone climbs into the front.

There's a knock at the door, and she gives a start. Her head snaps from the window to the door.

"Carmen." It's Tom's voice, calling through so she knows to let him in. "It's me."

26

Tom pushes Jonas into the room ahead of himself. Carmen stares at him, asks who he is. No doubt she recognizes the uniform.

Tom has the Beretta still sticking into Jonas's back. The gun is concealed inside his jacket, in his pocket. He kicks the door closed behind him. "Say hello to Jonas Pringle," Tom says. "An upstanding member of the border patrol agency. He's going to take us to Tucson." He remains behind Jonas, though he has pulled the gun from his pocket now and is pointing it at him openly.

"Tucson?" Carmen says. "Is that where she is?"

"That's where Madam Snow takes the girls she chooses."

Carmen frowns. "Madam Snow?" She shakes her head, guessing at who he means. She looks at Jonas. "Have you seen my sister?" she says. "Her name is Rosa. Rosa Hernández. Do you know her?"

Jonas shrugs. "I don't know," he says. "We get so many girls through."

Tom sees how Carmen's face changes, how her jaw goes a little slack as she processes what he's just said. She steps forward and slaps him. The noise resounds throughout the room. Jonas stumbles, caught off guard. He presses a hand to his face, rubs it.

Carmen glares at him. She takes a step back, calms herself. Tom notices how Jonas can't hold her eye. He looks down, still rubbing his cheek. Carmen wipes her hand on her jeans, like she's just touched something unpleasant. She turns to Tom. "There's a van outside," she says. "It's been there for a while."

Tom feels his face drop. He grabs Carmen by a shoulder and forces her down while he crouches. "Get down," he says. He's going to crawl to the window, to look for himself. He's not going to walk straight to it, leaving himself, or Carmen, exposed.

Jonas is still standing. He looks down at them, confused. "What – what are you –"

Tom gestures for him to get down, too, but before he can say anything, before Jonas can respond, Tom hears glass shatter and the sound of a bullet cutting through the air. There's a meaty thud. Tom looks up. Jonas falters, trying to keep his feet. He blinks repeatedly. Looks down. Tom sees blood blossoming on his chest. Jonas sees it, too. He doesn't look back up. He collapses, crumpling into a heap.

"Get in the bathroom," Tom says to Carmen, pushing her along the ground ahead of him. "Stay low!"

There are footsteps outside the door. Tom looks toward the sound. The footsteps have stopped. Tom raises his gun, ducking low behind the bed, staying out of view of the sniper who must be hiding either in or atop the building opposite. He lets off a few shots at the door to keep whoever is outside at bay. He hears them scatter into cover.

Carmen is in the bathroom. She's thrown the window open. It's on the side of the building and out of view of the sniper. Tom reaches the doorway, stands, Beretta raised. The hotel room's nearest window on the front of the building, directly in the sniper's line of sight, is six feet away from him. Nothing on his direct left but wall. The sniper cannot see him. "Climb down the pipe," Tom says, calling over his shoulder while he watches the door. "Get around the back of the building and hide there."

"What about you?" Carmen says, hesitating by the window.

"I'll be right behind you – go!"

Carmen starts climbing out, one foot on the edge of the bathtub and the other already swinging through the open window.

Tom doesn't watch her go. He turns back to the door, gun raised.

There is automatic gunfire from the hall outside the room. It blows the handle and the lock out. The door is kicked open. Tom fires, keeps them at bay. He steps back into the bathroom, throws the door closed. He turns the lock on the door, then grabs the towels from the railing on the wall nearby. It is not a strong lock and will not take much to kick through it. He throws the towels down to the base of the door, kicks them under the crack to wedge it closed. He goes to the window. Carmen is halfway down the pipe, shimmying as quick as she can. They're three stories up. Tom swings out the window. Behind him, the door's lock is kicked out of the jamb. The towels at the base slow it from opening.

Tom reaches for the pipe. Bullets start tearing through the door. Tom feels something hot tear through him, too, high up on his left shoulder. It skims him, it doesn't go deep, but there's enough force to knock him off balance. Blood bursts from the meat of his trapezius and splashes on the side of his face. He loses his grip on the pipe, begins to fall from the window. All three stories, nothing to grab onto. He makes himself as limp as he is able, knowing he's more likely to break bones if he's tense.

He hits the ground hard, the wind blown out of his lungs. He gasps for breath, tries to push himself up. Carmen reaches the bottom of the pipe. She runs to him.

Tom sees movement above, from the bathroom window. A face looks down, raising a gun. Tom grabs for his own, pulls it out and points it up toward the window. In the split second before he pulls the trigger, he realizes he recognizes the face smiling down at him. He blinks and fires, knowing he's unlikely to hit the person above, only hoping to force them back inside the bathroom, where they can't fire down at him and Carmen.

"Are you hurt? Can you move?" Carmen says, crouching by his side and reaching for his arm with tentative hands, scared to touch him.

"I'm fine," Tom says, but his voice is a croak, and he doesn't sound fine. Doesn't feel it, either, but nothing is broken, and he's not dead. They need to keep going. They need to keep moving. Because Tom is certain he recognized that face above them, the face of the man coming for them, firing at them.

Carmen helps Tom to his feet, takes some of his weight with her arm around her shoulder. "Around the back," Tom says, "around the back." His car is at the front, in view of the sniper. Jonas's car is at the back of the building, closer, and Tom has the keys. He looks over his bleeding shoulder as they go, and the face has returned to the window. The man isn't shooting. Hasn't even raised a gun.

Tom was right. He recognized the face.

It's Robert.

Captain Robert Dale.

He's watching Tom go. He's smiling. He's waving.

27

Cindy sits by her laptop, her legs cramping. She's hardly moved from this spot in days now. She stares at the screen, waiting for news, waiting for alerts. Chewing on her fingernails, feeling helpless. She's doing as much as she can, but she's six hundred and sixty miles away from Nogales, Arizona.

She thinks about Carmen, and her sister, Rosa. Can't get them out of her head.

In the past, Tom has paid her for the help she has given him. This time is different, though. This time feels almost personal for her. An older sister, trying to get her younger sibling to safety? It hits close to home. It brings back memories she'd rather not think about. Memories she grits her teeth against, blocks out. Memories she's never shared with anyone. Has kept to herself. Suffered alone.

Cindy knows too well the pain of losing a sister. She knows it's a pain that can never be healed. A pain she wouldn't want anyone else to have to go through. If she can help Carmen get Rosa back, she'll do everything she can to make sure it becomes a reality.

She's following the cyber trail of a man called Gerry Davies. He works for the FBI. From everything she's seen, it seems he works more directly for Eric Thompson. He's the one found the footage of Tom crossing over the Mexican border. He's the one hacking security footage.

He's good, Cindy has to give him that. He puts up firewalls around his work that it takes her time to break, and usually by the time she does, he's set up another one. It's time-consuming, and it's frustrating, and it makes her feel more helpless than before. She knows he's in Arizona, and she knows he's with another group of hitmen or mercenaries hired to take Tom out, but she doesn't know where exactly they are. She can't track them. Can't get ahead of them. She's playing catch-up.

Her fingers are aching from constant typing, and her legs are cramped from being crossed. She straightens her spine, rolls her neck. Hears it crack. She doesn't know what time of day it is. Her blinds are drawn, and she doesn't know whether it's light or dark outside. She's been lost in her work. It happens. It happens often. She gets so caught up in what she's doing she forgets to eat, to sleep, to stretch. She can go hours without drinking anything, then she comes up for air, and her throat is burning, and everything hurts.

An alert sounds. She stops stretching and zeroes in on it. It's a message, from Gerry to Eric. It's encrypted. She sets her jaw and gets to work unravelling it. More than likely he's checking in. Giving a status update. She hopes he gives his whereabouts – it may help her track them down faster. Give her a head start.

She feels her eyes go wide as she reads what it says.

They've tracked Tom to a hotel. He's been shot. Not dead. Injured. They'll find him.

Found TR's hotel. Shots exchanged. Creased him, didn't grease him. He's omega mike, but we'll find him.

Cindy feels sick, recognizing enough military slang to know that "creased him, didn't grease him" means Tom has been shot but not killed. In a panic, she grabs her phone and tries to call him. It rings out. She dials again. He doesn't always pick up first try, and she knows he's "omega mike," meaning on the move. And sometimes, the phone is buried deep in his backpack.

On the third attempt, someone answers. It isn't Tom.

"Hello, *Cindy*," the voice says. It makes her skin crawl. "And how might you know our dear friend Tom?"

Cindy hangs up. She dismantles the phone, snaps the SIM. Leaves her apartment on aching legs and tingling pins-and-needles feet, peering out her door before she goes. She leaves the building and deposits the broken bits of the phone in a dumpster three blocks away. She walks back to her building with hot sun burning down on her, though her arms are wrapped around herself like she's cold. She's wary of being watched. She keeps her face down and keeps walking. Gets back to her apartment and locks the door, puts the chain across. She takes deep breaths. Tom is in trouble. He's hurt. He needs help. Carmen needs help. Rosa needs help.

Cindy closes her eyes, tries to think.

It comes to her. Dark Claw 89. His cousin is Tom's friend. They know each other. They go back. *Way* back.

She hurries to her computer.

28

Zeke is out back of his house, grilling dinner, when his phone begins to buzz in his pocket. At first, he doesn't notice. Tre and Tamika are playing basketball with a kid-size set nearby. Tre is teaching Tamika how to shoot, and they're both laughing loudly at her failing attempts. Zeke's mind is on the steaks. It's only when Naomi comes out from the house, carrying two glasses of water with ice in them, and she says, "Can you hear that?" that Zeke finally feels it.

He reaches into his pocket, checking the caller ID. It's his cousin, James Greene. Zeke hands the tongs over to Naomi to keep an eye on the food while he steps to one side to answer the call. "James," he says, "long time."

"Almost seven months, now," James says. "When you called me for your buddy."

"Yeah, I remember." Zeke watches his children playing, and remembers how he got in touch with his cousin at Tom Rollins's behest. He'd needed some help, and he'd hoped James might know someone who could give him that help. Turned out James had.

"You asked me if I knew someone who could help your friend," James says.

"Yeah, I remember that." Zeke finds himself walking further away from his family, down the lawn.

"I put him in touch with Shriek. Now Shriek wants me to put her in touch with *you*."

Zeke pauses. "Why?"

James chuckles. "Tom Rollins again."

Zeke's spine stiffens. "Is he all right? What's happened?"

"I don't know. But let me say this – if she wanted to get in touch with you, she could find a way. Asking me to give you her number is either a courtesy, or a time-saver."

"A time-saver? Then maybe we should cut this conversation short, and I'll call her."

"Maybe so. I'll text you her number. Good luck with your friend, Zeke." James hangs up.

Zeke lowers his phone. Looks at the screen. A moment later a message comes through from James. It's a number. Shriek's number.

"Zeke?" Naomi calls over. She likely sees the look on his face. "What's up? Who was it?"

Zeke doesn't answer directly. "I just need to make a call," he says.

Naomi raises an eyebrow. "The steaks are nearly ready," she says.

"I'll be quick." Zeke is already dialing the number.

It's answered on the first ring. "Zeke Greene?"

"*Shriek*?" Zeke says.

"Call me Cindy. Listen – we don't have time for chitchat. Tom's hurt, and there are people after him."

"He's hurt? How bad?"

"I don't know, and I don't know who's after him or how many. I can't get in touch with him anymore. What I *do* know is that he's in Arizona, but he's probably on the move. I'm trying to follow the movements of the group after him, and I'm running facial recognition on security footage to try to get ahead of them, but that's as much as I can do. He needs someone on the ground, someone who can help him out, especially if he's hurt."

"And you thought of me."

"You're the only friend of his I know of."

"I'm flattered." Zeke bites his lip. He doesn't look back at his family. Doesn't look at Naomi by the grill, or Tre and Tamika still playing with the basketball. Knows that if he does, it will make his decision harder. "Okay," he says. "I'm gonna start heading to Arizona. You're gonna have to find him while I'm on the way, give me directions to where he is." A moment passes. "Let me know if he's still gonna be alive when I get there."

"I will," Cindy says. Zeke can hear relief in her voice. "Where are you now?"

"Home," Zeke says. "Shreveport."

"Louisiana?"

"Yeah."

"Shit – you're further away than I am."

"Then it sounds like I'm gonna have to start moving."

"I'll be in touch," Cindy says, and hangs up.

Zeke slides the phone into his pocket. He takes a deep breath, turns around, back to his family, and prepares to tell them that he needs to go.

Naomi is already looking at him. The look on her face is like she's read his mind. "Where you going?" she says.

"I have to go help an old friend," Zeke says, stepping closer.

"Who?"

"It's Tom."

Naomi looks down at the steaks, then back up at him. "You ain't got time to eat, do you?"

"I need to go now," Zeke says. "Right now."

She sets her jaw, but she nods. "Say goodbye to your children," she says.

Zeke kisses her on the side of the mouth. She strokes the back of his neck as he leans in. "Stay safe," she says.

Zeke hugs his children, kisses the tops of their heads, and then he leaves. He walks calmly through the house, not wanting to alarm them, but as soon as he steps out the front door, he starts running to his car. Jumps inside, and speeds away from his home. He doesn't head straight for Arizona. He goes downtown first, to his lockup. Other than a Beretta, he doesn't like to keep guns in the house.

Especially not guns like these.

He loads an AR-15 Tactical rifle into a sports bag, then an AK-47, and a couple of already loaded magazines for both. M18 smoke grenades on a nearby shelf catch his eye. He deliberates. Has no idea what he's going into. He grabs a few of them, puts them into the bag with the guns. The Beretta he keeps in the house, in a safe in the back of his wardrobe, is still there. He takes another one, checks it's loaded, tucks it down the back of his waistband. Again, not knowing what he's going into and wanting to be prepared for every possibility, he packs a couple of earpieces and microphones. Next, he grabs a pair of combat trousers and a khaki shirt, then a Kevlar vest. He doesn't have time to change right now, and he didn't have time to change when he left the house, but if he finds himself heading into a combat situation, he wants to be as fully prepared as possible.

He pauses at the door with the bag down by his side, looks over the lockup, making sure he hasn't forgotten anything. The weight of the bag is comforting, but simultaneously brings him butterflies. He swallows the anxiety. It's time to get to work.

He leaves the lockup, heads back to his car. Throws the bag in the trunk. Turns the vehicle toward Arizona and puts his foot down.

29

Tom is bleeding on the passenger seat. Carmen drives.

Tom realizes he has left his bag behind at the hotel, and it's likely been taken by Robert, covering up who was in the room, who his intended target was. Tom's not cut up about this. The picture of Alejandra, the Santa Muerte pendant, are both in his pocket. They are what's important, and he's glad he stopped traveling with the picture in the bag. He wants to reach for it, to comfort himself with her face, but he doesn't. Doesn't want to get blood all over her. Instead, he keeps his hand on his shoulder, keeps pressure on the wound.

Carmen is panicking. He can hear her muttering, "*Shit, shit, shit!*" under her breath, over and over.

"It's all right," Tom says. "Stay calm. Concentrate on your driving. Last thing we need right now is to get pulled over."

"Calm down?" she repeats, incredulous. "You're hurt! You're *shot!*"

"It's not as bad as it looks," Tom says. "It'll clean up. The bullet hasn't hit anything important. It hurts, but I can still raise my arm."

Carmen doesn't look at him. She swallows, trying to slow. Her eyes go to the mirrors, looking to see if the van she spotted earlier is following them.

"Are they there?" Tom says.

She shakes her head. "I don't see them. *If* it was their van. They could be in anything." She slams her hands down on the wheel. "Who were they? Did the cartel send them? The border patrol?"

"Neither," Tom says. "They either found me themselves, or Eric sent them."

Carmen tears her eyes away from the road and the mirrors long enough to look at him. "What do you mean? You know who they are?"

Tom grits his teeth, nods.

"Are they FBI?"

"CIA," Tom says. "Black ops."

Carmen pauses. "Like you?"

"Yeah. Like me. They're my old unit."

"You're sure?"

"I saw him. I saw Robert." Tom shakes his head, remembers his smile.

"You think the CIA sent them here after you?"

"No. This is too extreme. It's too personal. They're coming to kill me. Robert's doing this off his own bat, and he probably has Simon and Nathan along with him."

"Do you make enemies *everywhere* you go?"

"I try to be a friendly guy," Tom says. "But when you're adept at handling trouble, trouble always seems to find you." He spots a drugstore up ahead. "Pull over," he says, pointing.

Carmen does as he says.

"I need you to go in," Tom says.

She nods, already expecting this, looking at the blood

that is still leaking through the fingers of the hand on his shoulder, and the spatters over his face and arm.

"I need alcohol, wipes, a roll of gauze, and nonstick bandages. You got that?"

Carmen nods, starts to get out of the car.

Tom grabs her with his other hand. "I don't know how they tracked us down, but they could be using facial-recognition software," he says. "If they are, they'll have your face on record now, too. They'll have hacked security systems, and they'll get an alert any time either of us pops up somewhere."

Carmen's eyes are wide.

"Keep your head down," Tom says. "Cover your face as much as possible. Security cameras are usually in the upper corners of rooms, so don't look for them. Don't look directly into them." He winces.

Carmen looks at his bleeding shoulder. She nods. "I'll be right back."

Tom watches her hurry around the front of the car and into the drugstore. He turns his eyes to the mirrors, to the road. A car pulls in behind them. Tom reaches for the Beretta at his waist, his fingers at the handle, ready to grab it free and put it to use. The people in the car behind get out. A man and a woman. A young couple. The man wears blue jeans and a white T-shirt, and has his hair coiffed like James Dean. They both go into the convenience store next to the drugstore.

Carmen emerges, staring at the ground, her head still lowered away from the cameras. Her arms are laden with the items Tom sent her in for. She drops them into his lap as she gets back in the car. She starts driving, eager to get moving again after being stationary, if only for so short a time.

Tom pulls off his T-shirt and unscrews the lid on the alcohol. He stuffs the T-shirt into his mouth and bites down on it, then pours the alcohol over his wound.

Carmen's head flits from the road to him, watching what he is doing. "Jesus," she says. "Do you want me to pull over?"

The burning pain Tom initially felt is beginning to fade. Tom spits the T-shirt out of his mouth. "I'm not dressing it yet," he says. "Just cleaning it." He holds up the mostly empty container of alcohol. "This can inhibit the healing. Best I just get it out of the way now."

"Where am I even going right now, Tom?" Carmen holds up her hands on the wheel.

"Get out of Nogales," he says. "We'll find a motel where I can dress this, then we can pinpoint where it is we need to be in Tucson."

"We don't have Jonas," Carmen says.

"We don't need him," Tom says. "I remember where he said to go."

"Okay," Carmen says, tightening her hands around the steering wheel with a renewed sense of direction. The attack at the hotel, and Tom's wounding and fall, have shaken her. "Okay," she says again. "How are you? Are you all right?"

Tom lets his head rest. His eyes settle on the wing mirror and watch the road behind them. "Never better," he says.

30

Pedro pulls up outside the hotel. If it has a name, he can't see what it is. It's a cheap building offering cheap rates. A place where no one asks any questions. It makes him think of the motel, where Rollins first brought himself to their attention.

He likes these kinds of places, he thinks to himself. *The kind where no one bats an eye at a fake name.*

Pedro and Castillo go inside, one of their contacts in border patrol leading the way. The agent is the one who called them, told them about the shoot-out that occurred. How one of their men who didn't turn up for work that morning has been killed in it.

"We've been able to get a little privacy," the agent says, taking them up a flight of stairs at the back of the building, "because of what happened to Jonas. We've all got friends in the police, and they understand what it means when someone's killed one of our own."

Pedro doesn't care for the reasoning. He looks at this man who's trying to sound tough, like he and his buddies are going to hunt down whoever killed their comrade and make them pay, but he doesn't see a man of action. He sees a man who spends too much time in a coffee shop eating donuts. He looks at Castillo and Castillo smirks, and Pedro knows he is thinking the same. "You said there was some footage," Pedro says, "of the girl."

"That's right," the agent says. He's breathless already, though they've only gone up three flights. He stops outside the door that leads out onto the floor. "There aren't any cameras inside the hotel, but we were able to get some security footage from one of the neighboring buildings. The girl from the border's in it. Can't see the guy's face, though."

"He's ex-CIA," Pedro says. "He's not stupid. What about build? Did it look like him?"

"I think so, yeah. Plus, like I said, the girl was with him."

Pedro points at the still-closed door. "Let's look at the room, shall we?" He isn't expecting to find anything of use, but it's always worth covering all the bases.

There's a policeman standing guard outside the room. He side-eyes Pedro and Castillo as they pass with the agent, but he doesn't say anything. Pedro winks at him. The cop quickly looks away.

The agent stands over his fallen friend, looking down with his hands on his hips. He shakes his head, then covers his eyes with a hand. "Damn, shit," he says, stepping away. "Poor Jonas, man. Poor Jonas."

"Uh-huh," Castillo says, looking down. "Poor Jonas."

"They took his car, too, the bastards," the agent says. "Get him killed, then steal his damn car..."

Pedro steps over the dead body, looks the room over. "I don't see any personal belongings," he says. "Nothing of worth has been left behind."

"Nothing of use," Castillo says.

Pedro eyes the hole in the window. He sees glass in the carpet below. The shot has come from outside. He looks back to where Jonas lies. It lines up. He closes one eye and looks through the hole in the window to the roof of the building opposite. Imagines a sniper lying there in wait. Pedro doubts Jonas was his actual target. Jonas was just unfortunate.

"Have the forensics been in?" Pedro says, stepping away from the bullet hole in the window.

"Yes," the agent says.

"Did they find anything of interest?"

"I don't think so," the agent says. "Or if they did, they haven't processed it yet. We'll have to wait and see what they say."

"That'll take too long," Pedro says.

Castillo is in the bathroom. The window is already open. He's looking at the frame, then down into the alley below. Pedro steps up next to him.

"See anything?" he says.

"Some blood," Castillo says. "And where someone landed." He steps aside so Pedro can look down. He sees the blood spatters on the ground of the alley below, which have been cordoned off. There is blood on the frame, too. It looks like whoever got shot, it happened while they were climbing out the window.

"The trail goes that way," Castillo says. "Toward the back of the building."

"It's not a great deal of blood," Pedro says, pulling his head back inside. He remembers his time back on the force, seeing such scenes in many such rooms. He would talk to forensics. He learned a few things. "Some spatter, but not too much. It wasn't a kill shot."

"No," Castillo says. "Doesn't look like it."

"But someone is wounded."

"Yes."

"Good. It could slow them down."

Castillo nods.

The agent is still in the room, looking down at Jonas again. He keeps shaking his head. His lips are pursed.

"Were the two of you close?" Castillo says.

"Yeah," the agent says. "We...we were. We used to –"

Pedro cuts him off, uninterested. "We're going now," he says. "There are other places we need to be. Call us as soon as you hear anything worthwhile."

The agent blinks, then nods. "Okay," he says. "Okay. Sure."

Pedro and Castillo leave the room, head back to the staircase. "What do you think?" Castillo says as they head down.

"There's not much to be gleaned from an empty room with nothing but a dead border patrol agent in it," Pedro says. "But the footage showing that he's still with the girl is interesting."

"Mm," Castillo says, sounding like he agrees. "They've traveled far now. They're sticking together."

"She could've been one of the girls he freed from the motel," Pedro says. They reach the bottom floor, leave the hotel. They cross to their car. It's not Pedro's beloved R8. That's still at home, back in Mexico. He wouldn't travel across the border in such a vehicle, on such a mission. No, instead, it is a nondescript Ford that they picked up cheap before they came north. Perfect for a manhunt. "I think they're looking for someone," Pedro says when they're inside the car.

"Who?"

"I don't know. But to come here, together, and to stay together after he frees her from the motel – he hasn't kept the other girls by his side. He cut them loose. Wherever they went, they aren't with him now. They didn't cross into America with him and the girl. No, he's only with *her*. So why stick together for so long?"

"It's a good hunch," Castillo says. "But it's still only a hunch."

Pedro nods, turns on the engine. He slowly pulls away from the front of the hotel, starts driving. "Call Moreno and Mendoza," he says. "Tell them to search out the local pimps, the girls, anyone they can think of. Get them to flash the picture, see if anyone has been visited by them lately. Find out what they were asking."

Castillo pulls out his phone, sets to doing as Pedro has said. "What are we going to do?" he says, dialing.

"We're going to the brothels," Pedro says.

"This could be a time-consuming hunch," Castillo says.

"Leave no stone unturned," Pedro says, then Castillo starts talking on the phone, to Moreno, telling him what Pedro wants them to do. He's not talking for long. Moreno understands. When he's off the phone, Pedro gets him to call around, find out where the brothels are. He leaves him in the car and goes into a sandwich shop, buys lunch for them both. By the time he gets back, Castillo is waiting expectantly.

"I have addresses," he says.

Pedro hands him a sandwich. "We'll eat first, then we'll go visiting."

The first brothel they hit, they get lucky.

It's too early in the day for the establishment to be busy. The bouncer in the foyer is sitting around with a couple of bored-looking girls. One of them is filing her nails. The other is flicking through a magazine.

The bouncer gets to his feet. He's not smiling. Too busy trying to look tough. "Help you with anything, gentlemen?"

Castillo flashes the picture. "Been visited by these two lately?"

The bouncer looks at the photo, then he grins. "Yeah," he says. "We have."

Pedro cocks his head. "And what's so funny about that?"

"They went to two other places the same night they came here," the bouncer says. "My buddy Alan works one of them.

The guy –" the bouncer presses a thick finger to the picture, "– beat the shit out of him and took one of the girls."

Castillo looks back at Pedro, raises an eyebrow. "Sounds like you were right," he says, in Spanish.

It's clear from the look on the bouncer's face that he doesn't understand.

"What did they want when they came here?" Pedro says to the bouncer.

"Said they were looking for a third," he says. "And they were interested in Latin girls."

"Did they pick one?"

"Yeah."

"Which one?"

"You don't need to talk to her," the bouncer says. "After Alan got beat up, I already did, asked her what they all did together."

"And?" Pedro says.

"And they didn't *do* anything. They asked her some questions, and paid her extra to keep quiet about it."

Pedro stares at the bouncer, waits for him to continue.

The bouncer clears his throat, not trying to look so tough anymore. He looks at Pedro and side-eyes Castillo, and it's clear he's worked out who they are, and where they've come from. "They were asking her about girls who get smuggled up from Mexico," he says, "and if she knew anything about that. She didn't, though."

"Which brothel does your friend Alan work at?" Pedro says.

"It ain't got a name," the bouncer says, then gives them the address.

Pedro turns to Castillo. "This would have happened before the shoot-out at the hotel," Castillo says, beating him to it. They talk in Spanish. The bouncer takes a step back.

"And there wasn't another girl with them," Pedro says.

"And they kidnapped Jonas – to find out where else the girls are taken?"

"Tucson," Castillo says.

"Tucson," Pedro agrees.

"Tucson?" the bouncer says, understanding this.

"You don't have to concern yourself," Pedro says.

The bouncer is quick to nod.

Castillo reaches out, pats the bouncer on the arm. Castillo grins at the way the bouncer flinches. "You've been a big help," Castillo says. "Muchas, *muchas* gracias." He's still grinning.

They leave the brothel. "Call Moreno and Mendoza," Pedro says. "Tell them to meet us, and then we're going to Tucson."

"To Snow?" Castillo says.

Pedro bares his teeth and nods. The same place Miguel will be going very soon. "*Fuck*," he says.

Castillo knows what he is thinking. Knows why he curses. "Fuck," he says, nodding.

31

Tom and Carmen check into a motel halfway between Nogales and Tucson. They don't intend to be here long. Only long enough for Tom to dress his wounds, and to plot their route to where Carmen's sister is being held.

Where they *hope* she is being held.

As they pulled into the parking lot, while Carmen went inside to pay for the room, Tom made a mental note of the vehicles outside. Marking off in his mind everything already present. He squeezed the Santa Muerte pendant through his pocket as he did so, and thought of Alejandra.

Carmen returned to the car with a map of Tucson. She dropped it into his lap. "They had them in the lobby," she said, pulling the car around to their room.

They've been here an hour now. Tom's tattered T-shirt – the only one he has since he lost his bag – is soaking in the bathtub to get the worst of the blood out. He cleans his wound with the wipes, then flushes it out with water. While he does this, Carmen sits on the edge of the bathtub and squeezes the water out of his T-shirt. The water in the tub has turned pink. She holds the T-shirt up and inspects it.

"Better than it was," she says.

Tom nods. "It'll have to do. I need a hand with the bandage."

Carmen drains the bathtub and rinses it down, then heads through into the front room to lay the T-shirt out on the windowsill so it can dry in the sun. She comes back to the bathroom, to help Tom with the nonstick bandages. She dries his flushed wound with a towel, then presses the bandage down into place. She secures it with the gauze, unrolling it under his armpit and across his chest. Her touch is delicate and careful.

"How does it feel?" she says when she finishes. "Does it hurt? Does it sting?"

"It's numb," Tom says.

"Okay," Carmen says. "That's good, right? Better than it hurting. I should have gotten some painkillers while I was in the drugstore. I didn't think. I was too busy trying not to look at the cameras."

"It's all right," Tom says. He stands. Winces. Everything is aching after the fall.

"Your face says otherwise," Carmen says. "Maybe I should go to the reception, see if they have anything –"

"No," Tom says. "We stick together." He leaves the bathroom. She follows. He takes a seat at the table near where his T-shirt is drying and unfolds the map Carmen bought, searching for the location Jonas gave him.

"Are you sure he was telling the truth?" Carmen says.

Tom nods, remembering. "Pretty sure," he says.

Carmen wraps her arms around herself and stands by the window, watching the road, keeping an eye out. "We should get rid of his car as soon as we can," she says.

"We're going to," Tom says, without looking up from the map. "Okay," he says. "I've got it."

"You've marked it down?" Carmen says. She doesn't turn away from the window. Something catches her eye, and she leans forward.

"Committed it to memory," Tom says. "It's in here." He taps the side of his head, though she's still not looking. He grabs his T-shirt from the windowsill, feels it. It's hot from the sun, but still damp in places. He hesitates before he pulls it on, looking at Carmen's back, at the way her head is twisted to one side like she's seen something. "What is it?"

"It's the van," she says.

Tom pulls the T-shirt on, then stands next to her.

"Down the road there," she says. "It's trying to be inconspicuous, but it's them."

Tom sees the black van pulled to the side of the road, crawling along. They probably think it's out of view. Tom never saw the van back at the hotel. "You're sure?" he says.

"I'm sure," she says. "They've found us."

32

Gerry has followed the car's license plate. They've followed the road it escaped on, and he's searched ahead, to wherever he's been able to find security footage. He's seen them sitting outside a drugstore. Saw the girl emerge with her arms laden with bandages and other items for cleaning and dressing wounds. He's seen them pull in at this motel, only a couple of hours ahead of them.

"I see the car," Nathan says.

"Where's the camera?" Robert says, looking at Gerry.

"Above the reception door," Gerry says. He does not look up from his laptop. It feels like from the moment they first got him to open it, he hasn't raised his head, and his fingers have never ceased their typing.

"How much can you see from it?"

"The parking lot, mostly. The fronts of some of the rooms."

"Uh-huh. We can see the parking lot from right where we are. Are they still here? Do you know that much at least?"

"No sign that they've left," Gerry says, sounding defensive.

"They might've been subtle about it," Robert says.

"None of the other cars have left since they got here either," Gerry says. "So unless they left on foot, they're still in room twenty-three."

"Then gear up, boys," Robert says, biting his lip. "We're going in. And remember! Rollins is mine. Subdue him, but don't fucking kill him. The girl – well, I don't give a shit about her. Do whatever you want with her."

Nathan and Simon both grin and nod.

Gerry clears his throat. "Is that why you didn't shoot him in the alley?"

Robert raises an eyebrow. "What's that?"

Gerry avoids looking up. He swallows, and there is a click in his throat. "You had him back in the alley. I could see. You could have killed him right there after he fell, but you didn't take the shot."

Robert doesn't answer straight away. He stares at Gerry. Runs his tongue over his teeth. Watches him until he starts to squirm. "Is that a problem for you, Gerry?" he finally says.

Gerry swallows, still doesn't raise his eyes.

"I'll kill him how I want to kill him, Gerry," Robert says. "If that's all right with *you*. And how I *want* to kill him is with my hands. I don't care if they're empty or if it's with a knife, but I'm going to look him in the eye when I snuff him. You got that?"

Gerry gives a slight nod, looking like he wishes he'd never brought it up.

Nathan stops the van. They pull on their body armor, field protective masks hanging from them, then load up their weapons. AR-15s. Robert hooks a smoke grenade to his vest. They get out the back of the van, Simon getting out first and covering them, rifle pointed at the motel.

Robert checks the road. It's clear. He signals to Nathan, sends him around the back. Nathan nods, sets off, ducking low with his rifle raised. Robert and Simon head for room twenty-three. Gerry stays behind, in the van.

Robert and Simon point their rifles as they approach, keep the door and the windows of the room covered. They get up against the wall without incident. Robert pulls the smoke grenade from his vest. Simon takes a step back, rifle raised, covering the door. They look at each other, make eye contact. They nod.

33

Tom stuffs pillows under the blanket on the bed so it looks like someone is sleeping there, then he and Carmen head to the bathroom again. They leave the room via the window there. Tom knows at least one of the occupants of the van will be coming around the back of the motel, and he's ready to bump into them at any moment.

That moment comes at the corner, almost as soon as they reach it. The hostile is coming from the other direction, from the van. Tom knows it is likely to be either Simon Collins or Nathan Sapolsky, but he can't make out which it is at first. He's wearing body armor and carrying an AR-15. Tom is ready. Has his KA-BAR drawn for a quick and quiet kill. He grabs the man by the back of the head and drives the knife into his throat. Tom hears him gurgle, and looks down to see that it is Nathan. Tom tears the knife to the side and pulls it out, then lets Nathan drop. Tom takes his AR-15, hands it to Carmen. Her eyes go wide. "I can't use this," she says.

"If anyone comes at you, just point and shoot," he says. "Even if you don't hit them, it'll stop them in their tracks."

Carmen takes it, though reluctantly. The semiautomatic

looks out of place in her hands. She doesn't know how to hold it, or what to do with it, but now is not the time for a tutorial. Tom just needs her to have something that will keep her safe.

They round the corner, head to the next one. They can see the van. Its back doors are open. There's no one in the front. Tom pulls out his Beretta. He looks toward their room and sees Simon covering the door. Robert throws a smoke grenade through the window. They pull on their protective masks, and Simon kicks the door down.

"Get to the car," Tom says, then starts running.

He hears gunshots from inside the room, blasting the pillow form on the bed. As he reaches the room, someone is stepping out of it. Tom raises the Beretta while he runs, lets off two shots. They hit the person in the torso, thudding into the body armor. Tom can tell from the shape and body language that it is Simon Collins. The impact of the shots makes him drop his weapon and stumble back into the room. Tom keeps charging. Robert appears in the doorway as Simon falls, AR-15 raised. Tom doesn't slow. Kicks Robert back into the room. His former commander loses his grip on the AR-15 with the blow. The back of his legs hit the edge of the bed, and he rolls with the shape of it, throws himself back over the mattress and the shot-up pillows.

The smoke is still thick in the room. Tom kicks the dropped guns behind him, out of the room and out of reach. Simon is on the ground, sitting up against the wall. He tears at his body armor, gasping. Tom kicks him in the face through the mask, knocks him flat. The mask's face cracks. Tom raises the Beretta for the killing shot.

Robert rounds the bed, charges. Tom sees him out of the corner of his eye, spins on him. Robert ducks low as Tom fires twice. The bullets are too high. They hit the wall opposite, bury themselves there. Robert tackles Tom, drives his full weight into him and throws him up against the wall. The impact is hard. Tom drops the Beretta. He doesn't waste motion trying to catch it. Instead, he brings down the point of his elbow into Robert's back. The blow is not as effective as Tom would like through Robert's body armor, but it's enough for him to feel it. He brings himself up and punches Tom in the ribs, then headbutts him.

The back of Tom's head bounces off the wall. He tastes blood, and feels it running from his nose. He's able to block Robert's next punch, then throws one of his own. Catches him in the mouth, feels how his lips scrape against his teeth. Knows that Robert is tasting blood now, too.

Robert clamps a hand down on Tom's shoulder, seeing the bandage through the tattered T-shirt. He slaps his other hand down on top of it. Squeezes hard, both hands. He grins. The blood on his teeth gives him an extra sadistic flair.

Tom feels blood running from the wound again. Out the corner of his eye, he can see how it blooms under his T-shirt, spreading throughout the fabric. Can feel it running down his body.

"You've made yourself some enemies, Tommy," Robert says, his face close to Tom's. "Someone who's ready to pay a *lot* of money to see you taken out."

Tom knows he's talking about Eric.

"Hell – I'd do this for *fun*." Robert chuckles. "Didn't tell him that, though. I always say, ain't nothing feels better than getting paid for doing what you love."

Tom spits in his eye, then brings up his knee and drives it into Robert's side, into his ribs. "You talk too fuckin' much," Tom says, realizing how much he'd hoped to never hear the sound of the man's voice again. Robert's grip on his wounded shoulder loosens enough for Tom to bring up a leg and kick him away.

Again, Robert rolls back with the blow. He pulls out his

Glock as he goes, and brings himself back up on a knee, pointing the gun at Tom. He's smiling.

Tom grits his teeth, stares him straight in the eye. Won't give him the satisfaction of backing down.

The front of the room implodes suddenly. Tom presses himself back harder against the wall as plaster and wood and shards of broken glass fly through the air. Tom coughs as choking dust is thrown up. It obscures his vision. He blinks hard and looks back to see Carmen behind the wheel of Jonas's car. She's screaming at him. "Get in!"

Tom doesn't get straight in. He grabs his Beretta from the ground and scans the room, searching for Robert. He can't see him. He's slipped out in the chaos, likely out the bathroom window, as Tom and Carmen earlier did. Simon is gone, too.

"Tom!" Carmen says. "Come on! Let's go!"

Tom gets in the car, and Carmen battles to reverse it out of the side of the motel. The undercarriage scrapes as it extricates itself from the wreckage. Tom looks around. There's no sign of Robert or Simon. He can see people ducking low at their windows, peering out from their rooms, but too scared by the sound of gunfire to leave them.

"Go by the van," Tom says. "Get up next to it."

Carmen looks at him, but she does as he says. The AR-15 is on the backseat. He grabs it and rolls down his window as they get alongside the van. He shoots out the wheels on the passenger side. The van crumples, lowers, loses height.

"Go," Tom says. He pulls the map from his pocket and points straight ahead. "That way."

Carmen slams her foot down. They kick up stones and dust behind them as they speed away from the motel.

34

Pedro and his men reach Tucson, and go straight to see Shelley Snow.

Her mansion is lavish, and Pedro can't help but think how much its size and layout reminds him of Miguel's own. The driveway is as long, though there is not as much security present. The interior is all tiles, and there is a water feature of a cherub pouring water in the foyer. One thing it is lacking, however, is Miguel's young mistress, who is more remarkable to Pedro than any of the numerous paintings Shelley has adorning her walls.

While there were only a few guards outside, there are more inside the house. They wear suits and carry Glocks in holsters under their arms. They have earpieces with which to communicate. They look very professional, though Pedro has no idea if they're any good at what they do or not. They escort him and the others through to Shelley's office.

Shelley Snow is known in Tucson as a well-respected investor. That is her public face. What most people don't know is how she first came into her money. She's the most prolific and successful madam in the state. Possibly in the neighboring states, too. She didn't get that way by smiling and glad-handing. She's vicious. Dangerous. Merciless.

"You're early," she says, looking up as Pedro and his men enter her office. There are two bodyguards standing behind her, flanking her. They eye the cartel men warily. "Wanting to take a look around before Señor Aguilar gets here?"

"Not quite," Pedro says. He motions to the seat in front of him, opposite her. "May I?"

Shelley waves a hand. "If you like."

Pedro sits down, clasps his hands and crosses one leg over the other. He clears his throat. "I don't suppose you've heard of a man by the name of Tom Rollins?"

Shelley holds a fountain pen. It hovers over a piece of paper she was studying when they first entered. She cocks her head. "No," she says. "Can't say that I have. Should it mean something to me? Is he coming tomorrow?" She raises her head, turns to the bodyguard standing near to the cartel, about to ask him if Tom Rollins is on the guest list.

Pedro holds up a hand. "Allow me to explain," he says. He tells her who Tom Rollins is, what little they know of him, and what he has done so far. Shelley listens with an impassive face. When he finishes, she lays down her pen and folds her hands together, rests them flat upon her desk.

"And you think he's coming here?"

"It's the theory we're working off, yes," Pedro says.

"Which girl is he looking for?"

"We don't know."

"What about the girl he's with? Could it be some relation to her?"

"Possibly," Pedro says. "But we don't know who she is."

Shelley sucks her teeth. She stares at Pedro, holds his eye. "Well," she says, finally. "This isn't exactly good news, is it?"

"I thought you should be made aware," Pedro says.

"Is that so? And why wasn't I made aware of the attack at

the motel and the freeing of the girls there?" Shelley arches an eyebrow.

"We were hoping to contain the issue," Pedro says.

"I wouldn't say it's been contained," Shelley says. "If anything, I'd say it's gotten worse."

Pedro sucks his teeth now, annoyed because she's not wrong.

"The timing of this is very poor, Pedro," she says. "I have a gathering tomorrow night, as you're well aware."

"I'm aware," Pedro says. The Nogales Cartel are providing security for the event.

Shelley leans back in her chair. Keeps her hands folded, her eyes locked on his. "Do you know who Councilman Foster is?"

"I'm familiar with his name," Pedro says.

"You should perhaps familiarize yourself with him further," Shelley says. "One day he will be more than a councilman, and he will be running for higher office on a platform of border control. A patch of Arizona border that *we* will control. Everything that comes in and goes out will be at *our* discretion. And do you know how Councilman Foster will get to go so far? With the backing of me, and Miguel, and all the other people who will be coming here, to my home, tomorrow night. The last thing we need is some fucking rogue bursting down the door, looking for a whore."

Pedro takes a moment before he answers. "I don't intend on letting Rollins disrupt your gathering," he says, making a show of picking a piece of lint from his trouser leg. "I'll be here tomorrow. Castillo, Moreno, and Mendoza will be here tomorrow." He motions to the men behind him. "But I don't intend on leaving it until the last minute. I plan to have eliminated the threat of Rollins and the girl before then."

"It's tomorrow night," Shelley says. "You'll have to be fast."

"And I intend to," Pedro says. "After we leave your home.

But, should things not go as we'd like before then, I wanted to make you aware of the potential threat."

"Mm." Shelley taps a fingernail on the desk. "Is Miguel aware of how near the threat is coming to us, and when it could get here?"

Pedro waits longer than he should before answering. "Not yet," he says.

"Mm," Shelley says again, still tapping. "Perhaps you should rectify that. I'm sure he won't appreciate the surprise, especially not when he's so close to making one of his rare trips north of the border."

"I will," Pedro says.

"Be sure to tell him how much I'm looking forward to seeing him again. And on my home soil this time – tell him I will be returning the gracious hospitality he has shown me all the times I have traveled south. I'm looking forward to the privilege of doing so."

"He'll be pleased to hear that," Pedro says, getting to his feet. He keeps his face neutral.

Shelley's eyes never break her hold on his. "One way or another, I will see you tomorrow, Pedro," she says. "I hope that it's sooner, and I hope you come bearing the gift of Tom Rollins's severed head."

35

They had to ditch the van at the motel. It was useless with its wheels shot out. Simon grabbed Gerry and the rest of their equipment out of the back while Robert broke into one of the cars in the parking lot and hot-wired it. When they escaped the motel room out the bathroom window after the crazy bitch drove a car through the wall, they came across Nathan's body facedown and bleeding into the sand. They dragged him around the building, and Robert stuffed him into the trunk of the car they stole.

They're on the road now, Simon driving, Robert riding up front. Gerry is cramped into the back with his laptop and the rest of their gear. He's pale and shaken after being in the van while it was shot at. Robert can see how his hands tremble as he struggles to tap the keys.

Simon is silent. His jaw is clenched hard, and he stares at the road ahead, blinking and sniffing like he's fighting back tears. He starts to say something, but he only manages to utter, "Nathan," before his voice breaks. He clears his throat and swallows.

"Let him fuel your fire," Robert says. "Think about how

you'll make Tom pay when you get your hands on him. He's killed Nathan – our friend. He *was* our friend, right?"

Simon nods, his mouth twisting.

"That's right. So now that motherfucker has made this more personal than it was before. We'll gut him. We'll mount his fucking head. We'll grind his bones. And *then* we'll grieve. You understand? We don't grieve right now."

Simon nods again, setting his jaw. "Got it," he says.

"He's hurt, but we know that won't necessarily slow him down. We gotta stay sharp. Can't let ourselves get all clouded with grief because we're too busy thinking about Nathan. We think about him after."

"After," Simon says. "First we get that son of a bitch."

"Exactly. That's exactly right." Robert twists in his seat, calls back over his shoulder, "Where is he, Gerry?"

Gerry doesn't answer. Robert can hear him typing. A minute passes, and Gerry still has not spoken.

Robert turns fully in his seat. "You didn't hear me?" he says.

Gerry's color has not yet returned. He's still pale. Looks like he's going to throw up.

"Gerry!"

"I'm looking," he says, his voice very low.

"Answer me when I'm talking to you, damn it."

Gerry nods, so imperceptibly it's hard to tell if he does it of his own will, or if it's caused by a bump in the road.

"Look harder," Robert says. "Look faster. They couldn't have gotten far."

Gerry doesn't respond. Robert watches his face. He can see tears in his eyes.

"You gonna cry?" he says.

Gerry sniffs and shakes his head.

"The fuck's the matter with him?" Simon says, sounding angry.

"Probably never been shot at before," Robert says.

Gerry swallows, wipes at an eye.

Robert's phone begins to ring. It's Eric. He answers.

"What the fuck is going on there?" Eric says. He sounds pissed.

"We ain't got him yet," Robert says. "But we will, so cool your jets."

"Cool my jets?" Eric says. "This was supposed to be quick and quiet – that's why I hired you, and that's why I'm paying you so damn much. But you're not being quick and quiet – this has already gone on longer than I expected, and you're making more noise and mess than I ever could have imagined."

"No one said it would be easy," Robert says. "Man like Rollins, he's liable to make a simple job difficult. Plus, he just killed one of my team."

"I'm aware."

"Oh, you're aware, huh?" Robert looks back at Gerry.

"Of course I'm aware," Eric says, spitting his words down the phone. "Gerry has been updating me every step of your journey. He's provided detailed reports of every interaction you've thus far had with Rollins. Let me tell you, he does not appreciate being shot at."

Robert chuckles. "Who does?"

"I understand you had a clear shot when you first found him at the hotel in Nogales," Eric says. "You could have shot him after he fell from the window, but you chose not to. For *pride*, apparently. For some sadistic desire to kill him up close and personal. Does that sound about right?"

Robert glares at Gerry. Gerry won't look at him. "How I handle things is no concern of yours," he says. "All you gotta worry about is that it *gets* handled, and it will." Robert exhales through his nose. "I'm upping our price."

Eric is silent. "Excuse me?"

"One of my men – our *friend* – is dead. Consider it hazard pay."

"How much?" Eric says.

"We still get his share, plus an additional fifty grand."

"Are you fucking kidding me?" Eric says.

Robert grins. He doesn't imagine Eric is the kind of man who curses very often. "Oh, I'm serious. The alternative is we stop right now and head on back home."

Simon shoots him a look, but Robert shakes his head. There's no way they're stopping now, not when they're so close to tracking Rollins down and taking him out. Robert is bluffing, using Nathan's death as leverage for more money.

It works. Eric sighs, says, "Fine. But next time you find him, don't go in all guns blazing, for crying out loud. Keep the noise down for a change."

"Don't tell me how to do my job, Eric," Robert says. "I know how to deal with Rollins, and I'll do just that. We clear?"

"I wish I could say we were," Eric says. "Sooner rather than later, Captain Dale."

"That's how we all want it, Eric." Robert hangs up.

"We good?" Simon says.

"Yeah, we're good," Robert says. He turns around in the seat again, looking at Gerry. "You found him yet?"

"Not yet," Gerry says, his voice meek. He knows what Eric has told Robert.

"Uh-huh. Lay off the reports and keep searching, maybe you'll find him faster, huh?"

Gerry doesn't answer. Robert turns back around, drops into the seat.

"What do I do?" Simon says. "Where do I go?"

"Just keep driving," Robert says. "They went this way, so we'll follow. Just keep driving until tech boy, in the back there, comes up with something useful."

36

Tom and Carmen spot a sign for a small town five miles out of their way. They go to it. Carmen finds a drugstore and buys some more bandages and wipes, and she cleans out and re-dresses Tom's wound in the backseat of the car. It looks worse than it did before. It hurts more, too. They're parked in an alleyway Carmen has reversed down, off the main road and out of sight.

"I got painkillers this time," she says as Tom winces.

"I hope they're strong ones," he says.

"I don't know about that, but they should take the edge off."

When she's done, Tom pops a couple, swallows them dry, and lies low in the backseat while she goes to find him a change of T-shirt. She comes back soon after with a black one. Tom pulls it on and throws away the tattered and bloodied one. "We need to find another car," he says. "They'll have the registration plate of this one."

"There's a used-car lot near the drugstore," Carmen says.

Tom inspects the front of the vehicle, where Carmen plowed it through the motel wall. It's dented and scratched, and one of the headlights is shattered, but nothing is hanging off, and the engine still runs. "Let's go see what we can get for a swap," he says.

They get back into the car. "How far are we from Tucson now?" Carmen says.

"This detour's only added a half hour," Tom says. The car isn't moving yet. "By the time we get a new car and back on the road, we should get there by early evening. Shouldn't take us too long to find the brothel."

"But you'll want to wait for dark," Carmen says.

Tom looks at her and grins. "I'm becoming predictable," he says.

"You'll want to check it out first," she says.

"Exactly."

"I'm learning."

"You're a pro," Tom says.

"I had a good teacher."

"You did, and I've taught you well." He winks at her.

She smiles, laughs, and Tom thinks how he has not seen her do this much. It's good to see, and to hear.

"Let's go to the lot," he says. "It looked like the kind of place that won't ask too many questions. Let's see what kind of piece of shit we can trade *this* piece of shit for."

37

Zeke is in regular communication with Cindy. He wears an earpiece connected to his phone. He's in Nogales now. They follow Tom's trail.

"Y'know," Cindy says, "this would all be a lot easier if he just got another burner phone and called me up. I could send you straight to him, then. Let him know you're coming."

"He's probably busy," Zeke says.

"Yeah, well, when he's not in touch, I can't be a hundred percent sure you're not just chasing after a dead man."

Zeke grimaces. Hopes this isn't the case.

Cindy is silent for a while, then says, "Sorry. I shouldn't have said that." She sighs. "I'm just...I'm worried, y'know?"

"I am, too," Zeke says. "But we'll find him. I know Tom, and I know that chances are good he's still alive. He's always been hard to kill."

Zeke goes by a hotel where Tom was staying. There's been a shoot-out. Cindy picked up on the news of it via police reports. She saw Tom and Carmen check into the hotel through security footage on the street. She looked over the names of the people checked into rooms, but couldn't find either of them. Not even David Thompson, the persona she painstakingly created for his return from Mexico, put to rest before he was ever put to use. They're obviously using fake names.

There are cops parked outside the hotel, and Zeke catches a glimpse of a forensic team in the alley down the side of the building. Zeke doesn't slow, and doesn't stare. Doesn't want to get the attention of the police standing around.

"You got anything?" he says.

"One dead body," Cindy says. "Worked for the border patrol, name of Jonas Pringle."

"Anything else?" Zeke gets past the hotel, puts it behind him.

"I can't see what happened during the shoot-out," Cindy says. "The security footage of the buildings nearby was cut – they're either in touch with that guy from the FBI, or they've got him with them."

"Can you get into the video that was cut?" Zeke says, crawling along the road with no idea where to head next.

"No, there's nothing to pick up on," Cindy says. "It was cut dead. But – oh!" Her voice brightens. "It doesn't matter anyway, because there goes Tom."

"What?"

"I've got him on camera down the road. It's not the car they were in before, it's a different one – let me check something."

Zeke waits. He can hear her typing. He finds a space to pull over and wait. He's in front of a grocery store. It's quiet on the sidewalk. He sees an old lady with purple-rinsed hair slowly walking along on unsteady legs.

"Okay, the car they're in now pulls up at the hotel and parks around the back shortly before all the footage gets cut," she says. "I've checked, and the car is registered to Jonas

Pringle, our dead border patrol agent. Tom and Carmen have taken it."

"So you've got a lead on them?"

"I mean, it's hours old now, but yes, I've got something."

"Then point me to it," Zeke says, pulling out of the space and getting back on the road.

38

Rosa is alone. It's rare for her to be alone these days, and she's sure this relative peace will not last for long.

She lies on her side with her back to the door. She's tired, exhausted, her body is bruised and feels broken, but she can't sleep. Fear keeps her on edge. Keeps her awake. A tension that runs through her body, waiting for the key in the locked door to turn, to open, for someone to come inside and join her on the bed.

Rosa doesn't know where she is. Again, like the last time, she was transported with a canvas sack over her head. It's another hotel room. It's nicer than the places she's been kept so far. Bigger, too. It has a king-size bed and plenty of floor space, though there is little to fill it with. There is a dresser pressed up against the wall next to her bed where the clothes she has been given are stored. The clothes are not things she would wear casually. There is lingerie and stockings, thongs and G-strings. Short skirts and dresses that barely cover her behind. Outfits for a male eye rather than her comfort. Most of the men who come to see her prefer her naked, though.

Rosa rarely bothers to get dressed, unless they demand it. Even now she's naked, though she's covered herself with the bed's blanket. There doesn't seem any point in putting anything on. She'll be told to strip upon the arrival of her next visitor.

There is a bathroom connected to the room. It has a toilet, a sink, and a shower. There is only ever one roll of toilet paper in there at a time. There are no razor blades, though Rosa is expected to keep herself well groomed. She is inspected every so often – she assumes it to be every two or three days, though she can't be sure – and then she is watched while she shaves in the shower. Her captors – her *owners* – will not take a risk on their property wounding or attempting to kill herself.

She doesn't know where Juana is. Hasn't seen her in a while now. Since they were brought here. She knows, though, that Juana is here in the hotel, somewhere. They were transported together. She could even be next door, but Rosa has no way of knowing. She doesn't know how long she has been here. It could be two days – it could be two weeks. The hours merge together. She sees no daylight. The only light she gets is from the shaded bulb that hangs over the center of the room, never switched off. The windows are bricked up, the curtains are always pulled closed.

She's fed on a similar schedule as when she was back with the others. Only a couple of times a day, and small portions. Rosa is growing accustomed to always being hungry. Sometimes it's so bad it hurts, and other times she only feels it a little.

Rosa wants to know how Juana is, if she's all right, but whenever the guards come to visit, they will not tell her. Won't answer anything she asks. They scoff, or glare.

"*Please,*" Rosa has begged. "She's young. She doesn't speak any English. I just want to know how she is."

"Don't waste your time worrying about others," one of the guards told her. "Just worry about yourself." Then he gave her a green salad, with a couple of cherry tomatoes for color.

Rosa moves her head, and her cheek feels a wet patch on her pillow. She realizes she is crying. Hadn't noticed she'd started.

The key turns in the door behind her. Rosa's breath catches. Her body stiffens. She wipes the tears from her eyes with small movements of her hand, not wanting to make what she's doing obvious.

The door opens. It doesn't close straight away, as it usually does when a customer comes to see her.

No one comes to join her on the bed, lying down behind her perhaps, wrapping an arm around her. Or looming over her, smirking as they look her over.

No one comes to her. She can't be sure they've stepped into the room beyond the doorway.

Rosa doesn't want to turn.

She doesn't want to look, to see who it is, what they want.

She lies very still. She's holding her breath. Someone says something, and she soon understands there are two men in the doorway.

"Is she awake?" one of them says.

The other grunts, says something mumbled and noncommittal.

"I ain't got a good look at this one yet," the first says. "I hear she's a pretty one, though."

"Just wake her up," the second man says, his voice louder this time. "You can get a good look at her when we're on our way over."

The first man grunts, though it sounds like something has amused him. "Yeah," he says. Rosa hears him begin to cross the room, coming to her. She closes her eyes. He comes around the side of the bed, so that he's standing in front of her. She can feel his eyes upon her, running over the shape of her body beneath the blanket, lingering on her face.

"Wake her up and get her dressed," the second man says, still standing in the doorway. "We don't have time for you to load up on jerk-off material. We need to get around the rest of the girls."

The first man, close to her, makes that same amused grunt. Rosa feels his hand upon her bare shoulder. He shakes her. "Wakey, wakey," he says. "We're going on a trip."

39

The outside of the hotel is run-down and nondescript. In one of the windows near the entrance on the ground floor is a flickering neon sign that flashes 'No Vacancy.' Tom is wearing a jacket they bought when they first reached Tucson. It helps to disguise his wounded shoulder, which is bulky where the bandaging is, and occasionally dots through his T-shirt with blood. He has rounded the block on foot a few times already, checked the building for its doors and windows, its entrances and exits. He figures they'll get inside, find Rosa, and leave with her the same way they left with Emilia. He gets back to the car parked opposite, where Carmen is waiting, watching the front of the hotel.

"No one's gone inside," Carmen says.

"You're sure?"

"It's been my one job," Carmen says. "Of course I'm sure. I've done nothing but sit here and watch the door. This is definitely the right place?"

"This is where Jonas said," Tom says.

"He could've lied."

"He could've," Tom says. "But I don't think he did. He knew I was going to bring him along. He knew I wouldn't be happy if he was lying."

Carmen takes a deep breath. "Let's just do this," she says. "Let's get inside and find out. Sitting here isn't doing us any good."

Tom nods. "You know the routine?"

"We've done it three times already," Carmen says, referring to when they were visiting the brothels back in Nogales, play-acting a couple looking to complete their threesome. "I've got it. Let's go."

They get out of the car and cross the road to the front of the hotel. The night is cool, though Tom can feel heat rising from the road and the pavement, stored up over the course of the day. He wonders, as they draw closer to the entrance, if the 'No Vacancy' sign is a signal of some sort to people in the know. He pushes open the door and they step inside.

The building is silent. The foyer is still, and mostly empty save for one bored-looking man. Tom figures him to be security. The bouncer. His muscles look steroid-fuelled, his T-shirt is too tight, and his head is shaved. He's almost a carbon copy of the bouncers they saw in the brothels back in Nogales. Tom thinks about Alan. This man could be his brother.

The bouncer looks up as they enter, seems surprised to see them. "Help you?" he says.

"We're looking for a girl," Tom says.

"Slim pickings tonight, friend," the bouncer says.

Tom sees how Carmen looks at him out of the corner of her eye.

"We're looking for a third," Tom says, sticking to the script. "A Latina, preferably."

The bouncer thinks, his eyes rolling up to the ceiling. "We ain't got any Latinas tonight," he says. "They ain't here."

Carmen steps forward. "Where are they?" she says.

The bouncer's eyes narrow. "We gave 'em the night off," he says. "We're nice like that."

"Bullshit," Carmen says, spitting the word through her teeth. Tom sees her back stiffen, her fists clench. So close, once again, only to miss her sister, yet again. It's getting to her. She's tired, angry, frustrated. She's pissed off. "Where are they? What are they doing?"

The bouncer looks the two of them over. "Looking for a third, huh?" he says. Much like Alan back in Nogales, he's bigger and taller than both Tom and Carmen. He steps forward now, closer to Carmen, closer to them both. Intimidating them. Used to people being scared of him. "We ain't serving tonight, friend," he says. "So the two of you can turn around and get the fuck outta here."

Carmen takes another step forward, defiant. "We're not going anywhere until you tell us where the fuck they are."

The bouncer smirks. He reaches for Carmen. Tom steps forward, fast, grabs him by the wrist and wrenches back on it. The bouncer is caught by surprise. His body twists with his arm, contorted into an uncomfortable position. "Jesus Christ!" he says. "What the hell!"

Tom applies pressure, ups the pain. "Where are the girls?" he says.

The bouncer is in pain, but he remains belligerent. "Fuck you!"

Tom looks at Carmen. She nods. Tom punches the bouncer twice in the face. Bloodies his nose and mouth. "Tell us where they are," he says.

The bouncer spits blood. He starts to laugh. "Fuck you twice," he says.

Carmen says something in Spanish, a curse, then grabs the KA-BAR from Tom's waist. He doesn't try to stop her. She presses the knife hard to the bouncer's throat, her other hand on the back of his bald head. Her face is close to his, their eyes only inches apart. Hers are wide and blazing. The bouncer sees the look in them. He swallows, his Adam's apple scraping against the blade.

"Tell me," Carmen says, speaking slowly, enunciating each word, "where the *fuck* the girls have been taken, or I swear to *God* I will slice you from ear to ear, and from gullet to gut."

The bouncer swallows again. He feels the pressure in her hands both at the front and the back of his head. His eyes flicker toward Tom, still twisting his arm and holding him in place. Tom looks back at him.

"Okay," the bouncer says. "Okay. Just ease off, all right?"

Tom twists harder, and Carmen presses the knife in closer. "No," she says. "*Talk.*"

The bouncer is trembling. Tom can feel it reverberating in his hands.

He talks. Tells them what they want to know. Tells them how the girls have been moved. They're getting cleaned up, dressed up, for tomorrow night. For a gathering at Shelley Snow's house. The girls are there to provide entertainment for the people coming.

"What kind of entertainment?" Carmen says.

"What kind do you think?" the bouncer says.

Carmen cuts him. A trickle of blood runs down his neck to his collar. "If we ask a question, just fucking answer it."

"All right, all right, Jesus! They're going there for the men to fuck them. To make them more amenable to whatever kind of business deal Ms. Snow and the cartel are trying to sell them on."

"The cartel?" Tom says. "The Nogales Cartel?"

"Yeah, probably, it's usually them."

"What business?"

"I don't know – I promise, I don't. I'm paid to sit around

here and watch the girls, make sure they don't try anything stupid, and none of the guys get out of line with them. I don't know anything that might happen with a cartel, and I don't wanna fucking know."

"You believe him?" Tom says to Carmen.

Carmen doesn't answer straight away. She continues to look into the bouncer's eyes. "Yeah," she says. "I believe him. When are they coming back here?"

"After it's over. Maybe late tomorrow night, maybe the next morning, I don't know. I just hold down the fort and look out for the few girls who are still here."

"Why'd they leave some behind?"

"Keep business here ticking over. They took the prettier ones to her house. They took all the Mexican chicks. Figured that might be where the cartel guys' tastes lie."

Carmen looks at Tom. "I need to know she's there," she says. "I can't go there for her not to be, not again."

"We can't give her name," Tom says. "They can't know who we're looking for."

Carmen bites her lip. She looks at the bouncer. "Name them," she says. "The Mexican girls who work here. The ones who have been taken. Name them all."

"Jesus," the bouncer says, thinking, remembering. His reaction gives the impression there are a lot.

"Start," Carmen says. "We don't have all night."

The bouncer starts listing names. Carmen stops him after a couple.

"First *and* last names," she says.

"I don't know their last names," the bouncer says. "I don't need to know. I only know them by firsts."

"That'll have to do," Tom says.

The bouncer resumes. Halfway through, he says *Rosa*. He keeps going. Tom watches Carmen. She doesn't betray anything. He's glad, though he also wonders if perhaps she's too busy fearing it's the wrong Rosa.

"Where's the house?" Tom says when the bouncer is done listing off the girls' names.

The bouncer hesitates. "Man, I can't tell you that," he says. "They'll kill me."

"We'll kill you if you don't," Carmen says, and she cuts him again.

"Jesus, *fuck*," the bouncer says, grimacing. He bares his teeth. He looks up at Carmen, and he's fearful. His tongue flickers out over his lips. He tells them where Shelley Snow's house is.

"You got that?" Carmen says to Tom without turning.

"Yeah, I got it," Tom says, committing the address to memory. He speaks to the bouncer. "When's your shift end, *friend*?"

"I'm here until the girls get back," the bouncer says.

"That long until you get relieved, huh? Short-staffed?"

"There's no one to relieve me. Everyone's at the house."

"Everyone, huh?" Tom says. "How many is everyone?"

"I don't know, man, I swear. Sometimes Ms. Snow brings in other guys. I can't give you a number."

"What we gonna do with him?" Carmen says.

"I won't say anything," the bouncer says, very aware of the knife still pressed to his neck. "I swear. I *swear*."

"Promises, promises," Tom says. "On your feet." Tom hauls him up, still twisting his arm. Carmen takes the knife away, but she keeps it in her hand. Tom marches him across the lobby, down the hall until they come to a door. There's a key in the lock on the outside. "See what's in there," he says to Carmen.

She opens the door. There's a room on the other side. A bed with tousled sheets. The air smells like sex. Tom sits the bouncer down on the ground, then strips the blanket and the sheet from the bed. "Hand me the knife," he says.

Carmen does. Tom uses it to cut the sheet into lengths. He uses the strips to bind the bouncer's wrists together.

"That's tight," the bouncer complains.

"Supposed to be," Tom says. He stuffs another piece of the sheet into the bouncer's mouth and ties it at the back of his head, then takes another and covers his eyes. He hauls him back to his feet, one hand on his arm, fingertips digging into the soft skin between the bicep and the bone. He leads him from the room. The bouncer mumbles through the gag.

"I think he's asking where we're taking him," Carmen says. "And I'm curious about that myself."

"We're gonna check him into a nice comfortable hotel room," Tom says. He talks so the bouncer hears, too. "Somewhere far from here. Then, we're gonna tie him to the bed. Hate to break it to you, buddy, but those bonds are gonna be tight, too."

They leave the hotel. Tom checks the way, makes sure no one's coming, then hustles the bouncer over to the car. He pushes him into the backseat, then climbs in beside him. Tells Carmen to drive. "But don't worry," Tom says, patting the bouncer's knee. "Once we've done what we've gotta do, we'll call the hotel, let them know you're there. All you have to do is make yourself comfortable for twenty-four hours. That shouldn't be so hard, should it?"

The bouncer says something. His words are too garbled to make out. Tom doesn't care enough to find out what he's said.

40

They can't drag the bouncer into the hotel, bound and blindfolded as he is. Carmen goes in, pays for the room, then Tom hauls him up the fire escape. They tie him facedown on the bed, securing his wrists and ankles to the frame with cable ties they picked up on the way. They leave the gag in and the blindfold on. Tom leans down next to the bouncer's ear.

"Behave yourself," he says. "Lie down here and ride this one out. You try to make noise, you try to break free and warn them we're coming, it ain't worth what I'll do to you if I've gotta come back here. You understand what I'm telling you?"

The bouncer nods.

"Good." Tom turns the television on, raises the volume so to anyone passing by it sounds like the occupant is passing his night and day in front of the box. They hang the 'DO NOT DISTURB' sign on the door, then take the key away with them.

After they've checked the bouncer into the hotel, they go straight to Shelley Snow's mansion. It's on the outskirts of Tucson, surrounded by desert and cacti. There are other houses in the area, but none of them close enough to be considered true neighbors. Tom drives past the house. It's walled in, with the tops of palm trees poking over the top of the white walls all around the perimeter. Shelley Snow likes her privacy.

Tom doesn't stop. He keeps going, parks further down the road where they won't be noticed. He looks back at the house in the side mirror. The way in is gated. Beyond that, he saw as they passed, is a driveway.

"When are we going in?" Carmen says.

"Not tonight," Tom says.

"What? We're so close. She's right there –!"

"No." Tom cuts her off. "We know she's *going* to be there. We know she's going to be there tomorrow night for the gathering. We don't know she's there now. She could be anywhere. They could be keeping the girls somewhere else."

Carmen works her jaw, but Tom can see she knows he's right. Her shoulders sag, and she deflates. She looks back toward the house. "All right," she says. "Tomorrow, then. But how? I don't imagine you're going to charge headlong in."

"There's going to be security," Tom says. "And there's only two of us." He looks at the walls in the rearview mirror, at the trees beyond them. "We'll have to sneak in. Sneak in, find her, sneak out. Avoid a firefight as best we can."

"What if they see us?"

"It sounds like there's going to be a lot of people there, and from what the bouncer told us, they're not all going to be cartel. Chances are good not everyone is going to know everyone else. I could pass for a local gangster, or a businessman, or one of the security detail. We'll pretend like you're one of the girls, and I'm escorting you back to the house. The girls will probably all be inside. We'll look for Rosa there."

"We'll need different clothes."

"Yes, we will."

"Do you think they know what we look like?"

"They might by now." Tom stares at the walls, wishes he could see the grounds beyond them. He doesn't like going in anywhere blind, without at least some kind of idea of what the layout is. He doesn't have time to watch the house for as long as he'd like. To scope it out. They finally know where Rosa is going to be, and when. They've come so close so many times already. They can't let this opportunity slip them by.

He realizes Carmen is looking at him. "What?"

"I think you're going to need a haircut," she says. "And a shave. Especially if there's a chance they know what we look like now."

Tom looks at her, raises an eyebrow. "Are you planning on cutting your hair?"

"If I have to. But I don't think it'll come to that. I think I could style my hair, apply some makeup, slip into a dress and walk right by this car, and you wouldn't know it was me."

"Some other guys wouldn't, perhaps," Tom says. "Not me. I'd see you."

Carmen grins. "You're sure?"

"Of course." Tom winks at her. "I have an eye for details."

41

It's early in the morning when Rosa and the other girls, about a dozen of them, are lined up in the foyer of Shelley Snow's house. There's a water feature nearby. Rosa can hear its gentle splashing.

The girls are dressed in baggy clothes. Tracksuit bottoms and loose gray T-shirts. Their hair is scraped back into ponytails, into buns. They were kept elsewhere overnight, and have been brought here this morning in the usual manner with a canvas sack over their heads.

Last night, wherever it was she was kept, Rosa lay on the most comfortable bed she has ever felt in her life. Despite that, she couldn't sleep. Her mind raced and her stomach fluttered with the knowledge of what was coming. And then, after that, what will come next. A relentless onslaught of man after man, the monotony perhaps broken by another occasional party such as this one, but all of it stretching out into her future, without end.

Now the girls are lined up, on display. Shelley Snow walks up and down their line, inspecting them. It reminds Rosa of when she first saw her. The way she strode like a military commander, inspecting prospective troops.

There are men with her. Bodyguards, Rosa thinks. They stand nearby, hands clasped in front. They have guns on their hips. Rosa stands very still and looks straight ahead, tries not to be seen looking at the bodyguards, or at Shelley herself.

Shelley finishes her pacing. She steps back, her legs spread slightly apart. A sneer plays over her lips, like she is not satisfied with what she has seen.

"Tonight is a very important night," she says. "It's important for me. It's important for my associates. And it is important for all of you."

Juana is in the lineup. Rosa rode with her in the minivan on the way over. They sat together. Juana whispered her name after they'd been sat down, uttered it as a question: "Rosa?"

Rosa recognized her voice, though she didn't know how Juana had been able to guess it was her through the sack. They didn't say a word after that. They clasped hands down by their sides, out of view of their guards. Rosa could feel how Juana was shaking beside her. How her palms were sweating. How she kept sniffing like she was on the verge of tears, fighting them back.

"*Because* it is important to me, it is important to all of you," Shelley goes on. "I want you all to remember that. Tonight, you are here to ensure my guests are kept happy. You are here to make sure that they have smiles on their faces, and thus, with those smiles on their faces, they feel more inclined to align themselves with our ambitions." She looks them over, makes sure they're all listening. "Allow me to make myself very clear – if they are smiling, *I* will be smiling. I'm sure you all want to see me smiling, hmm?"

No one says anything. No one dares.

"Of course you do," Shelley says. "You don't want to see

me unhappy." She begins to pace again, though not as close as she was earlier. She clasps her hands behind her back. Stops walking as abruptly as she started. The men guarding her stand very still, watching the gathered girls with bored, half-closed eyes.

"If I haven't made myself clear enough already," Shelley says, "tonight is a very, *very* important night. I cannot stress this enough. With that in mind, if any of you think you cannot do what is expected of you, if you're worried you might let me down, then now is the time to say so." Shelley raises her eyebrows, cocks her head, turns an ear toward them.

No one says anything.

For a long time, no one says anything.

Then Rosa hears a whimper.

Shelley hears it too. Her eyebrows remain raised, but her head straightens up. She looks the line over, trying to find where the sound came from.

Rosa grits her teeth and hopes it wasn't her. Hopes it wasn't some involuntary noise coming up through her throat and escaping without her even realizing it. She feels cold sweat run down her spine. Feels it burst at her temples.

Shelley stops scanning the line. Her eyes settle on someone. Rosa doesn't dare turn her head to see who it is.

"It sounds like someone is having doubts," Shelley says. "Would you like to verbalize those doubts, my dear?"

Rosa hears a sharp intake of breath. Then she hears a voice. It speaks in Spanish, rapid-fire. Rosa knows the voice. It's Juana.

She's begging. Pleading. She says she just wants to go home. Rosa hears how her voice breaks. She's close to tears, if she isn't crying already. Still, Rosa does not dare turn her head.

Shelley looks on, nonplussed. She turns her head to the nearest bodyguard. "Do you understand what she's saying?"

The bodyguard's eyes remain half-closed, languid. He shakes his head. "Nope," he says.

Shelley turns back to the girls. "Translate," she says.

One of the girls, her voice sounding like she's standing next to Juana, says, "She wants to go home."

"I see," Shelley says. "Is that all she says?"

The girl hesitates. Juana has stopped talking now, but she's openly sobbing. "She...she says she's only seventeen. She wants to go back to her mother."

Rosa feels her lip tremble. She bites it to keep it still.

"Well," Shelley says. "Only seventeen, eh? And you feel as though you won't be able to perform to the best of your abilities tonight, is that right?"

Juana manages to stammer out a response in broken English. "Please," she says. "Puh-please, Senorita Snow...I want to go home...*please*..."

Shelley doesn't say anything. She looks at Juana. Watches her cry. She turns back to the bodyguard she spoke to and holds out her hand. The bodyguard pulls the gun from his holster and puts it into her palm. Shelley turns to Juana. She shoots her.

Rosa feels a jolt run through her body. The way the other girls stiffen, she knows they feel it, too. Some of them cry out. Juana hits the ground with a thud. Shelley steps forward. She shoots her three more times. Rosa closes her eyes tight. They're burning. Tears roll down both cheeks.

Shelley clears her throat. "Look at me," she says. Rosa doesn't open her eyes. "All of you, look at me," Shelley says.

Rosa does. Shelley is looking up and down the line. She settles on Rosa, sees that her eyes are open now. She checks the others.

"Now then," she says. "Does anyone else feel the same

way? Does anyone else feel like they may not be up to participating in tonight's event? Does anyone else want to go home and see their mother?"

No one answers. No one makes a sound.

"Good," Shelley says. She turns to her bodyguards and waves a dismissive hand toward Juana's fallen body. "Clean this up."

42

Tom and Carmen have bought new clothes and are lying low for the day in the cheapest hotel they could find. Unsure of the dress code, they've kept things as plain and simple and innocuous as they can. Dress pants and a white shirt for Tom, and a black dress for Carmen. They figure if Carmen is going to pass for one of the girls, it's more than likely they will at least be wearing dresses or skirts. In case things are *very* casual, they'll also be taking their regular clothes along.

Tom knows they're entering a potentially very dangerous situation, and part of him is uncomfortable at taking Carmen into it. Unfortunately, he needs her. She's his cover. She'll pass for one of the girls, and if they're lucky, they'll be able to move through the grounds without suspicion. With luck, it won't turn dangerous at all. In and out.

The other part of him knows full well there's no chance Carmen would allow him to make her sit this out.

Carmen has wedges to go with the dress. Heels are a no-no, in case they need to run. "These are flat," she said, inspecting the wedges in the store.

"Try them on," Tom said. "Make sure you can move in them."

She did. Walked up and down while Tom watched.

"Well?" he said. She looked steady to his eyes, but it was how she felt that was important.

"I'm not going to win any sprints," she said. "But I can manage."

Tom is in the bathroom, standing before a cracked mirror spattered with water stains and splashes of soap. He trims his beard with scissors, then lathers it and shaves it off with a razor. He splashes water over his face when he's done. His face stings, unaccustomed to the touch of the razor blade. He leaves the bathroom. Carmen sits by the window, watching the road below. She turns at the sound of him.

"So that's what you look like under all that hair," she says.

"Almost," he says. "You said something about a haircut."

"I did," Carmen says, getting to her feet. "Take a seat."

With the same scissors he used to trim his beard, Carmen cuts his hair. Locks of it fall about his shoulders. Land in his lap, and on the ground beneath the chair. It feels like she takes a lot off. It is thicker and longer than he realized.

"How'd you learn to cut hair?" Tom says.

"You've waited until we're a long way through to ask that question," Carmen says. "You didn't worry I'm just making this up as I go along?"

"You told me you'd cut it with such confidence, I saw no reason to doubt you."

"I appreciate the trust."

"You still haven't answered my question, though."

"I've picked it up over time," she says. "I cut my own. I'd cut Rosa's and our mother's. And I've cut the hair of ex-boyfriends, too – the ones who were too cheap to go visit a barber."

"Here I was thinking you were a schoolteacher on the

weekdays and moonlighting as a hairdresser on the weekends."

She laughs. "Oh, no. Recreational haircuts only." She snips a few more strands. "This would be easier if we had clippers. Even a beard trimmer would do."

"Just make me look as handsome as you can."

Carmen is standing in front of him, and she sees his grin. She smiles back without looking at him. "Well," she says, "that doesn't take too much effort."

She cuts a few more times, then steps back, tilting her head from side to side, inspecting her work. "Okay," she says. "I think we're done here. Go take a look."

Tom gets to his feet, brushing himself off. He heads back through to the bathroom, to the mirror. He looks himself over. Carmen has done a good job.

"You look different," Carmen says in the doorway behind him. "If there's anyone there who's seen your picture, I don't think they'll recognize you."

Tom nods. "With that in mind," he says, "I look forward to seeing your transformation."

She smiles. "Take a shower, and then I'll get started."

There are bits of hair and stubble clinging to Tom's shoulders and his bare torso. They're on his dressing, too. He'll have to change it again when he's out of the shower.

"I'll leave you to it," Carmen says, stepping back out of the bathroom. Her eyes meet Tom's. They hold. She hesitates. She smiles again, then turns and walks over to the window.

Tom watches her go. He closes the door and starts the shower running. It takes a while to warm up. The pipes rattle and clang, and the water sputters at uneven points while he's standing under it. Sometimes it runs icy cold for a few seconds, and then boiling hot. He gets clean. Gets out of the shower and dries himself off. He washes his hair out of the sink so that it's clear for Carmen. He pulls on a pair of underwear and leaves the bathroom. The rest of his clothes are on the bed.

"All yours," he says. "Be careful of the shower. It's temperamental."

"I could hear it," Carmen says. "It sounded like the pipes were going to come rattling through the walls." She stands. She's been sitting by the window again, keeping watch. Tom notices that she has cleared the floor of his shorn locks. He touches his smooth cheeks and runs a hand back through his now-short hair. He smirks.

"What?" Carmen says.

"Nothing," Tom says. "Just everything feels a lot...cooler, all of a sudden." He grabs a pair of socks from the bed.

Carmen crosses the room, toward the bathroom. She passes close by. She stops when she's next to Tom. She looks at him over one shoulder. He looks back. She turns to him. She bites her lip. Steps closer. Tom places his hands on her waist. Carmen raises her tentative hands, places them, one on his unwounded shoulder, the other on the back of his neck.

"Tom," she says.

She doesn't get a chance to finish her sentence.

There's a knock at the door.

They freeze. Tom's head whips in the direction of the door, expecting it to be Robert, having tracked them down. The knock is a taunting announcement of his arrival, right before he kicks the door down and once again charges in, guns blasting.

The door is not kicked down. Instead, there's another knock.

Tom lets go of Carmen. He grabs his Beretta. "Get in the bathroom," he says. Carmen does, though she stands close to the doorway to see.

Tom creeps toward the door on his bare feet. His back is to the windows, though he's not worried about a sniper.

There are no buildings opposite tall enough. He presses himself up against the wall next to the door, gun raised. He knows it's Robert – or Simon. There's no one else it could be. No one else who would come looking for them in this room. No one else who knows they're here.

Tom presses the barrel of the gun against the wood. "Robert," he says. When he answers, Tom will start firing. He's not expecting to hit him. If he does, that's a bonus. If not, it will scatter him, give Tom a chance to get the door open and get a clear shot.

"Try again," comes the response.

Tom freezes. He knows the voice. It isn't Robert. Isn't Simon, either.

Tom grits his teeth. He doesn't move. Doesn't take the gun away. "What are you doing here?" he says.

"I'm hurt, man," the voice says. "I give you the courtesy of knocking, and you stand there worrying that I might've come here with those assholes – and likely with a gun pressed to the other side of this door, am I right?"

Tom doesn't lower the gun.

"Cindy sent me," the voice says. "She told me they're looking for you, tracking you. She heard you might be hurt. Thinks you could maybe use some help. I mean, if you don't think you do, if you reckon you've got things well in hand, I can just head home right now –"

Tom opens the door. Zeke is grinning. Tom lowers the gun. He smiles.

43

Tom closes the door and relocks it once Zeke is inside, then they embrace. They squeeze each other tight. Carmen emerges from the bathroom, confused. Tom turns to her. "Carmen, this is Zeke," he says. "He's a friend. A good friend."

"Well, y'know, I *try*," Zeke says. "When I hear my buddy could be in trouble, and I drop everything and cross more than eleven hundred miles, does that make me a good friend? Does it make me a *best* friend?" Zeke holds out his hands. "Who am *I* to say?"

"Hello," Carmen says, still looking confused. She turns to Tom. "Did you know he was coming?"

"No," Tom says. "Cindy sent him."

"Ah," Carmen says. "The mysterious Cindy."

"Mysterious indeed," Zeke says, nodding. "I've never met her myself."

"Pleased to meet you, Zeke," Carmen says.

"Pleasure to finally meet *you*, too," Zeke says, holding out his hand. He and Carmen shake. "Feels like I've been looking for y'all for a long damn time now. Every time I get close, seems like I just missed you." He looks down, sees Tom naked save for his underwear. "Am I interrupting something?"

"Just grooming," Tom says, putting the gun down. "How'd you find us?"

"Cindy's been tracing security footage. She got a hit on the two of you checking into this hotel. Said she couldn't see either of your faces, but the builds looked about right, so we took the chance. She's erased that footage she found, by the way. She's figured that whoever's tracking you, they're doing so because they've got a guy with them who can do all the things she can. Guy by the name of Gerry. Erasing the footage oughtta slow them down."

"You know who's coming after me?" Tom says.

"Well, I'm guessing from the fact you said *Robert* when you came to the door, it can only be our illustrious Captain Robert Dale and friends."

"Friend," Tom says. "Nathan's dead."

Zeke absorbs this without emotion. He nods once. "Asshole had it coming," he says. "They all do."

"You knew they were coming?"

"If I had, I would've come sooner," Zeke says. "I had an idea they were up to something, though. I suddenly came into some unexpected vacation time, and they were real secretive as to the reason why."

"How's Naomi?" Tom says. "The kids?"

"They'll be a lot better when I get back to them," Zeke says.

"You can go right now if you want to."

"Now, I didn't come all this way to turn around less than five minutes after I finally find you." He puts his hands on his hips. "So brief me. What's the mission? I can see that you haven't found Carmen's sister yet."

"Take a seat," Tom says. He grabs the trousers off the bed,

pulls them on. While he dresses, he tells Zeke what has been happening. What they've done, and what they've found out. What they know of tonight. Tells him the plan.

Zeke listens intently. When Tom finishes, he nods once. "And you're going in there, up against a cartel – maybe more than one – and who knows what else, armed with your Beretta?"

"And my KA-BAR," Tom says.

Zeke rolls his eyes. "It's lucky for you I came prepared."

"You're going to help us?" Carmen says.

Zeke looks at her, like he's offended that this was ever in question. "Of course," he says. "Like I said earlier, I didn't come all this way just to say hi."

"Only problem is," Tom says, "I haven't seen any black guys among their crew. I don't know who's coming tonight, but if it's an all-white and Hispanic gathering, you could stick out."

"Then I'll be outside," Zeke says. "Backup. Getaway driver."

"Do you have earpieces, microphones, a way for us to keep in touch?"

"Never leave home without them." Zeke grins.

"All right," Tom says. "We haven't been able to do as much recon as I'd normally like, and we have no intel as to the layout of the grounds inside."

"So you're going in blind."

"Yes. Apart from what we can see of the other side of the wall. I think I've picked the spot where we're going to go over, where the trees on the other side are thickest and should give us enough cover when we drop down."

"Sounds like we've got as much of a plan as we're gonna get," Zeke says.

"Thank you for helping us," Carmen says. They both look at her. She looks back at them in turn. "Thank you both. I don't know..." She shakes her head. "I don't know how I would have done this without you."

"You'd have found a way," Tom says. "I'm confident of that." He tilts his head toward the bathroom. "Go shower, get ready. It's not long now."

44

Robert paces the floor, growing agitated. Simon is lying on his side on the bed, but Robert knows he feels the same way. Can see it in the way he glares at Gerry, and how his hands fidget.

Gerry sits at the table by the window, fingers frantically typing away. He's lost the trail.

They've checked into a hotel while Gerry searches. A chance to regroup. It's taking longer than Robert wanted.

"Speak to me, Gerry," he says. "Give me good news."

Gerry swallows. "I..." He sounds scared to continue. "I can't find them. I've lost the trail. I...I don't know what's happened. It's like they've just disappeared."

"Have they switched cars again?" Simon says.

"Maybe. I just, if they did, I can't –"

"What about the facial recognition?" Robert says. "Why aren't you getting hits on that?" He stops pacing, stares at Gerry.

"I'm not getting any hits on them," Gerry says. "Tom's always been difficult to trace like that anyway, we only ever get him by accident – but it looks like the girl's getting savvy to it now, too. Tom's maybe realized that's what I was doing, and he's smartened her up."

"You don't just need their faces," Simon says. "You know their bodies – search for those."

Gerry looks away from the laptop for the first time. Turns to Simon on the bed. "You want me to look through all the footage from all the streets in *Tucson* and see if I can recognize their body types strolling along the sidewalk?"

Simon sits up fast, not appreciating Gerry's tone.

"Calm down," Robert says. "He's right. That'd take too long."

"It's impossible," Gerry says, turning back to his computer. His hands hover over the keyboard, but he doesn't type.

Robert resumes pacing, trying to think. The room is silent without Gerry's relentless tapping. He can feel both of their eyes on him, waiting for him to come up with something.

He stops by the window, looks out through and across the top of the buildings opposite. He closes his right fist and presses it into the palm of his left. Pops his knuckles. Repeats it with his left hand.

"Broaden the search," he says without turning.

"Broaden it to *what*?" Gerry says. "When Eric finds out we've lost them, after we were so close *twice*, he's gonna be pissed off, he's gonna –"

Robert turns, and Gerry's voice breaks. His mouth clamps shut.

"They're trailing someone," Robert says. "They're looking for someone. Down in Nogales, they kept visiting brothels. Find the connection. Find who owns the brothels. Find what Rollins and the girl are looking for and send us there. Find out who the fucking *girl* is and why *she's* here."

Gerry takes a deep breath through his nose. "That's... that's a lot of searching. It'll take a while."

Simon stands, steps up behind Gerry, places a hand on his shoulder. "Then you'd best get started right away," he says. "And go as quick as you fucking can."

"Uh-huh," Robert says, stepping forward too. They box Gerry in, surround him. "Just imagine how upset *Eric* will be if he finds out you didn't do all that you could to find his man. That you were too busy complaining about how *hard* it all is."

The corner of Gerry's mouth twitches. He's breathing hard, harried and uncomfortable at the way they've surrounded him. Robert and Simon don't move. They loom over him. Gerry turns back to his laptop and gets to work.

"Thatta boy," Robert says.

Simon squeezes his shoulder, then pats him on the back. He returns to the bed, lies down on it.

Robert returns to the window. "Quick as you can, Gerry," he says as he goes. He looks back out over the buildings, as far as his eyes can see. "Find my boy, Gerry. Find my boy."

45

The girls have been ushered into the bathroom, one after the other. They've showered, having been told to wash themselves thoroughly. After they dried themselves, they were seated in a room and waited to be attended to by hairstylists and makeup artists.

Rosa sits and waits her turn, wrapped in a towel. She doesn't see the point. She knows, from experience now, that it will not take long before her hair is mussed and her makeup is running.

She stares straight ahead, but feels nothing. She's numb. She hears Juana crying, the sound echoing in her ears. Hears her begging to go home.

Hears Shelley Snow shooting her to death.

Rosa closes her eyes. She never saw Juana's body, but she can picture it in her mind. Lying flat and splayed, bloodied. Her eyes open, vacant.

Rosa is signalled into the chair. Her hair is curled and swept back from her face. Makeup is applied to her features, especially around her eyes. All the while, she thinks of Juana. Her stomach is a pit. Her arms feel like lead weights. She stares into the mirror opposite while the woman works on her and watches herself transform into someone she has never seen before. As bright and beautiful as they make her, her eyes remain dead.

When it's done, she's accompanied by one of the men who stood near Shelley Snow when she killed Juana. He takes her to a bedroom. "Bring your first to this room," he says, opening the door and waving her inside. "After that, take any room that's available. Get dressed and make yourself comfortable for a few hours. You'll be working soon."

Rosa steps inside, and he closes the door behind her. The door is not locked. They're not concerned about her trying to escape – they know she can't get out. There's nowhere to go, and no way of slipping out past the guards.

There is a dress laid out on the bed. It's waiting for her. There is a thong next to it. No bra. High heels on the floor. Rosa stands in the center of the room, does not go to the dress, not straight away. It is green and it sparkles. She imagines Juana wearing it. She closes her eyes tight.

She pulls on the underwear and the dress. She slips on the heels. There is a full-length mirror on a nearby wall. She looks at herself in it. The dress is figure-hugging. Rosa feels like she is looking at a stranger. A glamorous, beautiful stranger, with empty eyes.

She sits down on the edge of the bed, and she waits.

As the evening approaches, a guard comes and retrieves her. The girls are lined up in the foyer again, as this morning, for Shelley to inspect. Shelley has not changed. She wears the same pantsuit, radiating power. She looks more pleased with their appearances now.

"That's better," she says with a slight smile. "You all wash up very well."

She flicks a wrist, and the bodyguards transport the girls out of the foyer and into a room at the side of the house.

Some of them sit, and some of them stand. The men stay with them, guarding them. Rosa is near a window. She can see the courtyard. She watches as it begins to fill with cars, attended by valets who take the keys and the vehicles and park them around the side of the mansion. Men get out of the cars. She doesn't see any women.

The other girls around her begin to realize that people are arriving. They stand, lean toward the glass, trying to get a better look at the clientele they will be servicing tonight.

Rosa doesn't get up, doesn't go closer to the window, like some of the others. She's seen enough already. A lot of the men looked like cartel. The others, the white ones, they had hard edges and hooded brows. They looked dangerous, like criminals. Gangsters. There was one among them, though, who did not look so hard-edged. He was younger, fresher-faced, and surrounded by security. Men in suits and shades, who looked as uncomfortable as he did to be in such a situation.

"Get yourselves ready," says one of the guards. "You'll be going out soon."

"They're coming in," says one of the girls at the window, moving away from it and sitting back down.

Rosa grits her teeth and clenches her fists. She thinks about Juana. Wonders what they did with her body, where it is. If they perhaps buried her in the desert behind the grounds of the house. Her eyes burn. She blinks. Tears will cause her makeup to run. The guards, and Shelley, will not be happy if they see her in such a state. She has to get to work first. Has to earn what Shelley has paid for her. Only then can her makeup smudge, can it run, can her face be a mess. Only then can she cry. Before, and she'll end up wherever they've dumped Juana.

Minutes pass. The girls, one by one, leave the window. Rosa can see outside again. There are only the valets out there now. The guests have come inside. She notices some security come into view. Cartel men, armed with automatic rifles. One of them stops to talk to a valet, then laughs about something.

They are not escorted from the room as fast as Rosa expected they would be. The men are probably getting acquainted, talking shop, before the girls are paraded out and the party can truly begin.

Rosa sits still, awaiting the inevitable, but she notices how the girls around her are becoming antsy. She sees bouncing knees and tapping fingers. Chewed lips and fingernails.

Someone comes to the door, speaks to the guard nearest it. Rosa can't hear what they say, but she can guess at the content. Sure enough, the guard nods at the messenger, then turns to the girls. He doesn't bother closing the door. "All right," he says. "On your feet. Let's go."

The girls stand. They get into single file. Rosa finds herself somewhere in the middle.

"Remember to smile," one of the other guards says. He's grinning, looking them over.

"Pout and preen," says the one by the door.

"Peacock, baby," says another, laughing.

The one by the door chuckles, then speaks up again. "Remember what Ms. Snow said – make them happy. Big smiles. Let them know you're into it. You don't make them happy, well, you're gonna end up like your friend from this morning."

The girls are led out of the room and back toward the foyer. They're arranged on one side of the water feature. The men who have come to the house are gathered on the other side of it. They're talking among themselves, but they gradually fall silent as the girls file in. They turn their way, watch them. Some of them begin to smile. Rosa sees teeth, and flickering tongues. She can sense their hunger.

"*Smile*," one of the guards hisses at them. "*Pose.*"

Rosa smiles, though she does not show her teeth. The smile does not touch her eyes. She puts one leg forward and places a hand upon her hip. She feels the girls shuffling around her, doing the same.

Shelley Snow appears suddenly. Rosa does not see where she comes from. She stands in front of the water feature on the men's side. "Gentlemen," she says. "The evening's entertainment." Some of the men clap politely. Shelley raises a hand, motions to one of the men. Rosa recognizes him as the younger one she saw outside surrounded by all the security. "Councilman Foster," she says, "as the guest of honor, perhaps you'd like to take the first pick?"

The councilman's eyes flicker side to side. He looks like a deer in the headlights. One of the other men nearby, he looks like an older cartel member, perhaps a leader, grins and pats him on the back, motions for him to step forward.

The councilman does so. One of his security detail goes to step with him. "I'm sure he doesn't need his hand held," Shelley says. "You know what to do, don't you, Councilman?"

The councilman clears his throat, waves for his bodyguard to stay back. He steps up next to Shelley at the water feature and looks the girls over. Rosa keeps the rictus smile on her face and stares straight ahead. The older cartel man who patted the councilman on the back is smiling at her, ogling her. He winks. Rosa's skin crawls.

"There's no need to be shy, Councilman," Shelley says. "If your first choice isn't all you hoped for, you can always pick another later."

The councilman steps forward, still looking. Finally, he points, says, "Her."

Rosa isn't looking. She doesn't know whom he's selected.

"Take her by the hand, Councilman," Shelley says. "She'll do the rest."

The councilman comes forward. A moment later, he is in front of Rosa. He reaches out, takes the hand from her hip. Rosa's vision returns from the distance. She sees how Shelley is staring at her.

She hears gunshots. Hears Juana whimper.

Hears her die.

Rosa looks at the councilman. She flashes her teeth now. She takes his searching hand and leads him from the foyer, toward the stairs, back to the room she has been assigned. As they go, she can hear Shelley speak up behind them.

"Now," she says. "I'm sure there's something here for everyone."

The conversations they earlier walked in on, silenced by their presence, resume. She hears footsteps, too. Hears the men approaching the girls.

The councilman clears his throat as they reach the top of the stairs. He hurries to keep up behind Rosa as they make their way down the long hall, Rosa trying to remember which room she was told to use. "Um," he says. "What's your name?"

"No hablo inglés," Rosa says. It's a lie, but it's one he can't disprove. She doesn't want to speak to him.

He doesn't attempt to engage her in Spanish. "Okay," is all he says.

They reach the room. Rosa takes a deep breath. She pushes the door open and guides him inside.

46

Carmen wears the black dress and the wedges, which make her taller than Tom. Her hair is curled, and she has applied makeup. "Well?" she says, stepping out from the bathroom.

Tom tries not to stare.

"Tell the lady she looks beautiful, Tom," Zeke says, nudging him.

"I'm not trying to look beautiful," Carmen says, "though I'll accept the compliment. I'm supposed to look unrecognisable."

"I haven't known you long enough to judge that," Zeke says. "Tom?"

He nods. "It's like a different person has entered the room." This isn't entirely true, though. Tom can see her, under the makeup and the dolled-up hair. But he can see the transformation, too. Can see how anyone who might have seen her from a photograph, or security footage, will struggle to know it is her.

Carmen smirks. "Well, between your haircut and shaved

face, and this dress, we should pass as strangers to anyone who might have seen our picture."

"Here's hoping," Zeke says. "I'm sure none of us want this to get messy."

Tom fixes a small, round microphone to his cuff, and an earpiece that passes for almost invisible in his right ear. Zeke is set up in the same way, though he is dressed very differently. Combat trousers and a Kevlar vest over a khaki shirt. He pulls on a loose jacket and zips it up to hide the bulk of the vest. His weapons are in the car. "We ready?" he says.

Tom nods.

They leave the hotel. Zeke takes point. Tom walks next to Carmen. He glances at her out of the corner of his eye. "How do you feel?" he says.

"Nervous," Carmen says, then laughs lightly. "I bet that sounds foolish to someone like you."

"No," Tom says. "Sometimes I still get nervous."

"Is this one of those times?"

"Yes."

"I bet you're saying that to make me feel better."

"I wish that were the case," Tom says. He's going into a hostile situation lightly armed, surrounded by an unknown number of enemy targets. He doesn't know the layout of the building and its grounds, and Robert and Simon are still on his trail. "But we'll get through it. I've been through worse."

"I find that oddly comforting."

They leave the building, and Zeke leads them to his car. Tom and Carmen sit in the back, ready to duck low as they near the house. Zeke sets off, Tom directing him.

As they get near, Carmen's hand reaches across the backseat, finds his. Settles over the back of it and squeezes. Tom turns his hand around, grips hers. He looks at her. She looks back. Neither of them says anything.

"I'm gonna see how close I can get us," Zeke says. "I can see guards outside, but they're all congregating by the gate."

"We might have to park down the way and continue on foot," Tom says.

Zeke grunts in agreement as he passes by the grounds. Tom and Carmen are flat in the back, Tom covering Carmen. Their faces are close.

"I'm not gonna be able to wait as close by as I'd like," Zeke says, the car still rolling. "I'm gonna park down the side of this next house, out of view. It ain't close, though. If there's an emergency and you call me in, I'll come as fast as this engine will let me. If not, and you're able to get Rosa out without incident, head this way, and I'll meet you in the middle."

"Got it," Tom says.

"You can sit up. They ain't gonna see you this far down."

Tom does, looks back toward the house as they round the corner of the nearest neighbor. "Not too far," he says.

"Less than one klick, I reckon."

Carmen looks back. "I'm glad I got the wedges," she says. "That's a lot of ground to cover."

"And you're gonna have to be careful covering it," Zeke says, parking the car. "I'm sorry I can't get y'all any closer."

"It'll do," Tom says, opening the door. He turns to Carmen, holds out his hand. "Stick close to me, and do as I say."

"Listen to him, Carmen," Zeke says, turning back in his seat to see them. "Tom is the only man whose hands I'd put my life in, and that means a lot. He'll keep you safe, and he'll get your sister out of there."

Carmen places her hand in Tom's. "I already trust him," she says.

47

"All right," Gerry says, sitting back. "*All right.*" There's relief in his tone. He's almost smiling, fighting against it. Doesn't want to look too pleased with himself in front of Robert and Simon.

Robert sits in the chair opposite. He's been drumming his fingers on the tabletop, providing a background tattoo for Gerry's work. Gerry didn't seem to notice over the sound of his own typing. Robert raises an eyebrow, waits for him to explain.

"I've got something," Gerry says. "Jesus Christ, I've fucking *got* something."

"Are you gonna share it with the rest of us?" Robert says.

Simon is behind Gerry, lying on the bed. He sits up now, swings his legs over the side. Tries to see the laptop screen over Gerry's shoulder.

"The brothels are owned, indirectly, by the Nogales Cartel," Gerry says, drumming his fingers on the table now, in unconscious mimicry of Robert. "I've searched long and hard, man, and I'm pretty damn sure they're the ones supplying the girls to them, too – the Mexican ones, anyway. And get this, I'm searching stuff in Mexico, and there's a bar called La Perrera, in Nogales on the Mexican side. It's a hangout for a gang called Los Perros Locos – a little while ago it got attacked. A few of them were killed. Then, before that, there was a motel near the border, and some of them got killed there, too. Some girls they were waiting to transport over the border, probably to one of these brothels, they were all set free."

"Where you getting this information?" Robert says.

"You know those guerrilla journalists down in Mexico, the kind who go after the cartels and keep their identities secret? Well, *that's* where I'm getting this information from. They're the only ones who'll cover this kind of stuff down there. And get this – Los Perros Locos work for the Nogales Cartel."

"I'm wishing you'd get to the point," Robert says.

"Let me finish –"

"We ain't interested in listening to you jerk yourself off over how smart you are," Simon says.

Gerry ignores him, ignores them both, continues with his story. "La Perrera had security footage – I manage to break into it, *boom*. Who do I find? Rollins and the girl walking in right before the men get killed."

"See, *now* it's starting to get interesting," Robert says.

"Uh-huh," Gerry says. "So now we might have a lead, right? They've gotta be looking for a girl, right? Why else are they hitting up a cartel bar and checking out brothels? And it's probably something to do with the girl traveling with him – they have her sister, her cousin, her fucking mother, I don't know."

"How does this lead us to Tom?" Robert says.

"Well, I saw something else interesting, too. I just need to look into that further."

"Then stop blowing hot air and look into it. Find where they're going and point us that way."

Gerry nods, the look of satisfaction quickly fading from his face. He starts tapping again.

"What *is* the interesting thing you found?" Simon says, leaning closer.

"Well, not a some*thing*," Gerry says, not looking up. "A some*one*."

"Some*one*?" Simon says. "Who?"

"Let him work," Robert says.

Simon shoots him a look, then makes as if he's about to lie back down. He doesn't, though. He stays up. Gets to his feet. Starts pacing, as Robert did earlier.

"Okay," Gerry says. "*Okay.*"

"You ready to tell us *who*?" Simon says.

"I am," Gerry says. He looks up. "Shelley Snow."

"Should that mean anything to us?" Robert says.

"Probably not," Gerry says. "But her name's come up in connection to the brothels. There's a news report here talking about how she's been investigated for possible connections to the Nogales Cartel via sex trafficking and prostitution, but all charges were dropped. And guess what else? There's some more reports about her from those Mexican sources I told you about – that's where I first saw her name. They reckon she's buying up some of the girls."

"And is she?" Robert says.

"Well, she wasn't charged," Gerry says. "But that doesn't mean anything. Could just mean she has good lawyers, or good friends. Do you know who runs the Nogales Cartel?"

"Of course I don't."

"Miguel Aguilar. He's on the FBI Top Ten. And, according to those Mexican sources, an update they made *today*, he's on the move. They don't know where he's gone, but they say it's rare for him to leave his home, and even rarer to leave

Mexico, but he's done it before. And guess who he went to see on his last visit to the States?"

Robert shrugs.

Gerry sighs, his enthusiasm fading. "Shelley Snow."

Simon walks around the back of Gerry. Looks down at the laptop. His eyes narrow. "I can't make sense of this," he says.

"Then it's a good thing *I* can," Gerry says.

Simon slaps him around the back of the head. "Get to the fucking *point*," he says. "Tell us where to fucking *go*."

Gerry rubs his head. "There's chatter online – people are going to Shelley's house tonight. *Now*. Some kind of gathering."

"People?" Robert says.

"The kind of people who might be interested in doing business with a cartel," Gerry says. "I've checked footage. I've seen them heading to her house."

"So you have an address?"

"Yes. And from the footage I've seen, it's got to be full of gangsters and cartel right now."

Robert looks at Simon.

"So we go there," Simon says, "grab one of the cartel motherfuckers, flash a picture of Rollins and the girl, and see what *they* know about it. Find out what they're looking for."

"Find out what they're looking for, and get it ahead of them," Robert says. "Bait. Tom and his little girlfriend can come to us for a fucking change."

Simon claps his hands together. He claps Gerry on the back. "You took the long way around, but you got there in the end, man."

"The party, the gathering, whatever it is – it's happening *right now*," Gerry says, not for the first time.

"Then let's get ready," Robert says. "And let's go. Plot the route, Gerry."

48

At the party, Pedro stands to the side, his back against the wall, hands clasped below his waist. He knows that Miguel will find him eventually, but he is in no rush to hasten the process.

Shelley finds him first. "Señor Ruiz," she says, stepping up next to him, smiling.

He nods. "Ms. Snow." He was hoping to avoid her as long as possible, too. Isn't sure which of them will be worse – Shelley or Miguel.

"It seems you have not captured Mr. Rollins," she says. She holds a drink. A martini. There's an olive in it, skewered with a cocktail stick. She pulls it out and puts the olive in her mouth. "Weren't you planning on neutralizing his threat *before* tonight?"

"That was the plan," Pedro says, his mouth set, his face grim.

"And I assume, since I have not seen a corpse, or even a head, that all did not go according to plan?"

"He's a hard man to find," Pedro says. He turns his attention fully to her now, braces himself. "But that's no excuse."

Shelley arches an eyebrow. "Indeed, it's not." She looks over his shoulder, out of the house toward her grounds. "I assume your men out there are aware of him."

"They are," Pedro says. "And so are yours. I've shown them his picture."

"Well." She starts walking away, pats him on the shoulder as she goes. "I certainly hope Mr. Rollins doesn't turn up this evening. Both for his sake and yours. By the way, have you seen Miguel? He's looking for you."

Pedro grunts. "I'll find him."

"I imagine it's best that you do," Shelley says over her shoulder, leaving him. "You don't want to make him any more upset than he may already be."

Pedro watches her go, his teeth grinding together. Someone bumps into him as they pass, one of Shelley's guests from the local area. Drunk already. He waves a brief apology in Pedro's direction without looking back, then continues on, laughing at something only he knows. Pedro shakes out his shoulder, straightens his sleeve. He looks across the room and sees Castillo. Castillo tilts his chin, then crosses the room to him. "What did she say?"

"I'm sure you can guess," Pedro says.

"Have you seen Miguel yet?"

"I'm going looking for him now."

"We might get lucky," Castillo says. "He could be in a good mood."

"That's doubtful."

"Not entirely. He could be drunk."

Pedro grins, pushes himself off the wall.

"Do you want me to come with you?" Castillo says.

Pedro shakes his head. "I'll do this alone."

He makes his way through the gathering, through the men in huddles talking business, enjoying the drinks, and sitting or standing to one side with some of the girls they've managed to corral. Pedro has to push his way through some of them. Already, they all seem drunk. They can't handle their alcohol.

He spots Miguel amidst a group of white men, nodding along to something one of them says. Miguel is flanked by two bodyguards. His young girlfriend is not with him. He's left her at home.

Pedro steps up to the edge of the group, waits to be seen. It doesn't take long for Miguel to notice his presence. He nods, once, with hard eyes, then returns to his conversation. Pedro half-listens. Miguel is extolling the virtues of a stretch of border controlled only by a select few. The men are all making the right kind of agreeable sounds.

"Excuse me, gentlemen," Miguel says, taking a step away. "I hope to continue this conversation later." He walks straight past Pedro, motions for him to follow. Pedro does. The bodyguards are at their heels.

Miguel takes him outside. He lights a cigarette. The grounds outside the house are as busy as inside, men coming out for fresh air and smokes. The Nogales Cartel are working security, armed and patrolling the perimeter, bolstered by Shelley's own men. Pedro would rather it was solely cartel. He doesn't trust the gringos as much as his own soldiers. Doesn't know what they're made of, what they have to offer. He can understand Shelley's insistence on their presence, though.

"So," Miguel says, blowing smoke. "Tom Rollins. I have seen no body, been brought no head, and yet I was assured this would all be taken care of before I came to America."

"Señor Aguilar," Pedro says, lowering his head, "I apologize, but I swear to you –"

"I'm not interested," Miguel says. "It's too late now for excuses or promises. You already made me a promise, and it has been broken. Shelley has told me you made her a similar promise, and that too has not been kept."

Pedro stares at Miguel's Italian leather shoes, doesn't dare to look up to meet his eye.

Miguel goes on. "If I'd sent up Los Perros Locos instead of you, they'd have torn Nogales apart to find him. He would not have made it to Tucson. They would not have stopped, would not have rested, until the deed was done. I'm disappointed in you, Pedro."

"I'm sorry," Pedro says, making sure he sounds suitably chastised.

"Mm." Miguel takes a step back, looks over the grounds. "Your men are all aware they need to keep an eye out for Rollins and the girl?"

"They are," Pedro says. "They've all seen his picture."

Miguel grunts. He looks to the trees, and to the wall behind them. "I can't see him getting in with ease."

"No, sir."

"Still." Miguel turns back, blows smoke in Pedro's direction. "Don't think that means you can rest easy. Stay alert. Keep your men alert. Try not to fuck this up, too."

Pedro winces. "I won't, sir. I promise."

"Promises, promises..." Miguel waves his cigarette in the air. "Did you see the girls earlier?" he says, suddenly changing the subject.

"Some of them." Pedro had been at the back of the gathering when they were paraded out, shown off. He'd caught only glimpses.

"Did you see the one the councilman chose?"

"Only the back of her," Pedro says, remembering the sight of them heading up the stairs together.

"I've noticed he's come back down, but I haven't seen any sign of the girl," Miguel says, narrowing his eyes. "I've been keeping an eye out for her. I think someone else may have gotten in before me."

"Would you like me to find her for you?"

Miguel smirks. "No," he says. "Your current duties are far more important than that, and your searches lately have left a great deal to be desired. No, I'm sure I'll be able to track her down myself." He looks at Pedro, reaches out and raises his chin with a finger, so Pedro is finally looking him in the eye. "Don't fail me on this, Pedro," he says. His face is hard. He flicks the remnants of his cigarette and walks away without another word, his bodyguards following him back into the party.

Pedro remains where he stands, outside, jaw clenched and fists balled tight.

Castillo appears beside him. "How'd it go?"

"It could've been worse," Pedro says. "But he was right. That's the worst thing. I failed. I made promises, and I did not keep them." He shakes his head.

"There is still time for us to redeem ourselves," Castillo says. "Rollins may show up tonight. If he does, we're ready for him."

"I need some air," Pedro says, turning on his heel.

"We're already outside," Castillo says.

"Away from the house," Pedro says, and he walks away, puts some distance between himself and the conversations, and the laughter that bites at him and puts his nerves on edge.

49

Tom and Carmen reach the wall. They pause for Carmen to catch her breath, then Tom laces his fingers together and boosts her to the top. She scrambles up, lies flat, and waits for him. Tom takes a few steps back, runs, presses his boot to the wall to propel himself, and scurries up the rest of the way. The tips of his fingers catch the edge of the top of the wall. Carmen grabs his arm, helps him. He pauses at the top. They've chosen the point where the trees on the other side are at their thickest. He peers through them, checking what he can see of the grounds. There's a guard nearby.

Tom drops down the wall first, then catches Carmen at the bottom. He ducks low at the edge of the bush, looks out again now that he has a better view. He can see guards dotted around the property. Some of them are pacing, but most are standing still. Some converse. Most of them look like cartel. The one closest to them has his back turned. He's white, and Tom wonders who he has arrived with, or if he's in the employ of Shelley Snow.

Tom speaks into the microphone on his cuff, his voice lowered. "We're in. You hear me?"

Zeke's voice sounds in his ear. "Copy. Good luck."

Tom turns back to Carmen. "There's a guard nearby," he says. "Ready to put on a show?"

Carmen nods.

They tug at their clothes, loosen them, scuff them. Tom pulls a corner of his shirt out of his trousers. Carmen leans on Tom's arm as they emerge out of the bushes. Tom deliberately stumbles. Carmen giggles. Tom grins like he's drunk.

The guard turns, looks back at them. They don't look directly at him. They keep going, heading up toward the house, unsteady on their feet. Tom watches out of the corner of his eye as they go. Waits to see what the guard does. Tom is ready to move. Ready to put him down if he tries to raise the alarm.

The guard watches them, his head following their movement. He grins, chuckles to himself. He thinks they've been making out in the bushes, perhaps doing more, unable to find a room inside the house. His eyes remain on them. Probably watching Carmen's ass now.

Tom stays in drunken character. Barely walks in a straight line. Carmen acts like she's holding him up. Keeps giggling like he's said something funny, or else she's humoring him. Tom takes the chance to look around the grounds. Checking out the guards. Some of them glance over their way, but not for long. No alarms are sounded. They're too far away to be recognized, and the new clothes and hairstyles seem to be enough to throw the guards off. The real test will come when/if they have to go inside the house.

There are people outside who don't look like guards. They look like they're at the party. Some of them have girls with them, hanging off their arms in much the same manner as Carmen. The girls are mostly Latina. Some of them are white. None of them look like Rosa.

"Do you see her?" Tom says, leaning close to Carmen.

"No," she says. "I'm looking."

"She might be inside."

"Let's get closer."

They're stepping through the knots of people now. Around them, past them. Some of the men nod at Tom, say hello. Everyone is beaming, having a good time. Tom returns the smiles, the nods. They get closer to the house. It looms up before them, a spacious mansion purchased with ill-gotten gains.

Tom pretends like he's scratching his forehead, raises the microphone to his mouth, lowers his voice to speak into it. "We're going inside."

"Copy," Zeke says.

They step into the foyer, staying close to each other. Carmen's arm is hooked through his. Tom sees a water feature. A cherub pouring water.

Someone reaches out for Carmen, tries to take her by the hand. "You done with this one, buddy?" he says, flashing Tom a sloppy grin.

Carmen tries to keep the smile on her face, like this doesn't bother her, but it falters at the corners. Looks forced. Luckily, the drunk guy doesn't notice.

Tom takes the man's hand off Carmen. He doesn't handle him as roughly as he'd like. Makes sure to keep smiling. "Not yet," he says. "I'll be sure to give you a call when I'm through."

The other man keeps smiling. His eyes are glassy. He flashes Tom a thumbs-up. "I'll be listening," he says. He winks at Carmen. "I'll come running."

Tom and Carmen move away from him, from the others. They find an opening where they can look around. Check out the girls who are present. There aren't as many in the foyer as they saw out on the grounds.

"Where they keeping them?" Carmen says. "There must be a room somewhere, right?"

"Let's keep moving," Tom says. "We stay still and we're gonna draw attention to ourselves."

They start circulating through the foyer and the nearby rooms. Tom spots someone from outside coming in with a girl on his arm. He's telling her a story, waving his free hand as he does so. The girl nods along, trying to look interested. Tom watches them go. They reach the stairs, and they head up.

"Come on," Tom says. They follow them. The couple ahead of them go through one of the doors on the right-hand side of a long hallway.

Carmen grips his hand, squeezes it tight. "She could be in one of these rooms," she says. "Right on the other side of one of these doors." She bites her lip.

"Let's find out," Tom says.

50

Simon drives. Robert sits in the back of the car with Gerry. They park down the road from Shelley Snow's mansion. There aren't many houses in the area. No one they need to worry about seeing them and becoming curious as to why they're just sitting there. Robert gets out of the car, stretches his legs. "I don't suppose this bitch has security cameras on her property?" he says, leaning down to see Gerry.

Gerry has his laptop open. "Only on the gate," he says.

Robert straightens up. "A house this big and she doesn't have cameras inside?"

Simon remains in the car, though he has his window down. They're both kitted out, ready to move at the first chance they get. "Could be she gets up to some stuff in there she doesn't wanna take chances on anyone seeing the footage of," he says. "Like tonight."

"The thought had crossed my mind," Robert says.

"Maybe the lady likes an orgy," Simon says. "And maybe she *really* likes it with spic dick. You wouldn't want *that* kinda video to fall into the wrong hands."

Robert grins, looking toward the house.

Gerry says something, but Robert can't make out what it is. He bends over, leans into the car. "What?"

"The neighbors have cameras," he says, still tapping away. "They –" He stops talking, and his eyes go wide. *"Holy shit."* He taps a few more keys. "Look at this." He turns the laptop.

Robert leans in further. Simon twists in his seat to see.

An image is frozen on the screen. Security footage showing a man and a woman passing down the back of the distant neighbor's property, heading out of sight over desert ground. The man wears trousers and a shirt, and the woman is in a black dress.

Robert smiles. "He's had a haircut," he says.

"What the fuck, I can't see," Simon complains. "Turn it my way." Gerry does so. He studies the screen with narrowed eyes, but then his face breaks into a smile. "Well," he says, "don't they look lovely? They've really made the effort."

Robert looks toward the mansion, then to its neighbor further down. He points. "The footage is from that house?"

Gerry looks through the windscreen. "Yeah, that one."

Robert nods. He reaches into the open window and grips Simon by the shoulder. Squeezes him perhaps tighter than he needs to. "Fuck the cartel," he says. "Our boy has come to us."

Simon twists out of his hand. "What's the new plan?"

Robert chews his lip, feeling giddy, barely able to contain himself. He thinks of all those people inside, potentially armed to the eyeballs. He thinks of Tom and the girl among them all. He thinks of opening fire with his AR-15 and cutting down everyone in his path, not giving a fuck whose bodies the bullets tear their way through.

Then he thinks about finding Tom after it's all calmed down. After the gunfire has quieted, save for the distant *pop, pop* of Simon picking off the injured survivors. Perhaps Tom has fallen among all the dead, perhaps he's maimed. Maybe there's a bullet in his leg. He can't move. He can't escape, not this time.

And Robert thinks about getting down next to him. Getting close. Of pulling out his KA-BAR, and taking his time with it. Cutting him up, nice and slow. Sticking it into him, millimeter by millimeter. Cutting his head from his shoulders.

"Captain?" Simon says.

Robert snaps back to attention, a warm feeling in his chest. Realistically, he knows he won't have time like that, not on the grounds. Not after all the chaos they're about to cause. "We're going in," he says. "And, if possible, I want Rollins alive."

Simon leans out the open window. "Alive?"

Robert nods. "I have plans for him. Those plans are going to take time – time we won't have within those walls."

Simon shrugs. "Suit yourself. You give the orders, I'll follow them. But if that motherfucker gets close and it's him or me, I'm gonna waste him."

Robert squeezes his shoulder again, hard enough to leave a bruise. "I wouldn't expect it any other way."

51

Pedro stands with his hands in his pockets, his face turned up to the sun. It's lowering, but it's still bright and hot. He rolls his neck from side to side, popping it.

He feels a presence nearby, feels eyes upon him, and he looks to see one of the Americans standing close. There's a hesitant look on his face. "What is it?" Pedro says, no patience for the man's apparent worry.

The gringo clears his throat. "I need to... I need to see the picture again."

Pedro stares at him. "Why?"

"Because I've got something playing over in my head, and I can't shake it," the gringo says. "So I wanna check the picture again and see if I can put this thought to rest."

Pedro reaches into his pocket, pulls out the picture of Rollins and the girl from La Perrera. He watches the gringo as he studies it. Pedro sees the color fade from his face. "Well?"

The gringo coughs. "Um," he says.

"*Um?*" Pedro repeats. "Don't waste my time, white boy. Have you seen them, or haven't you?"

"I don't know," the gringo says.

Pedro blows air through his nose.

"The guy didn't have a beard, and his hair was shorter. The girl was wearing a dress and her hair was up, and she had makeup on. I figured she was just one of the other girls, right?"

"Picture him without a beard and with shorter hair," Pedro says, feeling agitated.

"That's what I've been trying to do," the gringo says. "It's, uh... It's hard to do."

"Where did you see them?"

The gringo points across the grounds, toward a corner. "I was standing guard over there," he says. "They came out the bushes, and they looked like they'd been fucking, y'know? I just figured they hadn't been able to find a room in the house, so they came out here. But then, when they were gone, I got to thinking, and there was something familiar about the guy. I just couldn't put my finger on it. I've taken a look around the party, tried to find him again, but I couldn't see him. Couldn't see either of them."

Pedro grinds his jaw. "How long ago was this?"

The gringo checks his watch. "About, uh, maybe fifteen minutes ago?"

Pedro wants to hit the man for taking so long. He doesn't, though. Doesn't want to make a scene, to draw attention. Instead, he silently curses, once again, that these stupid fucking white men were used on guard duty. "Did you see which way they went, at least?"

"Um...they're probably inside the house, right?"

"Gather up the men," Pedro says. "Fast."

The gringo doesn't move.

"*Now – go!*"

He jumps to attention, runs off.

Pedro looks around, searching for Castillo. He soon spots

him, standing with Moreno. He waves them both over. "Rollins is here," he says when they're close enough. "With the girl."

Castillo frowns. "How'd he get inside?"

"Useless fucking white boys, that's how."

Moreno rolls his eyes, unsurprised. Like he's been thinking the exact same thing as Pedro about having all these amateur gringos on guard duty with their own men.

"Spread the word," Pedro says. "Get everyone ready. He's not walking out of here. Oh – and apparently he's had a shave and a haircut, so make sure they're aware of that."

Castillo and Moreno nod, hurry off in different directions. Pedro watches them get the attention of the others, fill them in. Pedro turns back to the house in time to see Shelley Snow heading his way. She's noticed the commotion. All the guards suddenly rushing around.

"What's happening?" she says.

"Rollins is here," Pedro says.

"Are you *fucking* kidding me?"

Pedro knew she'd be pissed off. He doesn't have time to worry about that right now. "Where's Miguel?" he says.

"I don't know," Shelley says, looking like she has a bad taste in her mouth. "I was going to ask you the same thing."

52

Rosa is in the room. Since the councilman first brought her here, she has not left it. The second man was outside, waiting his turn. There was a lull before the third arrived. A brief respite wherein she was able to splash her face with water in the bathroom. Her makeup was smudged after washing, but she didn't care. She drank from the tap and ran water around the inside of her mouth, to get the taste of their kisses out.

Soon after, there was a knock at the door. The third man. He poked his head in without waiting for a response. "Good evening," he said in Spanish. He stepped inside without an invite and closed the door behind him. "How are you, my dear?"

Rosa didn't think there was any point in forcing a smile. It didn't matter anymore. He was already in the room, and his intentions were clear. "I've been better," she said.

He smirked, not caring. "Stand up," he said, "so I can get a good look at you." Rosa did as he said. "Do you know who I am?" He stepped closer, looking her up and down. Rosa hadn't bothered to pull the dress back on since the councilman. Hadn't bothered with her underwear, either. She was naked. There was no use attempting to hide it. The man licked his lips. He liked what he saw.

Rosa realized she hadn't responded. She shook her head.

"My name is Miguel Aguilar," he said, still smirking. "No? You don't know? That's fine. It's probably for the best. I don't make a habit of throwing my name around. I assume, however, that you *have* heard of the Nogales Cartel?"

Rosa knew her face betrayed the fact she had.

"That's right," Miguel said. "I lead the Nogales Cartel." He waited for her to look or sound suitably impressed.

"Oh," Rosa said. "Okay."

Miguel frowned. He quickly shook it off. "Well," he said. "Shall we begin?"

Miguel moves toward her. He's about to get what he wants. What he came here for. Soon, he will be on top of her.

He pushes her down onto the bed. His smirk has returned. He begins to undress. "I may need Los Perros Locos to begin sending me a catalogue of the girls they are sending to America," he says. "If I'd known you were among them, I would have insisted on our becoming acquainted sooner. I should not have to wait until I see my past wares in the possession of Shelley Snow."

Rosa says nothing. She rolls onto her side, her back to him. When he gets on the bed, he will position her how he wants her. She waits for that to happen.

She hears him begin to chuckle as he drops the last of his clothes. Hears him step toward the bed. Soon he will be on it, then he will be on her. Rosa closes her eyes.

His footsteps stop.

He doesn't reach the bed.

Rosa opens her eyes. She frowns, hears something else now. She hears him choking.

She turns back around, alarmed. There is another man in the room. She did not hear him enter. She does not recognize him, either. He stands behind Miguel, an arm clamped around his throat. Miguel claws at the arm, but the stranger's grip does not break. Miguel's eyes bulge. His tongue protrudes. His naked, sagging body trembles like jelly. His penis, hard but going flaccid now, flops around in his struggles.

Rosa pushes herself up. She looks into the stranger's eyes. The stranger looks back. She looks at Miguel. The whites of his eyes are turning red. He reaches for her with flailing arms, begging, pleading.

"Kill him," Rosa says, her eyes on Miguel's. "He's the head of the Nogales Cartel. Kill the son of a bitch."

The stranger does something, and she hears Miguel's neck snap. The stranger drops him in a lump on the floor.

Rosa realizes there is someone else in the room, behind the stranger, near the closed door. A woman, wearing a dress. Another of the girls. Rosa wonders what she's doing here, why she's with this man. Who they are. Her head is spinning. Her vision blurs.

The woman comes forward. "Rosa?" she says.

The voice is familiar. The face comes closer, clearer, into focus. Rosa closes her eyes tight. Shakes her head. This isn't real. It's a hallucination. Miguel Aguilar is on top of her, and her mind has gone far away, fantasizing a potential escape.

It's not real.

It can't be real.

Hands are on her shoulders, shaking her.

"Rosa, look at me," says the familiar voice.

Rosa opens her eyes. It's Carmen. She feels real. She looks so real, though Rosa can't comprehend why her hair is styled and she's wearing makeup. Why she's wearing a dress. Why she's *here*.

"Rosa, I've got you," Carmen says. "I've got you."

Rosa bursts into tears. She throws her arms around her sister.

53

Tom goes to the window while Carmen helps her sister to dress. He doesn't need to hurry them. Carmen is already aware of their rush.

The room is at the back of the house. The window looks down onto the grounds. The guards are rushing around below. They're mobilizing, searching. Tom thinks of the guard who saw them earlier, as they emerged from the bushes. Wonders if he's put two and two together, if it suddenly struck him that they looked familiar, or if perhaps it was one of the other guards dotted around the party.

"Shit," Tom says.

Carmen looks up. "*Shit?* That doesn't sound good, Tom."

"It's not good," Tom says. "Something's spooked them, and that something is more than likely us." He raises the microphone to his mouth. "Zeke?"

"I'm here."

"I think we've been made."

"I'm on my way."

Tom unbuttons his cuffs, rolls up his sleeves. Looks at the sisters. Rosa is ready. "Stay here," he says, his mind racing, formulating plans, means of escape. They can't stay put. Can't stay in this room and wait to be found.

He goes to the door, opens it a crack and peers out. At the end of the hall, one of the cartel guards is coming their way, looking in each room as he passes. He's armed with an AR-15. Tom falls back, pulls the KA-BAR from where he has concealed it down by his right ankle. He waits for the guard to get closer. Leaves the door ajar, and signals for Carmen and Rosa to get into the bathroom. Tom can hear the footsteps drawing near. A moment later, they're outside. The guard pushes the door open. He steps inside. Stops when he sees the body on the floor. He doesn't get a chance to react. Tom grabs him from behind, slides the knife between his rib cage and into his heart. It doesn't take long for the guard to go limp.

Tom moves the knife from his ankle to his lower back, within easier reach. He takes the AR-15 from the dead guard. Checks the magazine. It's full. He calls to Carmen, gives her his Beretta. "Stay close to me," he says, "and if it comes down to it, don't hesitate to use that."

Carmen stares at the gun in her hand, feeling its weight.

"We might still be able to get out of here without making too much noise," Tom says, "though it's a long shot." He looks at Rosa. "How well do you know this house?"

She shakes her head. "I don't. We got here this morning, and we've been shuttled from room to room."

Tom checks the hall again. It's clear. He can hear noise beyond, from downstairs and outside. He takes a deep breath. Knows the chances of them getting out are slim. Can only hope that with the AR-15 and the girls in tow, he'll pass for one of the white security guards.

He leaves the room, gun raised. Carmen and Rosa stay close behind. Tom keeps an eye on the doors to either side of them as they go, prepared should one suddenly fly open, one of the guards behind it. That doesn't happen. He reaches the top of the stairs and peers down. The foyer is emptier than it was before. Only a few stragglers remain, rushing back and forth.

Tom and the girls hurry down the stairs. He looks to the rear of the building, where they came in. Knows that's where most of the guards are. He looks the other way, sees an open door and the kitchen beyond. "This way."

He can hear car engines starting up outside, and still the shouting, the cries, the alarm. A voice cuts through it all, in English, but with a Mexican accent. "No one's going anywhere!" it says. "Get the fuck out of the cars! We have a situation here – the grounds are on lockdown!"

They're almost at the kitchen. It's next to the front door. The front door is thrown open. A cartel member steps inside. He's armed. He freezes. Tom's group freezes. They stare at each other, Tom waiting to see if he passes for a guard.

The man begins to raise his weapon. Tom releases two concentrated bursts into his chest. The man is thrown back against the door.

"Here!"

Tom spins. The call comes from behind. He sees another of the cartel at the back door, which promptly fills with more of them.

"In the kitchen!" Tom says, pushing Carmen and Rosa ahead of him.

Then the shoot-out begins.

54

Outside, Robert hears the gunfire.

"Sounds like the party's starting without us," he says to Simon.

"You know I do hate to miss out," Simon says, grinning.

Robert checks his magazine, then slams it home. They're ready to move in.

Gerry gets out of the car. "Why go in at all?" he says.

Robert and Simon both look at him.

"Just wait," Gerry says. "That place is filled with cartel, and who knows who else? Just wait. Let them deal with him. Go in when it's over and pick up the pieces, make sure he's actually dead. They can do the dirty work."

"Get back in the car, Gerry," Simon says. "You get to sit this one out."

"I'm telling you, man, this is *insane*," Gerry says. "And it's unnecessary!"

"Yeah, well, compose another email to Eric," Simon says.

Gerry starts gesturing toward the house. "Just let them kill him!"

"Fuck that," Robert says. "That motherfucker is *mine*.

Those Mexican sons of bitches don't have the right." He turns to Simon. They exchange nods, then walk towards the house. Robert glances back on the way. Sees Gerry still outside the car. He shakes his head, throws up his arms, then gets back inside.

55

Zeke is on his way, but they need to stay alive until he gets here.

They're pinned down in the kitchen. Tom returns bursts of fire to keep the cartel at bay, but he's unable to poke his head out long enough to get a proper aim. Anyone he manages to hit, if at all, is pure luck.

Carmen covers the kitchen windows with the Beretta, holding the gun up in two hands with trembling arms. Rosa has grabbed one of the knives from the counter, is holding it close to herself. There's a way out of the kitchen, a side door onto the grounds, which is locked from the inside, but Tom knows the area beyond is swarming. "We're pinned down here," he says into the microphone. "We're gonna need some kind of distraction to get out."

"I've got smoke grenades," Zeke says.

"That'll help. How far out are you?"

"I'm nearly at the wall, man."

Tom sticks the AR-15 around the corner, releases another burst of suppressing fire. The cartel returns it. Their bullets tear chunks out of the doorframe and the wall. While this happens, Tom checks the magazine. It's running low. He grits his teeth.

"Something's happening outside," Carmen says. She takes a step toward the window.

"Stay away from the window!" Tom says.

Carmen freezes. Outside, he can hear gunfire. Shots. The sounds of mass confusion. Looking to the window, he sees smoke billowing across the grounds. He speaks into the microphone. "That you?"

"What?" Zeke says. Tom can hear him breathing hard, like he's running, or climbing. It doesn't sound like he's driving anymore.

"I see smoke."

There's a pause. "That's not me."

Tom listens. Hears the sound of automatic gunfire outside. "Robert and Simon," he says. "It must be them. They're here."

"I've just thrown my smoke grenades in," Zeke says. "I'm gonna climb the wall now. Same place you and Carmen went over. Meet me here."

"We're on our way."

The gunfire in the foyer has calmed. Tom turns his ear to it, listens. Waits. After a silent moment, he hears the crunch of something under someone's shoe – a piece of plaster, or glass, it doesn't matter. Something torn out of the walls, the ceiling, or the ground. Tom swings the rifle out of the doorframe, zeroing in on the sound. One of the cartel is creeping up. He's looking down at his feet, aware of the noise he has just made. Tom blasts him. The man stumbles back, falls into the water feature. The water soon darkens with his blood.

Tom raises the rifle, looking beyond the bullet-chipped cherub. Sees two more men beyond, still sheltering in the doorway. This is less than there were before. The commotion outside has drawn the rest of them out. Tom's able to hit one of the remaining men. The other slides deeper into cover.

Someone starts kicking the kitchen's back door. Bullets tear into the area around the handle. Carmen points the Beretta toward it, braced for the door to break down and men come spilling in. One of the kitchen windows high up to her left smashes. A white guard tries to climb inside. Carmen swings the Beretta back, shoots three times. Two are on target. The third goes high. Doesn't matter. The two that connect drop him.

"With me," Tom says, one eye on the door.

He leaves the kitchen, sighting along the rifle to where the cartel member is taking cover behind the door. He purposefully stands on some rubble, crunches it. The man hears. He swings out. Tom is waiting. He shoots him through the face.

Tom drops the AR-15, grabs another from one of the fallen. He checks the magazine, then takes a spare from one of the other men's gun. "Stay close to me," he calls back to Carmen and Rosa. They head for the door. The confusion outside is in their favor, it's the distraction they needed. They reach the door and finally get a good look at the chaos. Smoke is sweeping across the grounds. People rush through it, becoming invisible. There are bodies on the ground, bleeding out. Gunfire is loud and constant. There are screams, too. Pained screeches. Dying cries.

Tom heads down the side of the building, away from the center of the grounds and the thickest area of smoke, the worst of the killing zone. They'll head the long way around the grounds, where it's clear. The guards have rushed away from their stations to engage in the firefight, have left the route open.

They round a corner of the house and bump into a man and a woman. The man is Mexican; the woman is white. The man's eyes blaze. "Rollins!" he says.

Tom doesn't know who he is. He puts a bullet in his knee to disarm him, then raises the rifle up to his face.

"Pedro!" the woman cries.

Her cry is cut short. Rosa leaps forward, buries the knife she has taken from the kitchen into the side of the woman's neck.

"Rosa!" Carmen says.

Blood sprays up into Rosa's face. "This is for Juana," she says, spitting the words through her teeth. She pulls the knife out and stabs the woman again, through the chest this time.

Tom guesses the woman is Shelley Snow. He can't imagine how anyone else could elicit such a visceral reaction. Snow drops to her knees. Her hands turn to claws and scratch at the handle of the knife, too scared to pull it out. It wouldn't matter if she did. It's too late for her. Blood gurgles in her throat and bubbles out past her lips. It pours from the gaping wound in her neck. She falls onto her back. Her eyes stay open.

Pedro, on one knee, watches it happen. Shelley's blood has splashed onto his face, too. He turns back to Tom, sees the rifle. He reaches to his waist, presumably for a gun. Tom's finger prepares to squeeze the trigger, to shoot him right in the face.

"*Pinche puta!*" The scream comes from behind, and is accompanied by gunfire. It's high and wild, and the bullets slam into the wall above and behind them. Tom drops to the ground, dragging Carmen and Rosa down with him. Rosa is stiff, eyes wide. She's covered in blood.

Tom looks back to see who's coming. Cartel are rushing toward them, eyes blazing. Four of them. Hurrying to save Pedro. Tom rolls through, gets to his knee, raises the rifle.

56

Pedro watches, helpless, as Rollins mows down Castillo, Moreno, Mendoza, and another whose face he doesn't get a chance to see before it disappears in a burst of red mist. Once they're down, he knows Rollins will turn back to him, finish him off.

The pain in his left knee is excruciating. It feels like the lower half of his leg is hanging off. This is nothing, however, compared to the pain of watching his men, his oldest and only friends, his most trusted confidants, gunned down. Soldiers come and soldiers go. He knows this all too well, and he's disassociated himself over the years. But this is different. This is Castillo. This is Moreno. This is Mendoza.

Pedro throws himself at Rollins as he begins to turn. He reaches to his waist for his gun, manages to pull it out while he keeps Rollins's automatic rifle crushed between them, useless. He raises his handgun, aims for Rollins's face. Fires. Rollins is able to twist his head to the side, to avoid it, though his ear is no doubt ringing now.

Pedro swings the gun. The barrel connects with Rollins's temple. Blood bursts, runs down the side of his head. Rollins gets a hand up, manages to grab Pedro's wrist, to angle the gun away from his face.

"I've been hunting you for a long time," Pedro says, his face close to Rollins's. "And now you're here, you're so fucking *disappointing.*" He grins, fights back against Rollins's grip, starts angling the gun back toward him.

Rollins moves. His head shoots up, his face coming closer to Pedro's own. Suddenly, Pedro feels a sharp pain in the center of his face. Feels warm blood burst from either side of his nose and run down his face. Rollins is biting him. Is biting so hard it feels like he's going to tear his nose off. Instinctively, Pedro tries to pull away, but as he feels his nostrils begin to tear, he realizes this is the worst thing he can do. He tries to swing the gun again, aiming it for Rollins's scalp, but the other man's hand still clasps his wrist, keeping it away. Keeping it high. Pedro lets off a couple of useless rounds.

Then he hears more bullets fired. Closer. Feels the impact of them in his side, punching through his ribs. Pedro's body contorts, and he tears his face away from Rollins's. His nose rips off. Rollins pushes him to the side and gets back to his feet.

Pedro lies on his back. He coughs blood. Can feel it running down his face, too, from where his nose used to be. He looks. Sees the two women, both in dresses. One of them is holding a gun. He thinks how similar they look. They must be sisters.

Rollins turns to them. "Keep moving!" he says.

The smoke is spreading across the ground, carried on a breeze. Pedro hears the older of the two, the one who has shot him, coughing. She holds the other, her sister, a hand on either side of her as she hurries her along.

Pedro looks to the sky. Through the drifting smoke, he sees how it has darkened. One by one, the stars are beginning to shine. He closes his eyes.

57

Zeke crouches low, stays by the bushes and near to the wall. The car is parked directly on the other side, ready for them to climb over, drop down, and make their escape.

Zeke stays on one knee, AR-15 raised. He has the AK-47 he brought on the ground next to him, ready to switch to it should he run out of ammo, or to pass it to Tom when he arrives. Whichever comes first. He's pulled the collar of his shirt up over his mouth and nose against the smoke. He sights through the rifle, sees silhouettes moving through the murk. He waits until the last moment, until they come stumbling out of it, coughing and blinded. He makes sure it's not Tom, or a girl, and then he fires. Picks the men off as they emerge one by one, cartel and white alike, secure in the knowledge that they're all criminals here. He can hear gunshots throughout the grounds, and in his earpiece. Tom has not been in communication for a couple of minutes now. Soon, the smoke will begin to clear. It will blow away. It's already thinner than it was before.

"Where you at?" he says.

It's a moment before Tom responds. "We're nearly at you," he says. "Hold tight."

"How far out are you?" Zeke says. He can hear tinny gunfire through his earpiece, coming from Tom's end.

"We're on our way to you," he says. "We're just having to be careful about it."

"Yeah, well, me too, so hurry up. You coming through the smoke?"

"No – we're coming around the outside."

Zeke's eyes flicker to the right, then the left. Someone from the cartel emerges directly in front of him, rifle raised. Zeke fires, drops him.

There are currently six dead bodies lying near him. He thinks there'll probably be a few more by the time Tom reaches him.

58

Robert and Simon move effortlessly through the smoke. They wear masks. They breathe with ease, and they can see better than the people fleeing blindly around them. Robert is aware there is more smoke on the grounds than he and Simon could have caused with their grenades, but he doesn't concern himself with it. Not right now. For now, he's shooting at anything that comes close.

They move calmly, and they fire in short, concentrated bursts. They're professionals. They're not wannabes like these guards running around, losing their minds. Robert and Simon wade through the dead, watching each other's six, keeping each other safe, knowing that the only people they need to look out for are each other. Everyone else is open game.

A girl rushes past, dress flapping, long black hair flying out behind her head. Robert hears Simon laugh as he shoots her down, lacing her back with bullets. She hits the ground on her front, skids to a stop.

"Almost seems a shame," Simon calls over to Robert. "She was hot."

Robert ignores him, sees a shape up ahead. He gets closer, shoots some older white guy through the face.

There is more gunfire coming from around the grounds, but so far none of it has come close to them. Robert thinks it's likely to do with Tom, but there's a chance the guards are panicking and firing at nothing. Spooked by shadows. They're probably killing each other and not even realizing it.

The smoke, much like the still-living people on the grounds, is beginning to thin. There isn't much left of either.

Simon pulls his mask off first. "That fresh Arizona air," he says. His face is alive, animated. He's giddy, bouncing on his feet. He's enjoying himself.

Robert knows the feeling. He pulls off his own mask, grins back. "Ain't many of them left," he says.

"We might've got Tom already," Simon says.

"*Might*," Robert says. "We'll keep sweeping the ground, then we'll check back."

Simon smirks. He checks his magazine, then throws it back over his shoulder. Pulls a fresh one from his belt and slides it home. "Let's go kill some more Mexicans," he says.

59

Gerry wishes he could see what is happening within the grounds.

He checks the camera on the gate, but there's nothing to see. His leg stress-jiggles, his knee bouncing the computer around on his lap. He puts it to one side, gets out of the car.

He can hear the gunfire coming from the house. The sound carries, still loud even at this distance. He can hear screaming, too. Sweat runs down his face. His feet begin to pace, kicking up sand. He covers his mouth with his hand.

He feels himself start to step forward, to go closer to the house, to try to see what's happening, but he stops himself. Shakes his head. Foolish. Stupid. He's not going to get himself killed for this.

"*Shit,*" he says, muttering under his breath, his hands laced atop his head. "*Shit, shit, shit, shit...*"

He stands and stares at the house, and his stomach fills with knots.

He throws up.

60

Tom's left ear is ringing from where Pedro's gun went off so close to it. Blood from his temple gets into his eye. He wipes it away with the back of his hand as they go, staying ahead of the sisters, covering them, looking back to make sure no one is in pursuit. Rosa's shoes were high heels and not as suitable for crossing the ground. She's kicked them off, is running barefoot. Carmen had to drag her away from the scene after killing Shelley Snow, but she's moving freely now, without assistance.

"I see you," Tom says, speaking into the microphone. "We're on your three, so don't fucking shoot us."

He sees Zeke's head turn, spot them. Zeke stands, rifle still raised, still sighting along it, covering the rest of the area. "I don't hear as many gunshots as before," Zeke says as they reach him. "Think most of these motherfuckers've been wasted." He's holding an AK-47. He sees the AR-15 in Tom's hands and slings the AK over his back.

They step back through the bushes, toward the wall. Tom swings the rifle back over his shoulder, then boosts Zeke, sending him over first so he can catch the girls on the other side. They send Rosa over next. Tom braces his back against the wall and laces his fingers. She steps into his hands while Carmen steadies her from behind, hands on her waist. Tom lifts her up. She's very light. They see her at the top, swinging her legs over the side, then dropping down into Zeke's arms.

Tom looks at Carmen. She doesn't step straight into his waiting hands. She places her hands either side of his face and kisses the corner of his mouth.

Tom grins. "That couldn't wait?" he says.

"If I didn't do it now, I might not have done it at all." She steps into his hands, and Tom lifts her. She's light, too, though not as light as her sister. A healthier weight. He wonders, briefly, how little they were feeding Rosa during her captivity.

Tom pushes himself away from the wall as Carmen reaches the top. He turns, takes a step back, readies himself for the run up. Carmen swings her legs over the top, prepares to drop down. She looks up. Through the trees. Into the bushes. Her eyes go wide.

Tom sees. He spins, pulling the AR-15 off his shoulder and raising it, firing it instantly, knowing it can only be a hostile.

It is. It's Simon.

The bullets cut through his face. The back of his skull blows out. He crumples. Tom knows that wherever Simon is, Robert is sure to be nearby.

He promptly makes himself known. Slams the butt of his rifle across Tom's jaw. Tom hears something click near his ear with the impact. The blow knocks him to the ground. He tries to raise the AR-15, but Robert kicks it away.

Robert looks pleased with himself. "Was that Zeke I saw?" he says, laughing. "Oh, boy. Two birds with one stone, huh?"

Tom rolls back, gets out from under Robert. He charges him, wraps his arms around his waist and forces him back. Tries to lift him up, to throw him overhead and slam him down, but Robert plants his feet. He raises a knee into Tom's chest, does it again, then slams a forearm down over his back and grabs him by the head. He brings his knee up again, this time into Tom's face.

Tom stumbles back. He tastes blood. Robert is showing his teeth. The expression could almost pass for a smile. "I ain't gonna get to take as long with this as I'd like," he says. He shrugs. "Shame. I'll have to make up for it with Zeke."

Tom throws a punch. Robert blocks it, then throws one of his own. Tom is able to avoid it, then block the next, then he lands one in Robert's side, to his ribs. Robert twists with it, but throws one of his own, hitting Tom high in the chest. Robert drops his arms, ducks down like he's going to follow through with an uppercut. Tom braces for it. Robert doesn't bring his fist up. Instead, he seems to grab something from his side, and then his arm shoots out, straight ahead. There's something in his hand. Tom feels it slide sharply into his midsection. Robert pulls the hand back. He's holding his KA-BAR. It's dripping with blood.

Tom looks down. Sees red blossoming low under his shirt. Feels warm liquid run down his leg.

Robert punches him in the stab wound, doubles him up. Tom falls to a knee. Robert kicks him onto his back. The knife is gone from his hand. Tom didn't see where it went. Robert kneels down over him. He wraps his hands around Tom's neck, and he begins to squeeze.

"This'll have to do," he says. "Satisfying in its own way, I guess. But I had big plans for you, boy. I was gonna peel the skin from your body. That's right! Was thinking I might make myself a belt outta it or something."

Tom struggles against the grip. Feels the air restricted from his lungs. Feels the blood running out of him. The edges of his vision are blurring. Robert's face comes up close, remains in focus.

"I ain't gonna get to do the things I wanted to do to you,"

he says, "so you're gonna have to make it up to me by doing me this one little favor, all right? I need you to keep your eyes open – c'mon now, boy, that's right, keep those peepers open. That's it – I need you to keep them open, and I need you to look deep into mine."

Tom lets go of his hands, searching the dirt for something of use. His KA-BAR is digging into his back, his weight pressing down on it, making it hard to reach. He doesn't have the Beretta. He tries to squeeze his fingers under himself, to get at his knife. Robert presses his weight down onto him, stops him from moving.

"Stay still, Tommy," he says. "Be a lot faster for you if you do. Hell, makes no difference to me. I'm having the time of my life right now."

Tom reaches for his face. It happens almost in slow motion. He has to finger-walk his hand up Robert's cheek. Robert feels it happen. Dismisses it as the last desperate grasping of a dying man. The tips of Tom's fingers make it to Robert's left eye. He claws at it, sticks his fingers in as far as he can get them.

Robert cries out. His grip loosens, though doesn't leave Tom's neck entirely. His face twists away. His body shifts. His weight lifts. Tom reaches under himself, grabs the handle of his KA-BAR. He pulls it out and buries it in Robert's side.

"Jesus, *fuck*!" Robert falls away. His hands are off Tom's neck now.

Tom pulls the knife out, and he gasps for breath. Robert is nearby, trying to push himself away, both hands cupped over the wound. Tom gags, coughs, but manages to crawl toward his former captain. He sees his own blood dripping from his body and soaking into the ground as he goes. He grabs the top of Robert's shirt when he reaches him, pushes him down flat on his back.

The KA-BAR appears in Robert's hand again. He slashes

with it, manages to catch Tom across the ribs. Tom grabs his hand, twists his thumb back. Hears it snap. Robert drops the knife. Tom pins him to the ground again.

When he speaks, his throat is raw, his voice sounding like it has been scraped with gravel. "I won't get to take my time with this," he says, putting his face close to Robert's. "So you're gonna have to make it up to me by doing me this one little favor, all right? I need you to keep your eyes open."

Robert tries to say *Fuck you*, to curse him out, but Tom silences him. He sticks the point of the KA-BAR into the fleshy skin under his jaw, and he pushes it up inside his skull. Into his brain. Robert's eyes roll back in his head.

Tom pulls the knife out and falls back. He tries to get to his feet and stumbles. The strength is leaving his body. He looks to his left, through the trees, and he sees what little remains of the cartel and the gangsters hesitantly coming toward the bushes.

Gunfire comes from behind Tom. He manages to turn his head, to see Zeke laying down suppressing fire, keeping the men away. Tom feels his eyes closing. It's getting dark around the edges again, like when Robert was strangling him. He manages to get his hands to where he was stabbed. He puts pressure on the wound, but he's growing weaker.

He sees Carmen. She's dropped back down the wall. She's running toward him.

Tom's eyes close.

61

Gerry stands bent double at the side of the car. He's thrown up twice more. He's sure he doesn't have anything left, but his stomach continues to cramp. His nerves are fraught.

He straightens, wipes the corner of his mouth with the back of his hand. He spits. Laces his fingers atop his head. Looks back toward the house. He can't hear gunfire anymore. Everything has calmed. He watches, waits for Robert and Simon to re-emerge, perhaps with Rollins in tow.

They don't appear. Gerry shifts his weight from foot to foot. His stomach rumbles.

"Jesus Christ," he says, running his hand down his mouth.

He pulls his laptop out of the car, rests it on the roof. He checks the cameras on the gate one more time, like he expects the view to have changed. He starts searching the security footage from the neighbors' houses, checking to see if they have anything of worth.

He hears a car. Turns his head, and sees it speeding from around the corner of the house. It comes toward him, kicking up dust in its wake. Gerry looks inside as it passes. A black man is driving, and there's a Mexican woman in the front beside him. He's only able to glimpse briefly into the back as it speeds by, but he sees another Mexican woman, and a white man with his head in her lap. Gerry thinks he sees blood, but it's all gone in a flash. He looks back toward the house. There's still no sign of Robert and Simon. He starts to bounce on his feet.

Gerry begins to think they aren't coming.

"Fuck this," he says. He goes to the back of the car and throws open the trunk. He holds his breath as he reaches in and drags Nathan's body out, dumps the corpse by the side of the road. He hurries back around the front and climbs behind the steering wheel. He puts his foot down and keeps it down, speeds past the house, and keeps on going.

62

Cindy sits by her laptop, hands locked together beneath her chin. She's cross-legged in her chair. Her knees bounce up and down, tapping against its arms. She refreshes the news feed over and over, but it doesn't tell her anything new. It talks about the gunfight at the house of local businesswoman Shelley Snow, between members of the Nogales Cartel and various local gangsters. No one knows what sparked it, but more than one journalist is going off the theory that they'd met up to discuss a business arrangement, then tempers began to fray, and things grew volatile between the two dangerous groups of people.

It tells of how Miguel Aguilar, head of the Nogales Cartel, and number nine on the FBI's Most Wanted, was also present. How he's dead now. How Shelley Snow is dead. How Councilman Foster was found wounded, wandering near the house hours later in a seeming fugue state, conveniently unable to remember anything that had occurred.

It talks of the girls who were found, too. Most of them trafficked into the country. Some of them had been killed in the battle. All of them told the same story – they'd been taken there against their will.

All those names, and no mention of Tom Rollins. No mention of Zeke, either, or Carmen, or Rosa.

Cindy chews a thumbnail. She doesn't like being in the dark.

She's lost contact with Zeke. Hasn't heard from him in over a day now. She's tried calling. It would ring out. She's tried a couple of times since, and it went straight to voicemail, like the battery had died.

She's checked beyond the news. Checked deeper. In the FBI. In the CIA. Nothing is coming up.

Part of her wonders if Tom is dead. She wonders about Carmen and Rosa, too, how they are.

Her phone rings, interrupting her thoughts. It's on the desk in front of her. She grabs at it. It's Zeke. She hesitates before she answers, remembering when she called Tom and someone else answered. "Hello?"

"Cindy." It's Zeke.

"What's happened?" she says. "I've been trying to get in touch –"

"Tom's hurt," he says. "He's been in surgery."

"Holy shit – how's he doing?"

"It was touch and go, but he's stable now."

"Which hospital are you in?"

"It ain't a hospital. It's a backstreet operation run by a couple of doctors who lost their licenses. We were short on options. If we took him to an actual hospital the cops would've been called."

"Shit. Is he awake?"

"No, not yet. Listen, we're hidden, and we're out of the way, but he's a sitting duck here. If the FBI or the CIA, or whoever the fuck else, find out where he is and show up, it's like we're serving him on a silver platter."

"You can't move him?"

"No, not with his injuries."

"What do you need me to do?"

"Tom needs an ally right now," Zeke says. "Someone who owes him a favor, and has the power to get him out of this situation a free man."

Cindy thinks. She gets the impression Zeke is referring to someone in particular. "Someone from Texas, perhaps?"

"Exactly. Do you have a number?"

"No, but you know I can get it."

"Okay. Fast as you can."

"I'm on it. What about Carmen and Rosa?"

"They're safe. They're together."

Cindy breathes a sigh of relief. "That's good." She smiles. "When Tom wakes up, tell him…"

Zeke waits. "Yeah?"

"Tell him…that I hope he's all right. I'm gonna go now."

"Good luck."

"Same to you."

Cindy hangs up the phone. She laces her fingers, forces them outward until her knuckles and joints pop. She gets to work.

63

Tom wakes.

The light hurts his eyes. He blinks against it, then looks around the room. There's a drip beside him and a catheter. He sees people present, but their faces are blurred. He counts four.

"Sleeping Beauty, that you waking up?" It's Zeke's voice. He comes closer, and Tom sees his face clearly.

"I think so," Tom says. His voice is a croak. "How long have I been out?"

"Couple of days now. You lost a lot of blood, man." Zeke stands by the side of the bed, squeezes his arm. "You need a drink?"

"That would be good," Tom says, rocking his body side to side, shifting his weight around.

Tom's vision has cleared now. Carmen and Rosa stand at the other side of the bed, looking down at him. They've both changed out of the dresses they were in for the party. Carmen is in jeans and a shirt, like she wore shortly after he first met her. She slips her hand into his and smiles at him. "We've been worried about you," she says.

Tom squeezes her fingers. He notices how the paint on the room's walls is peeling, and he can tell he's not in a real hospital. He looks up at Rosa. She's wearing a loose sweater and a pair of tracksuit bottoms. "We haven't met yet," he says to Rosa. "Not properly."

She smiles, though there is a sadness in her face that never fully goes away. "My sister speaks very highly of you," she says.

"We're glad you've woken up," Carmen says. She strokes the back of his hand.

Zeke reappears beside him, holding a glass of water with a straw sticking out of it. He puts the straw between Tom's lips. Tom drinks. While he does, he looks toward the fourth person in the room, holding back. It's a man. He's wearing a suit. There's an American flag pin on his lapel. He's familiar, but Tom's head feels fuzzy, and he can't place where he knows him from.

Zeke sees where he's looking. He turns to the stranger. "I think he's all right to talk," he says.

The man steps forward, to the foot of the bed. "Mr. Rollins," he says, "I'm glad to finally meet you."

Tom studies him, knows he's seen him before. Knows he's seen him in person.

The man sees the look on his face. "My name's Seth Goldberg. I was there the day you stopped the attack in Dallas. We spoke, briefly. Do you remember?"

It comes back to Tom now.

"You saved my life, Tom," Seth says. "And, more importantly, you saved my family's lives. You saved a lot of families that day, and kept many others from heartache. I feel like I've been looking for you for a long time since that day. I wanted to say thank you. I want to shake your hand." He holds his own out.

Tom pushes himself up to a seated position. He takes Seth's proffered hand, and they shake.

"I also understand you're in a bit of a jam at the moment," Seth says, looking around as if to illustrate their less-than-savory location.

They let go. Tom shuffles up the bed, rests his back on the pillows. "I guess that depends on which jam you're referring to."

"I've looked into you, Mr. Rollins. May I call you Tom?"

Tom nods.

"I know your past, Tom. I know who you are, and what you do. What you *used* to do. That's not a job you're just supposed to walk away from the way you did. You're a wanted man."

Tom shrugs one shoulder. "It's not ideal," he says.

"Uh-huh. I'm sure. But you saved Dallas from a terrorist attack. I know all about what happened down in Brenton, too. And now this. A businesswoman in Tucson, trafficking women over the border with the aid of the Nogales Cartel – and now the head of that cartel, one Miguel Aguilar, number nine on the FBI's Most Wanted, is dead."

"Are you getting to a point?"

Seth chuckles. "I am. I have some sway, Tom. I've called around, and I've pulled in some favors from friends in the NSA. They're going to clean up your history, get rid of your record for going AWOL. You won't be a wanted man anymore."

Tom tilts his head. "Is that possible?"

"You've killed a lot of people, you've caused a lot of damage – but the ends have justified the means. For that, the NSA is willing to turn a blind eye to your participation in recent events. The death of Miguel Aguilar has helped in that regard, too. And with your background, serving your country, that also plays in your favor."

"I appreciate the help, Senator," Tom says.

"Call me Seth."

"I guess we're even now, Seth."

"I wouldn't say that," Seth says. "I'm not sure I can pay back the debt I owe you for my family's lives, but I'll do what I can."

"When's this all come into effect?" Zeke says. He stands to one side, his arms folded.

"I just need to make another call," Seth says.

"Maybe when you make that call, you can do me another favor," Tom says.

Seth looks at him. "Name it," he says.

"There were girls at that house," Tom says. "There are others, too. Most of them are in Nogales, and there's one called Emilia hiding out in a motel near the border. I'll give you the address. They all want to go home." He looks at Carmen and Rosa. "A couple of my friends want to go home, too."

Seth nods. He looks at the sisters. "I can organize that," he says. "No problem."

Tom nods.

"My wife will be disappointed she wasn't able to come here and thank you, too," Seth says. "But I got the call, and it sounded urgent, so I came straight here."

"The call?" Tom says.

"Mm," Seth says. He smiles. "A very strange call. Obviously from someone who doesn't want to be well known. They were using a voice modulator, whoever they were. They told me of the situation. Told me where you are."

Tom thinks of Cindy. He looks at Zeke, who nods.

"Well," Seth says, reaching into his pocket and pulling out his phone, "I have some calls I need to make." He starts to leave the room. He pauses by the door. "By the way," he says, "I've always wondered – the people who attempted the attack in Dallas, do you think you got them all?" He raises his eyebrows. "I'm not afraid to admit I've lost some sleep wondering if there's still anyone out there. Who's to say they might not attempt something like that again?"

Tom looks at him. "Sleep easy, Senator," he says. "They're all dead."

64

It's late when Zeke gets back to Shreveport. He's tired, but he's close to home now.

He hung around the hospital another couple of days with Tom. Making sure he was all right. Making sure he was safe. Making sure Senator Seth Goldberg followed through on his promise of help. Sure enough, he did as he said he would.

Tom Rollins is no longer a fugitive.

"So what you gonna do now?" Zeke asked him. "Now that you're a free man, free to do whatever you please."

Tom grinned. "I was already a free man," he said. "It was everyone else who struggled to accept that."

Zeke leaned back in his chair, feet up on the bed. "That don't answer my question, though."

Tom shrugged. "I don't know. I haven't given it much thought." He looked out of the room then. Toward the hall.

Zeke thought he knew what he was looking at. Carmen and Rosa were there. Sleeping in chairs, the younger sister with her head resting on the shoulder of the older. The older with her arm around the younger. They'd gone through hell to find each other. They weren't going to let go now.

"Travel, maybe," Tom said finally. "I might head north. I feel like I've been in the sun for too long."

"Uh-huh," Zeke said, seeing how his eyes were lingering out in the hallway still. "Sure you don't wanna go back down to Mexico?"

"There's nothing down there for me."

"There could be."

Tom shook his head. He pulled the blanket down a little and inspected the stitches low in his abdomen.

"Don't pick them," Zeke said.

"I'm not a child."

"Force of habit." Zeke laughed. "And don't go flashing your new scars, trying to change the subject on me."

"I know what you think," Tom said. "And you're wrong."

"I'm not so sure I am."

"They've already been through a lot. They don't need me around, complicating things further."

"And how you gonna complicate things?"

"You know as well as I do, Zeke," Tom said. "When you have a history of trouble, trouble always has a way of finding you."

Zeke rocked back on the chair and pondered this statement. "You really think that?" he said.

"I've lived it."

Zeke has thought about that a lot. It was the last real conversation he had with Tom. He fell asleep soon after, and Zeke did the same in the chair. This morning, Carmen and Rosa returned to the room.

"I think I should go home," Zeke said.

Tom nodded. He understood. "Give the family my love."

"The kids would like to see Uncle Rollins again soon."

"I'd like to see them, too," Tom said. "Maybe I'll make my way around to Louisiana some time."

They embraced, then Zeke said his goodbyes to Carmen and Rosa, and he left the hospital. He called Cindy from his car. "You did good," he said.

"Was there ever any doubt?" she said.

He chuckled. "Such modesty."

"It keeps me humble. How's he doing?"

"Good. He's supposed to be in there another week at least, but knowing him, he'll probably leave in a couple of days."

"I'm glad he's getting better."

"You should give him a call. I'm sure he'd be glad to hear from you."

"He has my number," she said. "I don't have his. Not anymore. Not since he lost that burner."

"Well, then, I'm sure he'll get in touch in time. It's been a pleasure working with you, Cindy. No offense, but I hope we don't have to do it again soon."

She laughed at that. "'Til next time. Whenever that may be."

Zeke has not stopped to rest on his drive home. He's made one pit stop, for gas and snacks. His body is aching. His lower back is stiff. He just wants to get home.

He's been thinking about his future. What it might hold for him. His unit is dead now. He's not sure what the CIA will do with him. Whether they'll put him with another, or if they'll put him somewhere else entirely.

He's tried not to dwell on it, knowing that whatever will come will come, but it's been a long drive, and he's had little else to do but think. The music on the radio, and the incessant prattle of the DJs, have done little to distract him.

He reaches his street, and spies his house at the end of the row. It's in darkness. He checks the time. It's midnight. His eyes feel heavy, and he wants to get to bed. Wants to curl up next to Naomi and feel the reassurance of her warmth beside him, the feel of her body curled into his. Wants to hear the gentle breathing of his children in their rooms.

He pulls onto the drive and gets out of the car, trying not to groan as he does so. Feeling how the various kinks and aches catch fire as he straightens up. He twists from side to side, hears things pop. He looks up and down the road. Everything is so still, so quiet. So peaceful. He takes a deep breath of the warm night air, then goes inside.

Zeke takes care to step lightly through the house, not wanting to disturb his family. Makes sure to step over the stair that creaks. He reaches Tre's room first. Looks in, and finds that Tamika has crawled into his bed. Tre has his arm around her. They're both snoring softly. Zeke kneels down beside the bed and feels himself smile as he strokes both of their faces. He pulls the blanket up to their shoulders, makes sure they're comfortable.

Naomi is curled on her side. Zeke tiptoes around the outside of the room to his side of the bed. As he undresses, she turns to him, surprising him. "I heard your car pull in," she says, yawning, sounding sleepy.

"I didn't mean to wake you," he whispers.

"You didn't wake me," she says. "Not really. I never sleep too well when you're gone." She yawns again. "How's Tom?"

"Still alive."

"That's good. You have to help him stay that way?"

"Eventually." Zeke slides into the bed beside her. She turns back over, presses herself up against him.

"Do you know when you've gotta go back yet?"

Zeke puts his arm around her. Kisses the side of her head. "Not yet," he says. "But I think I'm gonna hear something soon."

65

It's late in the non-hospital, but Tom can't sleep. It's hard for him to feel worn out when he's spending his days lying in a bed. He's restless. He checks his stitches for what feels like the hundredth time, trying to gauge how well he's healing. Working out in his head how likely it is for them to pop if he checks himself out tomorrow.

"You keep looking at them like you expect something to have changed."

It's Carmen. She stands in the doorway. He looks up at her. "I don't have anything else to do," he says.

She steps into the room, stands next to his bed. "I offered to get you a book," she says.

"I have guests," he says, referring to Carmen and her sister. "It would be rude if I were to lie here reading. Where's Rosa?"

"She's sleeping," Carmen says. She hesitates, then says, "We're going home tomorrow."

Tom nods. "I'm glad. I'm sure you both are, too."

Carmen nods, and the corner of her mouth tugs upward in a smile. "It will be good to see our parents again."

"I'm sure they've missed you both."

She nods. She looks around the room like she's seeing it for the first time. She looks out toward the hall. No one passes by. "It's so quiet here at night," she says.

"Everyone's asleep," Tom says. "Like your sister is. How come you're not?"

She shrugs. "I'm not tired. What's your excuse? You're supposed to be resting."

"I spend all day resting. I don't know how anyone can expect me to do it overnight, too."

She smiles. "What will you do here, all day long, when you don't have my sister and me to keep you company? Perhaps you'll have to find a book after all."

"I won't be staying here," Tom says.

Carmen raises an eyebrow. "No?"

He shakes his head. "When you get out of here tomorrow, I don't think I'll be too far behind you."

"Oh really? Where are you going to go?"

"There's something I need to deal with," Tom says, "and then, after that, I can go anywhere I want. Zeke was asking me the same question. I've given it some thought since then. I think somewhere with snow."

Carmen laughs. "Snow?"

"Uh-huh. Been a while since I last saw some."

Carmen grins, shakes her head. "Do you think you'll ever return to Mexico?"

"Never say never. If I do, I'll be sure to come by and say hello."

"You don't know where I live," Carmen says. "And even if I gave you the address now, what's to say I won't have moved by then?"

"I'd find you," Tom says.

"I don't doubt that." She falls silent, looking down at the bed.

"Do you want to lie with me for a while?" Tom says.

"There isn't enough space."

"I can move up." Tom shimmies along toward the edge of the bed to demonstrate.

"I don't want to hurt you," she says. "Your stitches –"

"My stitches are fine." He pulls the blanket back.

Carmen looks back toward the hall, to her sleeping sister. She looks that way for a while, deliberating, then she climbs onto the bed. She squeezes up close to Tom. He puts the blanket over her, and his arm around her shoulders.

"Are you comfortable?" she says.

Tom lies back, resting his head on the pillows. "The best I've felt all the while I've been in this fucking place. Longer, in fact."

She rests her head on his chest. It doesn't stay there long. She turns her face up to his. She looks at him. She leans closer. Tom lowers his face to hers. They kiss. Her hands hold tightly to his body. Tom pulls her to him, his arm still around her shoulder. With his other, he pulls the blanket higher, covers them both.

66

Tom Rollins is still alive.

Tom Rollins has disappeared.

All record of Tom Rollins's past, his being wanted for going AWOL, has been expunged.

Eric can't get a track on him. Rollins briefly appeared at that disastrous party, and then he just – *poof* – disappeared. He's gone underground, back off the grid, and he's not showing up anywhere. Facial recognition isn't getting any hits. It feels like a lost cause.

Eric sits in his office, and tries not to lose hope. He *can't* lose hope. If he loses that, then he's lost everything else.

There's music playing outside, in the distance, so loud he can hear it even here in his study, through the windows. Coming from the home of one of the new-money football players, his property filled with half-naked women jumping into his pool. He and his friends getting drunk, taking drugs. Likely taking photos and videos of themselves, posting them online for the world to see.

When Eric has the time, he'll silence them once and for all. Right now, though, he has bigger fish to fry.

He gets to his feet and paces the room, trying to ignore the distant muffled noise. It puts him on edge. Makes his head hurt. It causes him stress, which makes his stomach turn and his skin itch.

It has been a month since the battle in Tucson at Shelley Snow's house. A month since Robert and his team were killed. Gerry Davies has not returned to work since. He quit from the road, over the phone, saying he feared for his life and didn't want any part in things going forward. Eric doesn't know where he is now, or what he's doing, but it doesn't matter. Gerry isn't his concern. He can find or hire any number of people who can do what he did, who can even, perhaps, do it better.

All that matters is that he finds Rollins. Finds him, and ends him. He can't rest easy until this is done, no matter how long it may take. He cannot lose this determination. There's too much at stake, both personally and professionally.

Eric leaves his study, roams the house in search of Eliza. He finds her in her room. She's getting ready to go out. Sitting at her vanity table, applying makeup. Eric feels his stomach sink at the sight, though he's not sure why.

She turns at his entrance. "Eric," she says, "is everything all right?"

He clears his throat. "Have you heard the music?"

She frowns, listens. It's not so noticeable in this part of the house. She shakes her head. "What music?"

"They're having a party," he says.

"Who is?"

"I don't know." He waves his arm vaguely in the direction he heard it coming from. "Out there, somewhere. One of those football players. They've got their music so loud I can hear it in my study."

"I'm sure it can't be *that* loud, dear," she says.

"Come listen for yourself."

"I can't do that," she says, turning back to her mirror. "I'm busy."

Eric grunts.

She turns back to him, raises an eyebrow. "Are you all right, Eric?" she says. "You've felt...*off* for a while now. Is something troubling you?"

"Work," he says, without thinking. His standard excuse.

"Of course," she says. "Is it anything you'd like to talk about?"

He shakes his head.

"Perhaps you should book a vacation sometime soon. We could go to Vermont, perhaps? Or overseas, maybe? A rest would do you some good."

"Maybe," he says. "One day. There's just something... something I need to deal with first. I'll feel a lot better once it's all wrapped up."

"*Ooo*," Eliza says, making her eyes wide. "Sounds like a matter of national importance. Is my husband saving the country again, making democracy safe for all Americans?"

"What else?" Eric says. "Same as always, eh?"

She looks at him a moment longer without saying anything. Eric can feel her studying him, paying close attention to his face, to his tired eyes.

"They're working you too hard," she says eventually. "They have other agents, and they need to start utilizing them."

"I'll tell them you said so."

"Go get yourself a drink, dear. You look like you could use one. A *stiff* one. And have an early night, perhaps. You look like you could use one of *them*, too."

"I'll take your suggestions under close consideration," he says. He'll more than likely follow through on the former, but he knows the latter is impossible. He'll spend the night on his computer, searching for signs of Rollins, putting the call out for mercenaries who might actually be able to get the fucking job done this time. "Where are you going tonight?"

"Oh, just...out," she says.

"With whom?"

"Friends." She looks at him.

Eric can imagine the friends – or, more precisely, *friend*. "Will you be back tonight?"

"I'll have to see how the night goes." She takes a breath. "Eric, you know how this works. You don't ask me these types of questions. We have a tacit understanding. Honestly, you've been so *needy* lately. I've never seen you like this before. I don't know what to make of it. It's quite unbecoming."

Eric mumbles an apology. "I'll leave you to it," he says. "I think I'll go and get that drink you mentioned."

He leaves her room and heads downstairs. He pours himself a Scotch, neat, and takes it to the back door. He stands outside in the evening air and takes a drink. The music is louder out here. Clearer. He drains off his glass, staring into the distance, toward their nearest neighbor. Toward the noise.

The sky is getting dark. He doesn't think the night will silence them. They'll be going until the morning, and perhaps beyond. It wouldn't be the first time.

A thought strikes him suddenly, and he wonders if Eliza ever joins them. If it's maybe where she is going tonight.

He doubts it. Dismisses the thought as ridiculous. She was far too dressed up to be attending such an affair. His fraught nerves are getting the worst of him, making him imagine things that couldn't possibly occur.

He's still outside when Eliza comes down the stairs. She's wearing a low-cut red dress that accentuates her deep cleavage. She has her hair up, with a few loose strands hanging down the side of her face. "I'm going now," she says. "My taxi's here."

Eric can see the concern on her face as she looks at him, speaks to him. He forces himself to smile. "Have a good night," he says. He raises his almost-empty glass in a salute. "I'll see you...well, whenever you get back, I suppose."

She hesitates, torn between him and the front door. "Are you sure you're all right?" she says. "I'm not... I'm not sure... Would you like me to stay? I don't like seeing you like this."

"How many times can I say I'm fine?" Eric says, still forcing his smile. "Go. Enjoy your night. You'll be bored if you hang around." He holds up his drink again. "I'm taking your advice. A stiff drink and an early night. I'll be fast asleep before you even get where you're going, wherever that may be. There's no need for you to cancel your plans on my behalf."

Eliza continues to hesitate. "Are...are you sure?"

"I've never been surer." The smile is beginning to ache on his face.

Finally, Eliza relents. "Okay," she says. "Okay. If you're sure." She leaves the house. She looks back only once, when she's on the other side of the door, closing it. Eric continues to smile at her. He waves, and then the door clicks into place and she is gone.

He lets the smile fall from his face. He listens as the sound of her taxi idling out front pulls away. He steps back outside, through the french doors. Drains his drink. It burns on the way down, but he barely notices. He stares off toward the distant house, sure now it is where all the noise is coming from.

"Will you ever *shut up*?" he finds himself screaming into the night, across the expanse. His voice will get lost on the way. It cannot penetrate their wall of noise. It doesn't make him feel any better. He throws the tumbler in their direction. It doesn't reach. He never thought it would. It lands with a thump. The glass does not break. Some other time, maybe in the morning, when he feels up to it, he supposes he'll go and retrieve it. Not tonight, though. Tonight, it is a statement that no one knows about, that no one saw but himself.

He leaves the glass out in the dark, along with his hanging words. He steps back inside the house. Closes and locks the door. He turns around and finds that he is not alone.

Eric blinks, for a moment thinking that Eliza has returned to him. That she changed her mind in the taxi and decided that she couldn't bear to leave him alone.

It's not Eliza.

It's Tom Rollins.

Eric has to blink again to be sure. Rollins is dressed all in black, and Eric wonders for just a fleeting moment how he could have been so foolish as to mistake this outfit for his wife's red dress. Rollins is wearing gloves, too. He holds a gun down by his side. A Beretta.

"It's you," Eric says. He straightens up, clears his throat. "Our first meeting. Though we've spoken before, isn't that right?"

"That's right," Rollins says.

"Mm. How long have you been inside my house?"

Rollins doesn't answer.

"No," Eric says. "I suppose it doesn't matter. Care for a drink?"

"I'm not here for a drink."

"I suppose you're not." Eric looks down at the gun. "So what's the plan here, Mr. Rollins?"

"I'm sure you've worked out the plan, Mr. Thompson."

Eric breathes through his nose.

"Take a seat," Rollins says.

Eric does as he's told, moving to the nearest sofa. He sits in the center of it. Rollins steps around in front of him.

"Just get it over with –"

Before Eric can finish, Rollins raises the gun, pulls the trigger. The bullet plants itself between Eric Thompson's eyes. His head snaps back, blood spraying out behind it. It hangs over the back of the sofa, his body remaining upright.

Tom puts the gun away. He leaves the house, then walks a couple of miles down the road, his hands in his pockets. Walks back to where he left his car parked the night before. He's spent the last twenty-four hours in Eric's home. It wasn't hard to hide out. It's a big house.

He passes a neighbor having a loud party. A few drunken people are hanging out in front, laughing at each other as they try to stay upright. They don't see Tom as he passes. He walks on through the darkness. He reaches his car. It's all alone, in the driveway of an empty home, a For Sale sign out front. Waiting for its new owners.

Tom starts the engine. He turns on the lights. He pulls out of the driveway and turns the car around.

He heads north.

ABOUT THE AUTHOR

Did you enjoy *Hard to Kill*? Please consider leaving a review on Amazon to help other readers discover the book.

Paul Heatley left school at sixteen, and since then has held a variety of jobs including mechanic, carpet fitter, and bookshop assistant, but his passion has always been for writing. He writes mostly in the genres of crime fiction and thriller, and links to his other titles can be found on his website. He lives in the north east of England.

Want to connect with Paul? Visit him at his website.

www.PaulHeatley.com

Published by Inkubator Books
www.inkubatorbooks.com

Copyright © 2021 by Paul Heatley

Paul Heatley has asserted his right to be identified as the author of this work.

WRONG TURN is a work of fiction. People, places, events, and situations are the product of the author's imagination. Any resemblance to actual persons, living or dead is entirely coincidental.

No part of this book may be reproduced, stored in any retrieval system, or transmitted by any means without the prior written permission of the publisher.

ALSO BY PAUL HEATLEY

The Tom Rollins Thriller Series
Blood Line (Book 1)
Wrong Turn (Book 2)
Hard to Kill (Book 3)
Snow Burn (Book 4)
Road Kill (Book 5)
No Quarter (Book 6)
Hard Target (Book 7)
Last Stand (Book 8)
Blood Feud (Book 9)
Search and Destroy (Book 10)
Ghost Team (Book 11)
Full Throttle (Book 12)
Sudden Impact (Book 13)
Kill Switch (Book 14)

The Tom Rollins Box Set (Books 1 - 4)

Printed in Great Britain
by Amazon